DRAGON QUEEN

Dragon Queen

Dragon Monarch Book Two

Jason P. Crawford

Epitome Press Publishing

An Epitome Press Book

Special Thanks To:

Angelique Gunnels and Jentina for putting up with me while we write together;

Patricia Hankins for instilling in me a love of the written word,

Sara Hammons for always being supportive and helpful;

James T. Johnson for bringing Amalia to life in a such a perfect way;

and my wife, Cherrie, for being the reason I always want to come back home.

ACKNOWLEDGMENTS

I want to thank my readers. Every comment, every review, every time someone says "I really thought that this was good" brings light to my day that I didn't know could be there. Thank you all for everything.

CHAPTER ONE

"Gorman signals the buglers." The words echoed from the stone walls, measured and careful, the product of recitation rather than conversation. "Count to seven. Twelve steps, stop." Footfalls followed, one after the other, as the sound gave voice to the action. "Take the scepter in your right hand, bow your head. The crown goes on, they take your shoulders, say the benediction."

High Princess Amalia Therald took a breath. Her room felt stuffy; even with the windows open, the breezeless summer day made it into a semblance of a stone oven, and she could smell her sweat in the air, tangy and filled with nervous tension.

"That and dog." She turned her head to the side and let her mouth curl up in a small smile. "You're lucky that you don't have to worry about things like how you smell."

Marchen let out a small yip, his panting and heavy breathing showing that she wasn't alone in feeling the heat. His feet padded across the floor, then stopped; the silence disrupted by loud lapping, water being pulled from a bowl by a canine tongue.

Amalia shook her head. *That sound. Never ceases to drive nails into my skull.* Another laugh. *I remember the first time still, when Father brought him in, and...*

There it was again. No matter how hard she tried to keep her mind off of it, she couldn't escape. The emotions rolled up, the feelings of anger and guilt. Her skin flushed hot and her chest hitched as she succumbed to despair, sitting on her bed to avoid falling to the floor. Her muscles remembered the sensation of battle, of her sword blade clashing with that of High King Marcus as they fought. Remembered the anger that had driven her, the rage that had led to her challenging him.

Would I have killed him?

She didn't know, and that not knowing made it worse. Even though she hadn't taken his life with her own hands – that had been Glorianna – the guilt wouldn't leave her. Over and over again, Gorman and Destrick and Catlin had comforted her, telling her that it wasn't her fault...

But it was.

I can't even pretend that it was because of Mother. At the thought of her, Amalia's hand twisted in the sheets, clenching tight in a spasm of anger. Instead of the sadness and guilt that she felt when thinking about Marcus, thoughts of Elise engendered rage and frustration. *I didn't even know what he'd done before I left here to go after him.*

Marchen interrupted her spiral into the depths of her consciousness with a low whine and by nudging her left thigh with his muzzle. She reached out and scratched his head, feeling her muscles relax and some of the tension drain from her body.

"You're right." Amalia leaned over and kissed the top of her dog's head, making a face as she had to fish a hair out of her lips. "Doesn't matter how many times I go over it, nothing changes, does it?"

He pressed his head up into her hand, his nose brushing against her skin, and she felt the now-familiar tingle in the back of her brain as their minds connected.

Can you be happy? The concern in his mental impulse washed over Amalia's mind, drowning her in its depth and strength. *Can I help you be happy? I'm happy when you're happy.*

The mental contact brought flashbacks - soaring over the trees, the oceans. Diving down to catch a fish in clawed talons, the sea spray across her face. The oranges and pinks of the sunrise, streaking over the water. The visualizations reminded her exactly how tired she was, how fatigued, and she shook her head. *Gods, just to get away* again...

Another yip brought her attention back to her dog.

"I know you are, sweetheart." Amalia touched her forehead to the hound's, and laughed when he shifted away and licked her face. "It's not your fault, but—"

A knock interrupted her. "Your Highness?"

"Yes, Elsa?" Footsteps, soft leather carrying a light frame, stepped into the room. "Is something wrong?"

"No, your Highness. Just the Royal Councilor here to see you." She stepped to one side.

"Oh!" The High Princess took a moment to compose herself, standing straight. "Then admit him."

The creaking wood frame heralded the sound of Gorman's boots on the floor. "Your Majesty? Is something the matter? You're supposed to be in the Great Hall—"

"Rehearsing the coronation. Yes, I know. I was practicing it in here first." Another deep breath; the newcomer smelled of rose water and cinnamon, but another scent tickled Amalia's nose and intrigued her – the faint aroma of lavender. The door closed as the lady-in-waiting excused herself, leaving the two of them alone.

"You needn't worry about that." He stepped to her side, and the sound of fabric thumped against her bed, fluffing the sheets up.

Clothes?

"We'll go through it as many times as we need to for you to get it right. Just like when…" Gorman trailed off, then cleared his throat. "Like every time before. And it's just a formality, anyway. You needn't worry."

"You said that already, Gorman." Amalia took a step toward him and lay a hand on his shoulder. "When you repeat yourself like that, it becomes obvious to me that I *do* need to worry."

Gorman laughed, but it was a nervous sound, tremulous and shaky. "That's not what I meant, your Majesty."

"I'm not the High Queen yet." She moved around him, putting her hands out as she reached the bed. "You shouldn't be calling me 'Majesty.' It violates protocol."

Her fingers touched silk, and the brushing of her skin on the fabric brought forth a new wave of lavender. She picked up the garment, feeling its weight shift as it unfolded in her hands. "It's very heavy." She adjusted it, draping it over one arm and separating the folds with her other hand. "Is this what I'm to wear at the coronation?"

"Yes." Gorman stepped up behind her and gripped her wrist, bringing her hand to the bodice area of the dress. Amalia felt three gemstones, oval in shape, laid out around the neckline. The embroidery stood out against her skin, and the hips flared out into a double-layered skirt, with the outer layer parted in front and sweeping around the back. "The tailors made some adjustments to the fit of your…your mother's dress."

Elise. Amalia let her hand drop, and again felt the anger, the frustration. *I've looked forward to wearing this for so long, thinking I would be honoring your memory, Imagining Father's face, lined, maybe balding when he passed the throne to me. Imagining what you would have looked like if I could have seen you standing next to him, watching me, smiling at me.*

I miss her too, Sister. Glorianna's mental voice came like a comforting hand on the shoulder. **Her absence leaves a great hole in both our hearts.**

At least you were able to know her. The connection between the two strengthened as the things around Amalia began to fade from her awareness. *Can you show me—?*

"Princess? Are you—?"

Amalia started, putting a hand on her forehead to cover her distraction, taking a second to bite back her irritation. "Not that again, Gorman. Once more and I might lose my mind." She exhaled through her nose, inhaled, exhaled, the sudden separation from Glorianna like an open sore in her mouth. "It's not supposed to be easy, right? That's what everyone keeps telling me. I'm supposed to feel angry, hurt, guilty?"

She heard the cloth around his neck rustle and the skin fold as he nodded. "Of course. It's just..." He paused. "You'll have to forgive me for my concern, Princess. With…with your father gone, and all of the responsibility for the kingdom suddenly placed on your shoulders, I…I worry." He chuckled, scratching at his short beard. "I suppose it's one of the hazards of getting old, watching all of those you knew as children turn into adults."

Amalia sighed, feeling the weight on her increase, pressing her spirit down. "I…I don't think I can do this, Gorman. I'm not ready. There is so much that I still need to learn, need to know." She turned her face to her mentor's. "What if—"

"With all due respect, Your Majesty, you need to shove the 'What ifs' into a small box and lock them underneath your bed." He took her hand. "Listen to me. There hasn't been a single good King or Queen or Governor or what have you that had everything together. It's like being a parent – there are no instructions, no guidelines. You simply do the best you can…"

"Every day, every time." Amalia nodded, then stifled a yawn. "I remember the lesson. Thank you for reminding me."

"That, Princess, is both my duty and my pleasure." He stepped forward again, then reached down to Marchen. "Are you taking good care of her?"

An answering bark, and Marchen was on his feet, his tail wagging against the stone floor, making small scraping sounds as he panted. The image made Amalia cover her mouth to keep from snorting.

"Here you go, then." Another shuffling of cloth and a low, muted aroma of salt and meat. "How about some dried beef? I think you deserve it for being such a good dog."

Marchen's excited reply was all Gorman needed, and he dropped the treat, leaving the hound to inhale the meat and bolt it down, moving his jaws in huge scooping motions as he chewed. Amalia smiled, listening to him enjoy himself.

"For what it's worth, Princess." Gorman's interjection made her turn her head back toward him. "I think that you'll make an excellent High Queen. You have the benefits of your father's wisdom and your mother's strength." He took her hand again. "And, don't forget, you have us. We believe in you."

"And I'll need that support." Amalia listened as Marchen finished off his snack, coming over between herself and Gorman to beg for more. "No, that's enough. Time to go."

She snapped her fingers, and Marchen bounded over to her side, sitting at her feet as she knelt down and took hold of his leash. "I think I'm ready. As ready as I'm likely to be, at any rate."

"Very well, your Majesty." Gorman stepped to her side and threaded his arm around hers, then reached over and took the gown. "Don't want this to drag on the floor or fall down while we walk."

"Of course." Amalia squared her shoulders. "You signal the buglers. Count to seven. Twelve steps, stop. Take the scepter in my right hand. Lower my head. The crown goes on, they say the benediction."

Gorman patted her hand. "You keep your head down until it's over, then turn and bow to the court. Everyone kneels."

She reached out and opened the door. "The priest names me High Queen by the will of Junandar. Long…" Her voice hitched, and she swallowed it down. "Long live the Queen."

CHAPTER TWO

"That went very well, Counselor." The priest's words rasped in Amalia's ears like sandpaper, rough and worn by age. "I expect that the High Princess will conduct the ceremony honorably on the morrow."

"I would not anticipate any differently, your Eminence." Gorman's voice was filled to bursting with pride. "She has studied diligently over the years and acquitted herself well before."

Keep your mouth shut, Amalia. The Princess did her best to appear involved, her fingers tracing out the shapes of letters scored into a small board. Another letter of condolences, this one from Yensin Morganus.

The Kingdom of Karis offers our sincere well-wishes in this time of trial. Rest assured that we will spare no effort in answering any call to arms against the monsters that slew your father. We are at your disposal.

Of course you are. Amalia pressed her lips together to keep from speaking aloud. *You weren't there to see what actually happened, how I started the whole thing. Or how my mother-*

"Has everything been prepared for the banquet after the coronation?" Even while in the deep realms of thought, the priest's voice was enough to drag Amalia's awareness back into the present. "We would not wish to dishonor the gods and the Archprelate through inadequate offerings and celebration, would we?"

"We are quite ready, your Eminence." Pride gone, a hint of rancor now tinged Gorman's tone. Amalia ducked her head to hide her grin, and Marchen pushed himself against her side, startled by the sudden movement. "This isn't the first time that we've changed rulers, unfortunately."

"No, but it is, by far, the least auspicious." The priest's words followed him around the room, and Amalia could hear the sounds of clinking glassware and metal as he stopped to examine the settings. "And, therefore, it is vital that we keep the gods' favor during this transition."

"Your Eminence, if I may." Amalia stood up and, holding the letter to her side, turned toward the priest. "I think that Junandar and Porir will be most honored if we serve as rulers should – care for our people, work to make life better for them, and cooperate amongst ourselves."

She gave a smile. "As High King Marcus would say, the rest will work itself out after that."

Gorman nodded, and the priest cleared his throat. "While that may be true, etiquette and ceremony must be upheld or their favor may turn against us. And regardless of your best intentions, your Highness, one cannot fight against the will of the gods, should it turn sour."

"And, of course, keeping their favor should prevent that, should it not?" Amalia felt the anger begin to rise again, heard it in the swelling tide of her voice. "Keeping the traditions holy would prevent the horrors of, say, losing the High King to a dragon's attack? Or the Queen?"

She felt Gorman lay his hand on her shoulder, but she shook him off, pressing forward into the holy man's personal space, feeling the heat of his body as she approached. "Or perhaps we affronted them in some way, despite our piety, despite our—"

"Amalia!"

Gorman pulled her round, holding her with both hands, face-to-face. "You are smarter than this." He paused to let that sink in. "Think before you say anything else. For your mother's sake, and your father's."

"I…" She could hear the shifting behind her, the priest's robes and shoes changing position as he pondered what he should do, before he gathered himself and spoke up.

"Let us pray to Nome to assuage your grief, your Majesty." His compassionate words did a poor job of hiding the tremor beneath them. "Even royalty is not immune to the tribulations placed before us by the gods."

His words set a fresh fire in Amalia's heart, one that she only banked with difficulty. "You…you are wise, and I shall heed your counsel." She turned back toward him, inclining her head. "I shall make an offering and prayer to the Deathly One, that he might lift this anger from my chest and bring me peace."

"I shall as well." With a scraping bow, the priest let himself out, wooden soles clomping against stone until both the sound and his smell disappeared behind the door.

Amalia heard her tutor take a breath, and she raised her hand to cut him off. "Don't say it, Gorman. Please don't. I know I shouldn't have lost my temper."

"Actually, your Majesty." A deep, rolling chuckle started, low in his chest, gaining in strength as he fought his words through. "I was going to compliment you on making the Deacon of Junandar nearly wet himself with fear."

She wrinkled her brow, letting herself laugh a moment but then stopping, confused. "I…I don't understand. You aren't angry?"

"Of course not. And I hope you understand why I had to caution you." The laughter tapered off, and Gorman strode to the nearest window, throwing it open and ushering in the faint summer breeze. Quince and orange floated in on the wind from the royal orchard, mixing with apple and olive trees, causing Amalia to breathe in and smile. "It was entertaining. And, besides, he *was* treating you like a child. Trying to exert some sort of authority over you or Aetheria, or both, I expect." A pause in which Amalia could feel his gaze on her face. "You did exactly right in showing him his place."

"Still, you were right; I took it too far." Amalia didn't want to show it, but Gorman's approval did wonders for her mood, dispelling the self-reproachment she had been preparing. "I shouldn't have insinuated that the gods didn't care about my parents, that they caused it."

"No, perhaps not." Another snicker, and then Gorman took her arm again. "But it brought this old man a few minutes of entertainment."

She smiled one more time. "Then I suppose it may have been worth it, at least for the present." Then she leaned her head into his shoulder. "I'm scared, Gorman. What if no one will follow me? What—?"

"What-ifs do nothing but waste your time and concentration." He patted her hand and began walking with her out of the room, toward the orchard. "Enjoy the day. You've earned it."

Because the hard part is coming up. Amalia nodded. "Thank you, Gorman. What are your plans for the remainder of the day?"

"My plans? You flatter me. Men my age don't have the luxury of plans. We're simply called upon to give our advice on one crisis after another, all the while trying to hide the fact that we have absolutely no idea how to solve them." They both laughed. "At any rate, make sure you get some rest, your Majesty. The day starts early tomorrow."

Amalia nodded, and waited until she heard his footsteps recede across the chamber, through another door, and start down the hall before she snapped her fingers. "Marchen! Come!"

With a leap and a barking bound, the dog took his customary place by Amalia's side, waiting for her to reach down and grasp the leather leash that was bunched up in its holster on his collar. After she had it, Amalia stood back up and pushed open the heavy door to the orchard, feeling the sun on her face and hands as the door left its frame.

I remember when that door was almost impossible for me to open by myself. She stood a moment, flexing the fingers of her free hand. *I wonder exactly how strong I've become?*

The question sent another surge of guilt through her. She didn't have the right to enjoy these abilities, these powers – they were what caused her father to try his hand at filicide, what brought his later doom upon him. She shook her head to dispel the clouds that threatened to cover her consciousness again.

Amalia took a step out, down the stairwell and into the orchard, allowing the green smells, the leaves and shoots and ripening fruits, to wrap around her senses, to drown out her own thoughts and feelings in favor of pure sensuous inundation, like immersing her mind in a river of life. Her hand moved of its own accord, reaching up and plucking a ripe orange from a low-hanging branch, then bringing the large, round fruit to her nose as she inhaled. The sweet, citrus smell lit up her nerves, sending tingles down her spine and into her arms and legs.

"Holy Father of the Green." She whispered the prayer to Haphapshem, rolling the fruit between her palms. "Thank you for this gift, and all the other bounty that your soil provides."

"May you always find the rains when you thirst, and may your sister shine on you when you hunger." A deep voice joined in from her left, its sudden intrusion startling her. The tree rustled as the speaker pulled down another orange. "All that we are, we owe to you."

Amalia turned her head away. "I…I didn't hear you come out."

"I didn't." Lord Destrick's voice smiled at her. "I've been here for about an hour now, enjoying the day. It's so much nicer here than inside, especially in this weather."

"Yes." The small talk put Amalia on more familiar ground, let her get her mental feet under her while she tried to recover from her surprise. "I've been having difficulty getting moving in the morning, the heat is so oppressive. I don't remember another summer being this way."

"We've had worse, your H…your Majesty. I recall a day that led you to lock yourself in your bathing room for several hours, asking for fresh water every bell to cool yourself with."

Amalia flushed. "Did I truly do such a thing? How long ago was this?"

"We may have been ten, perhaps eleven." He turned and rested on one of the benches that lined the causeways in the orchard; his movements gave away the fact that he was, for once, not wearing his customary armor, but instead had chosen loose, light garments of cotton to ward off the heat. "I remember how exasperated the servants were, sweat pouring down their faces as they tried to keep the water flowing." A small laugh. "More than once, they spilled some of it on themselves, just to cool down, before dropping it into the reservoir for your bath."

She covered her face in shame. "Gods, I was so spoiled." She shook her head, still hiding behind her hands. "I can't believe they didn't just up and throw me out of the window instead."

Destrick laughed, sitting down beside her, a respectful distance away. "I won't pretend that a few didn't suggest it."

A few seconds of silence passed; Amalia licked her lips, hesitant. "Destrick? May I…may I speak with you for a moment?"

"I thought that's what we were doing." She felt him near, leaning forward without leaving his seat. "Is something wrong, your Majesty?"

"I…" She girded herself, forcing down the nervousness. "I have treated you poorly in the past, and I apologize."

The Knight-Commander said nothing, simply waited for her to continue. The feeling of his eyes bored into her face, and she almost lost her nerve. Her heart raced and she felt sweat breaking out under her arms, on her forehead, greasing her hands. "I was far too harsh during our last training session." She took a breath, straightened her spine. "You didn't deserve my anger, and I beg your forgiveness."

"Your Majesty." Destrick sighed, shifting a little in his seat. "You have nothing to apologize for. I was out of line, and I—"

"Stop trying to ruin my apology, Destrick!" Amalia exhaled through her nose. "You don't understand. Whether or not you acted intentionally, whether or not you were out of line, your actions did not warrant your dismissal." She twisted her fingers together, but kept her mien as composed as she could. "Is it…is it possible that we could resume our training?"

Three heartbeats passed before he responded. "Of course, Princess. But…but why? I thought that you were taking lessons from the huntsman." The pitch of his voice lowered along with the volume. "Learning how to fight dragons."

"Yes, but…" She shook her head, and the memory of wind whipping past her ears and face made her shudder. *I don't want to know how to fight them.* "His style isn't as helpful as yours was." Then she crossed her arms and tried a smile. "You said yourself what an excellent study of the sword I had become."

"It's true. I'd be glad to have you back in class…and not just because I enjoy your company." He let that hang in the air for a moment. "I've already noticed changes in your movements and your stances that need to be addressed. The huntsman has been a poor influence on you and your technique."

Amalia lifted her brow. "Truly?" Then she grinned, rising to her feet. "Perhaps we should determine the truth of your allegations on the field, Sir Knight."

He rose as well. "So be it, my Lady. I accept your challenge." His arm cut through the air as he performed a sweeping bow. "I shall meet you upon the field of battle in an hour. Be prepared."

She dipped in a curtsy, keeping one hand wrapped around Marchen's leash. "Very well. I will send your body on to your family for proper burial."

Before he could reply, Amalia swept out of the orchard, stopping only to grab her uneaten orange from the bench. As she walked out, head high, struggling not to grin, she heard the Commander breathe a laugh.

"We'll see."

Indeed we will. Away from Destrick, another wave of tiredness forced Amalia's mouth wide in a yawn. *But perhaps a nap first? I am so tired.*

"Bed, Marchen." Amalia flicked the leash lightly, directing the hound to attend to her words. "We have some time before we need to be seen again."

Marchen began to lead her on her way, toenails clacking on the stone floor with each step, the rhythm soothing, familiar. Amalia found herself almost drifting off, her feet carrying her of their own volition until she realized she was about to hit a corner, or veer into a passerby. Three times Marchen paused, and only the cessation of sound roused the Princess enough to avoid a collision.

"I *am* badly off, aren't I?" At the door to her chambers now, Amalia pushed them open with her shoulder, the effort insignificant even with her level of fatigue. "This nap will be good for me."

Stripping off her clothes and laying them at the foot of her bed, Amalia slid beneath the silk sheets, the fabric sliding smoothly over her skin, wrapping her in a cool embrace that shifted to warmth as they absorbed her body's heat. Her head hit the pillow, and her muscles relaxed; she felt the sleepiness creeping up, ready to bring her into dream.

But then she felt something else. The ever-present connection, ready and waiting for her.

...Glorianna?

Yes, Amalia? The Princess could hear the sound of surf, striking the rocks Glorianna rested on. **You beckoned?**

Can we...? Even after so many weeks, so many trips side-by-side, Amalia still felt ashamed, guilty at this pleasure. *...Please?*

As you will. The two minds joined, and the sensation of sheets and pillows vanished as if travelling down a long tunnel. *I've kept my eyes closed so I don't shock you. It's still full daylight, after all.*

The warmth of the sun played out on Amalia's back; she could feel the small spots, individual sunbeams. *But I want to see!* She couldn't keep the urgency out of her thoughts, and didn't try; the Link ensured that the two's minds held no secrets from one another. *Please? Let me see.*

Of course I will. Slowly, eyelids peeled back, revealing the morning sunlight fracturing into rainbows, spreading all around on the walls of Glorianna's cave. Crystals fragmented the incoming light into reds and yellows and greens, sending the colors in ribbons into the pool of water below and on the rocks around them. Once the light reached them, Amalia realized exactly why Glorianna had been trying to protect her; the intensity and sudden cavalcade of color almost overwhelmed the human's mind.

Is this better? The dragon stretched, standing and pushing her hindquarters backward while extending her wings; Amalia could feel the tension in each muscle and sinew, and she reveled in the sensations. *What do you want to see?*

My people. The answer came instantly. *If I am to be Queen, I must be able to see my people - how they live, how they love. What they do and how they feel.*

Much easier to rule dragonkind, my sister. Glorianna strode outward onto the small plateau outside her cave, with rivulets pooling into large puddles at her feet, water splashing as her claws cut through them. **I know what all of my subjects need and want. Always.**

I can hear them too. Beneath the Link, like an undercurrent, came the rising mass of whispers and murmurs that signaled the group-mind of dragonkind. *It probably would be easier if humans were like that, but I don't know if we could handle it.*

A common refrain, the flaws of people. Glorianna reached her jump-off point and stretched her wings out again; Amalia felt her heart hitch up into her throat in anticipation before the dragon threw herself over the edge, wind hurtling past her ears, her horns, and her talons as she pulled herself up and away from the water. In almost no time, the Aetherian coast came into view, a strip of sandy beach with rolling trees nearby. The ground tumbled beneath her, rolling like a boulder down a hill. **Where are we going?**

I don't know. Amalia settled in her sister's mind, allowing the sensation of vision to flood her own brain. *Why don't you surprise me?*

CHAPTER THREE

As the hours stretched on, the castle overflowed with people – visitors, guests, and guards wandered between the rooms and outbuildings, each preparing for the upcoming coronation.

Peasants and gentlefolk alike bowed and curtsied as she passed by, skirts brushing the floor and leather creaking. They gave the High Princess a wide berth as she stepped through the hallways, but didn't stop their conversations. She caught whispered mentions of excitement, nervousness. A guard ushered a crowd of curious onlookers out of the bedroom of one of the royal guests, and a tray of sweet breads and pastries passed within a foot of her, making her mouth water with its enticing aroma.

The buzz of excitement caught Amalia as well, sending her pulse upward and butterflies spiraling in her stomach despite the fatigue in her bones. *Time's running through the hourglass.* She turned a corner, putting her hand out just in time to catch a swinging door before it struck her. Her thoughts swam in her head, peeking their heads out like fish in a bowl. *I don't get to pretend to just be a Princess anymore. I have to be Queen.*

She swallowed, the lump in her throat tight and painful.

Another turn took Amalia deeper into the building; fewer wanderers crossed her path here, and the echoes of milling celebration faded behind her, giving way to cool stone and the soft padding of her shoes. She tried to focus on her upcoming meeting with Destrick, lips stretching in a smile as she anticipated the battle.

One last dance before everyone's watching my every move. The thought sent a frission down her spine, a tingling that spread through her core. *I just hope that—*

"Princess? May I speak to you a moment?"

Amalia sighed, irritation flaring, then turned, keeping her face as composed as possible. "Yes?"

The man before her spoke hurriedly, his words fumbling over one another. "Yes, um…your Majesty…"

Don't interrupt. Just let him get it out.

"My…my name is Donnen. Donnen Cooper. I'm…I'm terribly sorry to be interrupting your day, with your coronation coming up and all, but…" His nails grazed the back of his neck, and the wind brought the faint scent of dirt and sweat with it – the smell of a working man. "But back during…during the last Dragon Festival, y'met my wife and son. Thomas?"

The High Princess dipped her head, trying to remember, jaw locking to hold back another yawn. *That was when I told Father about Glorianna.* Her brow wrinkled. *Was there a…at the gates. Yes.*

Then she forced herself to give the man a smile. "Of course. He was a sweet boy. He wondered about my scars."

The relief rolling off the farmer was palpable. "Exactly, your Majesty. That's right. Well, my son, he…he wanted me to ask you something."

"Oh?" *Why is he so agitated? Is the request really that horrible?* "What would that be, then?"

"He wants…he wants to be up in the front when you get crowned. Wants to see it for himself." Then another rush of words. "I told him that only the royalty s'posed to be up there, but he wouldn't listen, insisted that I come and ask you myself. Said that it would be the only birthday present that he really wanted, if I could just come up here and tell you what he'd said." Folding fabric, crumpling over and over, reached Amalia's ears. "So I did, and now I'll just go back and let him know that we can't do that, that it wouldn't be right anyway."

"Hold on." Marchen sat down next to her, pressing his muzzle into her leg, and Amalia shook her head, laughing inside. "Not you, silly dog. Him." Ignoring the hound's questioning whimper, the Princess faced the peasant again. "Tell Thomas that I would be more than pleased if he would attend my coronation. As my guest of honor."

The man's gasp forced another smile from her. "Your Majesty, I can't…that's not necessary…I mean…"

"Please." She took a step toward him and reached out, the thin silk covering her forefinger pressing against his lips. "I won't take no for an answer. I expect that the three of you – more, if Thomas has any siblings – to be seated in the first row, to my right as I walk toward the plaza." Then she backed up, folding her arms and raising her brow. "If you aren't, I will be most displeased."

"Of…of course, your Majesty!" The man's feet scraped the ground as he knelt, pressing his forehead to the floor in full genuflection. "I…We'll be there. You have my word."

"Very well, then." The royal mask dropped over her features. "Will that be all?"

He rose again, but his voice pulled away as he backed toward the nearest passageway. "Yes, yes. Thank you again." He was near tears, his baritone cracking, his lips quivering. "I…I don't know what to say."

"You've already said it." And with that, Amalia turned and continued on her way, stopping only when she was sure she was out of the man's sight. Then she slumped against the wall, putting her hand to her mouth to stifle the laughter.

"I wish I could have seen his face!"

Marchen barked twice as if to answer.

"No one is going to believe him – his wife certainly won't. Think he's making things up to impress his son."

The laughter trailed off, bit by bit, as another thought crossed her consciousness. *I could* see *his face, couldn't I? It wouldn't be so hard, if—* .

"And he'll be that little boy's hero for years, I would think."

Amalia jumped at the intrusive voice, the guilt of her thoughts making it feel as if he had caught her in an indiscretion. "Cannot even find a place to hide after doing a good deed." Then she brought her head up. "And how can I help you, Greagor?"

The huntsman laughed, his warm, rich voice filling the chamber, seeming to raise the air temperature a degree or two. "Nothing you need do for me today, Majesty. This week belongs to *you*." He laughed again. "But I thought that I would compliment you on the way you handled that. Masterful."

"In what way?" Amalia almost snapped the words, irritable and tired; to avoid saying something further, she stepped past him, hearing his boots clomp against the floor as he fell into step just behind and to the side. "All I did was grant a simple request from a young boy who was kind to me once. Nothing that anyone else wouldn't have done."

"But you aren't just anyone else, Amalia. And you know it." The man's disregard for formality did not go unnoticed, but, unlike with many others, it didn't bother her. "You're about to be crowned High Queen of the entire realm, and you just let a family of peasants into the coronation. As honored guests, no less."

"What of it?" Amalia's humor began to worsen; Greagor's words weighed on her, judging her, making her doubt herself. "Do you think I should have done differently? I care not. Thomas is a good child, and I repay kindnesses when I can."

The huntsman slid past her to a nearby window, and the change in breeze told Amalia that he had stepped in front of it, his face blocking the portal. "Good words. I hope you can keep to them as you grow into your rulership."

"I have no intention of going back on them." The hallway grew close with the lack of airflow; instead of the smells from outside, Amalia became conscious of a faint mildew creeping in from the tapestries on the walls, a sour odor that made her want to curl up her nose. "The trust of the people is important to any ruler. Sacrificing that trust for short-term gain is folly."

"Well, I'm the last person that you need to be defending your choices of governance to, given that I'm not technically one of your subjects. I could always just go back home if you decide to dabble in tyranny." He pushed himself away from the window, and the breeze, weak though it was, began to clear the corridor once again. The increased pitch and volume of his words told her that he had turned back to face her. "So when will we be having our next training session?"

Amalia shook her head, grimacing. "I cannot say. I expect that the new requirements of office will demand much of my attention, unfortunately." She knelt down and scratched under Marchen's collar, causing the dog's leg to twitch. "Perhaps once things are settled, we'll be able to figure out enough time."

"…Of course, your Majesty." The change of tone was immediate and the change in the conversation's temperature palpable, causing Amalia to flinch mentally. "Please let me know when your schedule can accommodate your lessons. Your enemies will be more than content to wait until you give the word. I'm sure there's plenty of time to prepare."

The Princess didn't trust herself to respond; instead, she stood, nodded to the huntsman, then turned on her heel and hurried down the hallway as quickly as she could without running. Marchen jogged beside her, his nails clicking and the pads of his feet thumping against the ground.

What makes him think his priorities are more important than mine? She shook her head, kept moving, her muscles tense, her jaw pressing her teeth against one another. Every step seemed to slam into the stone floor, louder than usual. *He's a huntsman, skilled or not. He shouldn't be talking to me that way.*

"Is something bothering you, Highness?" Her lady-in-waiting, Elsa, stopped before passing her in the hallway. "You seem distressed. Perhaps you need rest."

"Mind your—" *Stop. It's not her fault.* "Nothing you need worry about, thank you." Amalia fought to keep her voice stable. "What are you about?"

The other woman shifted in place, and the aroma of rose water struck Amalia's senses. "Just finished making sure that your garments are ready for the coronation, and the festivities thereafter. Should I—?"

"Thank you, Elsa. That's...that's wonderful." Feeling her stoic veneer shaking, on the verge of shattering, she waved her left hand back the way she had come.

"Why...why don't you go see if Gorman has anything else for you?"

Then, without waiting for an answer, the Princess pressed on, her pace quickening with every step until she reached her destination. Her palms landed on the door to her chambers, deep in the center of the castle. Here, the hubbub on the perimeter was blocked by several layers of stone walls, allowing Amalia to lean against her door and, for a few moments, rest in near-total silence.

"Gods give me courage and wisdom." She relaxed against the wooden panels of her door, one hand sliding the bolt shut, and let the tension run out of her muscles. "I don't know if I can do this."

You don't have much of a choice, do you?

Amalia sighed, part of her mind thrilled by the mental contact and another part reluctant to acknowledge it.

What do you want? We just visited with one another.

The ripple of a laugh tickled Amalia's spine. ***I wanted to extend my congratulations to my dear sister. And to make sure that all is well in your waking world as well as in your dreaming one.*** The humor disappeared, leaving only a serious mental impulse. ***Transitions of power can be dangerous, especially for humans. Has anything happened? Has anyone made threats, or tried to act on them?***

Amalia broke her limbs from their stasis, her fingers undoing the ties of her dress and slipping the clothing off, folding it into small, neat piles to be laundered later. *Nothing like that. Everyone has been very kind, mourning Father but professing that they hope and wish the best for me and for our country.* She paused, her hands hesitating. *Why?*

Because you mourn for more than your father. You fear, and I worried that it was due to some outside cause. Amalia allowed her thoughts to drift, the perception of her room fuzzing out, replacing itself bit-by-bit with those from the dragon's mind: the stone floor turned to rolling grass, her skin tingled as she felt distant sunlight warming it, and the wind picked up, filling the air with the scent of honeysuckle.

Honeysuckle? Terror rose up in her heart. *Are you…at the Apina? Just down the hill?*

Perhaps. The images forming in Amalia's mind confirmed it – she could hear the river waters, see the silhouette of the castle just past the crest of the hill. **Don't worry about me. No one is here to see me, and even if they came, they wouldn't know where to look.**

Foolish and reckless. Amalia strode to the window, leaning her head out in the direction she knew Glorianna to be.

Maybe. Maybe I don't forget the stealth I use simply because you aren't Linked with me. Or maybe not. But I wanted to speak to you without my own subjects burdening me with their concerns and well-wishes.

The Princess shook her head. *Get you gone. I don't want some overzealous farmer or fisherman getting himself killed because he thought that he'd bring your head to the palace.*

How kind of you to think about that when you can't join me. Glorianna laughed again, and Amalia felt the connection stretch and attenuate, the sensory input fading out. ***Your concern for your family touches my heart.***

Don't say that. Amalia's fist tightened, and she felt the muscles in her neck and stomach follow suit. *I worry about you all the time, not just when we're together. It's just...* She sighed. *I still haven't figured out how to explain it to you.*

No you haven't. Another pause. ***I look forward to riding the wind with you again, sister. Tonight. Or whenever you choose.*** The last of the connection disappeared, leaving Amalia wholly within her own room again, her ears, nose, and the rest reeling as they struggled to adjust. She put a hand on the windowsill to support herself against the sudden wave of vertigo.

Marchen leapt up, his face brushing her hand and his paws landing on her upper thigh. She winced at the claws touching her skin, but then smiled at her dog.

"I hate that part, you know. The separation." She brought her other hand up to her breast, fist closed. "It leaves this empty feeling in my chest, in my heart, every time. Like something's been torn out of me."

Marchen whimpered, and Amalia went down on her knees to gather him up into her arms and lap. "Not everything, silly dog. You're still here. It's…I don't know." She got back up and moved to her armoire, opening one of the chests and inhaling the deep scent of lavender and clove. "It's like saying goodbye to an old friend that you never expect to meet again."

Another whimper, and the dog padded toward her another few steps. She turned her face his way a moment, then back to the clothes, her hands sorting through them to find her training gear. She stopped once she pulled them out, taking a deep breath; fatigue swam in her ears, threatening to unbalance her. "It seems ridiculous. She killed my Da. I should hate her. I *am* angry with her, but…"

Amalia slipped on her jerkin and breeches, strapped on her leather bracers. "You know what'll make me feel better?"

A questioning bark.

"Beating the tar out of Lord Destrick." She grinned and reached her left hand out, gripping the hilt of her sword, hefting its weight as she got to her feet. "I think that will put everything right."

~~~

"All right, your Majesty." Destrick's voice rang out from fifty feet away, and Amalia could imagine him pacing the line of the dueling circle, carved into the stone of the floor. She knew from experience that the practice dummies and spare weapons had been stacked to one side of the large room, out of the way of the combatants. "Are you sure you're ready?"

"Are *you*?" Amalia couldn't help but smile, holding her sword up, slanted over her head with the hilt high. The thrill of battle ran through her veins, a euphoria that seemed to slow time down and bring everything else into focus, battling back her weariness, her nervousness, her fatigue. "Because I hear a hesitation in your step. You haven't even lifted your sword yet."

"True." The air whistled as Destrick's blade swept upward. "I wanted to see where your feet were before I took up my own position. You've set them apart rather farther than I'm used to. Is there a reason for that?"
~~~

Amalia focused on her stance, shifting her feet without lifting them from the ground. "I…I'm not sure. I think it's to set me lower to the ground." Next she took stock of where her limbs lay, the set of her knees, the angle of her hips and thighs. Then she nodded. "Yes. I feel more stable here, like I have more power from this position."

"I can see that." He paced a little more, changing his position relative to her, and Amalia could feel his eyes on her limbs. Their last interaction, forgiven though it might have been, was not forgotten, and remembering that day, the way he had touched her, the way he must have been looking at her, warmed her to the core, threatening to distract her from the battle at hand.

Where is he? Her mind refocused, combing through her sense memory in a desperate attempt to locate Destrick, only relaxing once she realized that he hadn't gone anywhere. *What's the matter with me? Why am I so…*

"Amalia? Are you all right?" She realized that her head had been dipping, and brought it back up to face her opponent. "You're sweating. You know, we don't have to do this, if you're nervous. Maybe about tomorrow. It's all right if you want to cancel, and call it a day."

Despite the kindness of his words, Amalia could sense a hint of mockery, of laughter, behind them, and she compressed her lips together. "Thank you, Sir, but I expect that you will be the one begging off today." She firmed her stance. "Perhaps I will be kind, and leave you with enough dignity that you can still face your family come morning."

"That would, indeed, be kind." His feet stopped moving, and Amalia envisioned his stance, beginning at the head, where his voice emanated from, and sketching in the locations of his arms and legs, his feet and blade. He stood taller than she, with a longer reach, but his blade was lighter. "Begin."

The two began the slow, circling dance of combatants appraising one another. Without vision, Amalia relied on her hearing and her understanding of swordsmanship fundamentals to guide her. She tracked the length of each step, the timing of each footfall, and listened for the shift and creak of leather that would herald a pivot or a charge. Sweat tickled the back of her neck, and she spared it a momentary thought, a split-second of distraction.

That moment, Destrick lunged.

Gods damn it! Amalia caught the sound of his last footstep just in time, rolling to the side to avoid the strike. Destrick's blade whistled less than a foot to her left, close enough that she felt the wind of its passing on her outer thigh. She came up from her tumble at once, swinging her sword in a wide strike, a maneuver designed to push him back rather than do any damage.

It worked; his feet skidded on the stone, the movement setting him two or three paces back as she got back into her stance.

Was it two *or* three? Amalia struggled to be sure. *Why is this so difficult?*

"You're wavering." He wasn't mocking her now; his tone was serious, the instructor concerned for his student. "You don't have the confidence you used to. Your back leg is weak and your head is pivoting from side to side, like you aren't sure where I am."

Even through the frustration of the moment, Amalia let a small smile lift the right corner of her mouth. *He knows me so well.* The thought warmed her again, but she shook it off. *No. Focus. Concentrate.*

She tightened the muscles in her legs, then sprang out after him. Her first swing collided with his blade, sending tremors up her arms and the guard-Commander sprawling, stumbling as he tried to get his feet under him. Amalia bared her teeth and brought the sword back, gripping the hilt with both hands and slamming down, bracing herself for the impact with his weapon.

He wasn't there.

The attack overbalanced Amalia, leaving her open for Destrick's strike. Before she could track his movement, pull back or reposition, she felt his steel on the back of her neck, the sharp blade resting on her skin.

She froze. Her heart pounded, partly from the exertion...but not entirely. Something else sent her nerves quivering, made it hard for her to keep track of her limbs, her position. The room faded out of her perspective, wavering and twisting, and her mind could only latch on to one thing at a time.

Amalia fell to her knees, putting her hands out just in time to keep from slamming into the stone. The impact scuffed her hands, opening small wounds in her palms that left blood on the floor. She brought her knees under her to help hold herself up, taking the weight off her hands and moving into a sitting position.

What's happening to me? The world pulsed again, sounds distorting, some fading and others growing sharper. It felt like her mind had been tossed adrift on a raft, and she was clinging to every sound, every smell, like the last bit of flotsam in a storm. *I can't concentrate.*

"This isn't right." Destrick's sword clanged to the ground, and he knelt beside the Princess. His calloused hands grasped her shoulders as he came around to her front, facing her. He prodded her cheeks and forehead, coming in close.

She barely felt any of it.

"Amalia? Are you hurt?" Destrick's voice doubled, trebled; the fighting space became an echo chamber, each copy of the words coming just a split-second before the next. "I didn't think I'd hit you."

"…You didn't." Amalia tasted each word, her lips moving before and after the sounds left them. "I'm not harmed. But…but I don't feel right."

She felt Marchen press against her before she heard him move. Everything seemed delayed…except the things that were accelerated. The distortion kept her from pinpointing anything; her brain felt overloaded, a cup running over. She straightened her legs, standing upright, and put a hand to her head to combat the wave of dizziness and nausea that threatened to knock her down again. Her mind reached out toward her sister, almost instinctively, but her thoughts couldn't find their way.

Destrick slipped his arm under her to support her weight before she fell. "Amalia! Hold on." Grunting with the effort, he led her to one side of the room, away from the center of the circle.

Is it toward the benches, or the weapon racks? The thoughts nagged at her; for the first time in years, she had no idea which direction she was headed. *Are we out of the ring yet? I don't know how far we are.*

"Marchen? Come." Her words had no power, and getting them out of her mouth took effort. In the back of her mind, Amalia realized that this was wrong, that she needed help…but that's all it remained, a thought in the hollow of her mental landscape.

The dog jumped at her, almost knocking Destrick down, making the knight yell "Back!"

That roused some feeling in Amalia, cut through the growing fog that divided her perceptions. She reached out, stretching her fingers until they found Destrick's hair. For a moment, she realized *I forgot what color it is*, but the thought passed when she yanked on it, eliciting a harsh cry.

"What are you doing?"

"Don't be mean to my dog." She let go. Her fingers tingled, and she could still feel the strands between them. "He wasn't trying to hurt you."

"Right." Destrick knelt, laying the Princess on a hard wooden bench. "Stay here, please. I'll summon Gorman and we'll figure out what to do."

"Have I been poisoned again?" That was the only explanation she could manage, and it brought with it a vague sense of fear. "Is someone trying to kill me?"

"I don't know." His voice faded, wavering in and out. "But we're going to find out."

Don't leave me. Amalia moved her lips, but she wasn't sure if any sound came out. She wanted to move, but the environment felt endless, a vast sea of blackness that held no end. Even the warmth of her hound felt hollow, far away, a tiny flame in the nothingness. She tried to reach out for Destrick, to signal for him to stay.

Don't leave me.

CHAPTER FOUR

Amalia spun through the light, and it encompassed her whole being. Everything she was, everything she had ever been, and everything she felt she could ever be was held within this light. She stared into the radiance, and felt its power. The power thrilled her, enflamed her.

Frightened her.

The light cascaded in a rainbow of golden colors. Amalia had never seen colors with her own eyes, yet she remembered them from her psychic rendezvous with her sister – reds and blues and greens that spoke to her soul, warming her from within. They wrapped around her, and she felt safe, warm.

Then they burned.

The ropes of color caught fire, each their own hue, searing into her flesh, bonds of pain that she could not escape. Amalia struggled, fighting to free herself, but each movement just pushed the flaming colors deeper and deeper into her flesh. Her muscles shrieked in agony, but the ropes tightened, burning deeper and deeper. Crimson criss-crossed her chest, thin burns cutting through the breast and stomach alike. Blood coursed down from the wounds, and she cried out, begging for help, begging for forgiveness…whatever it would take to end this, to make everything the way it was, the way it had been.

The burning hues reached her bones, scorching her spine, her arms, her legs. Amalia felt tendrils of fire creeping between her ribs, seeking her lungs, her heart. The burning came from inside, tearing her apart, splitting her into thousands of pieces. *I'm still screaming*, she realized, but her throat burned just like the rest of her, and she didn't know how to stop it.

Amalia fell apart, separated from herself, but each piece's agony was still her own. She could no longer scream or cry, but the blood falling from her body pattered onto the unseen ground as darkness closed over her, and she knew that the world heard her death.

~~~

"Amalia?" The voice was familiar, echoing down a long corridor to the Princess's ears. Each second, the
~~~

speaker drew closer, closer, until he was beside her, kneeling at her head. "Are you awake?"

She winced as she tightened her muscles to move; the hard bench left her back and tailbone sore. She planted her hand on the wood and pivoted, swinging her legs around and planting her feet on the floor. A hand gripped her at the knee.

"Steady. Nice and slow. Any dizziness? Queasiness?" Another set of fingers palpated her ankle, then her right wrist. "Shortness of breath?"

"No." Amalia shook her head. "I did have those things, when I lay down…but they seem to have passed. I'm doing better now."

"Excellent." The man's voice maintained its professional quality, keeping an even tone as he pressed on certain points of her body. "Open your mouth, please."

Amalia did so, extending her tongue to allow the man access. After a few moments, where she could feel his posture shift as he changed his angle of observation, he grunted. "It'd be easier if I could check your pupils and the color of the whites of your eyes, but it'll have to do."

Amalia sighed. "Many things would be easier if that were an option, I think." She ran her right hand through her hair and took a moment to appraise the situation. There were three people in the room, besides herself and the medicus. Marchen sat at the end of the bench, panting, his head turned toward her, and the whole room was much cooler than she expected it to be.

"What's the last thing you remember, Princess?" The medicus gripped her wrist with two fingers and began tapping the bench with his other hand, in time with her heartbeat.

"Ummm…" She sought the answer in her memories, digging through the jumbled mess of fever-dream that she vaguely recalled to the real world. "I…I came down here to spar with Destrick. We fought for a little while, but…" She shook her head again, massaging her temples with her hand. "Everything's clouded. I can't remember clearly."

"That's not surprising." He continued with his examination, releasing her wrist and bending the cartilage of her ears in his hands. "You seem to have been in quite a state when we found you."

Amalia rolled her head on her neck, waiting for a twinge or other indication of injury. "Do you know what happened?" The breathing of the people in the room was ragged, spiking Amalia's hearing like a small hammer on a nail. "Was I poisoned? Am I ill?"

"As best I can tell, your Majesty…" The medicus pressed the back of his hand against Amalia's forehead. "You're suffering from a case of stress and fatigue. How has your sleep been lately?"

"Umm…" She fidgeted, her head dipping. "It's…"

"That's what I thought." The medicus stood, turning toward Destrick and Gorman. "She's been overworking herself lately, with the coronation and armed practice. She may be seventeen, but her body and mind are facing stresses that she's never had to deal with before." He began to place metal and glass instruments into a leather bag. "She needs to rest and have someone else deal with matters for a while. Get some sleep. Insomnia is quite common in this sort of situation, and can be just as debilitating as consumption or plague."

But I have been sleeping. It just… Amalia couldn't say the words aloud. *It hasn't been normal sleep.*

Gorman was the first to speak. "But the coronation is tomorrow. She can't just…just not attend!" He started to pace, his bare feet (*he must have been caught off-guard*, Amalia noted) padding on the stone.

Destrick cleared his throat. "But isn't it possible to postpone? In the interests of Amalia's health, I mean." A slight shuffle, and she knew he had turned to look at her. "Her health is more important than ceremony."

"The royals will be there, and the people are expecting their new ruler." Gorman tapped his foot on the ground, and Amalia could almost hear him chewing on his own tongue. "They might see an illness as an indication that the gods are displeased with her."

"Superstitious stupidity." The medicus almost spat the words as he finished packing up. "But my recommendation doesn't change based on the idiocy of the peasantry. She needs rest, or you'll be finding yourself searching for *another* ruler to sit on the throne before she passes twenty summers." The disgust in his voice spilled over the gathering, coating their ears in it. "And then where will you be?"

Everyone was silent for a moment, and Amalia sighed, mustering her energy to stand. *I suppose it's up to me, then.* Taking a deep breath, she pushed up with her legs, the motion drawing everyone's eyes and attention.

"I believe that the physician's concerns have merit. I do need to slow down and monitor myself more. That much is apparent."

"Amalia—"

She raised a hand to forestall Gorman's protest. "But the coronation goes on tomorrow as planned. You are correct in saying that we can't wait or postpone it. I will retire to my chambers for the remainder of the day and do my best to relax." She turned to face the two other men. "If one of you would be so kind as to see that my meal is brought up to me, I would appreciate it greatly."

"That sounds like an excellent idea, Princess." Destrick strode toward her, covering the distance in three steps; the force of his sudden arrival startled Amalia's senses for a moment. "May I escort you to your room? I'd feel more comfortable knowing that you had made it there safely, rather than passing out in the hall on your way."

"Actually, Lord Destrick." Gorman put a hand on his shoulder.. "I think it better if you bring her to the Royal Chambers, rather than the Princess's room." He laughed. "I suppose they're going to be yours tomorrow, anyway, so I don't really need to distinguish anymore." Then, more seriously: "Amalia will be more comfortable, and have better rest there."

"Of course." Then Destrick held out his hand, his fingertips grazing the back of Amalia's glove. "Is that all right with you, Princess?"

No. Amalia wanted to say no. The idea of going into her father's room, of living in the same chambers that he had, searching through his things…it terrified her. She hadn't crossed the threshold in the three months since he'd died

(been murdered)

and she didn't know how she'd handle it.

"Of course." She proffered her arm, and the guard-Commander took it in his own. "Gorman, please do your best to make sure I'm not disturbed by anything except the most important business."

"It shall be as you say, your Majesty." Gorman stepped aside to allow the two of them to go past. "Thank you,

Almetri; your services and advice are always welcome." He paused. "I'd be interested to know how you diagnosed her exhaustion. The symptoms seemed to me like they could have been caused by an imbalance in the ear. I've seen that before, amongst some of our soldiers after their training, and it was most onerous to treat."

"No troubles." Amalia and Destrick stepped between the two older gentlemen, who continued their discussion. "Vertigo can have several causes. The apparent one here is a lack of sanguine humor."

"Blood?" Their voices faded as the two younger people strode from the arena, toward the door. "How did…"

The door closed behind them. Amalia allowed some of the steel to leave her spine, relaxing again now that fewer people were present. She replayed the medicus's advice in her mind, taking a deep breath, then another, as she took stock of herself.

"He can't help the chance to learn something new." Destrick's voice interrupted her introspection, almost startling her; the words carried a little too far, echoed a bit too loudly.

The Princess nodded, allowing a fond smile to appear. "It doesn't even matter what's going on; he does that every time."

"I know." Destrick shook his head. "I remember, years ago, when I had gotten injured by something that the King was working on, a new type of catapult. One of the counterweights came down on my foot and I had to have it set."

"That was horrible!" She rocked back and forth a little, moving Destrick along with her. "You screamed so loud that I heard it in the orchard. Scared me half to death; I went running to Father, trying to figure out what was going on."

Destrick patted her hand. "While the medicus was seeing me, Gorman kept asking me about the weapon. How it was built, how much weight had fallen on me, all sorts of things. I didn't want to be rude to him, but I couldn't really concentrate on the questions he was asking he had to repeat himself several times."

"That's exactly like him." Amalia laughed as well. They turned left, and her senses sharpened, the map of the castle springing to her mind. "He can't help himself."

The next few minutes passed in silence, the two walking side-by-side, passing by the few servants and guards that populated this area of the castle. Gusts of wind blew through the windows, cool on her face.

"What time is it?"

"9th bell, or near enough."

She turned her face to him, her brows creasing. "I was asleep that long?"

"Indeed." She heard his tongue pass over his lips. "Gorman was quite beside himself. First he thought I had injured you somehow; once I convinced him otherwise, he was terrified that another attempt had been made on your life."

"Thank the gods that isn't the case." She smiled again, but this one a little more melancholy. "I have enough to worry about without madmen trying to kill me."

"I imagine so." Another pause; the two crossed a large, carpeted hallway, the separation between the castle and the private chambers of the royal family. Destrick nodded then reached forward and swung the heavy wooden door open.

Amalia's heart caught in her throat, and her foot stopped before crossing the threshold. Why was this so difficult? She had come into this room countless times as her father's daughter, knew it almost as well as she knew her own. She could imagine the furnishings, the wood grains, could hear the crackle of the fire in the hearth, stoked by the servants, as High King Marcus read yet another tale of heroism and romance to his breathless girl, her head nodding with every sentence, fingers clutching at his clothes as the heroes fell into danger.

The memories came, faster and faster, one upon the other as if someone were pouring them into her mind: running her hand along the walls in the middle of the night after waking from another nightmare, blinding fire and pain; hiding inside one of the footlockers as Gorman sought her attendance at another lesson; the first barks of the hound she loved so dearly, startling her with their earnestness and energy.

But those moments now lived only in her memory. Never again would she hear her father's voice; never again would she be able to ask his advice or seek his council.

And it's her fault.

Amalia felt the grief and rage she had been fighting, putting aside, invading her veins and infiltrating her heart. Her muscles tensed, her hands clenched, and her teeth ground together. *How could you trust her again so easily, after what she did to you?* Her mind trembled, warring with itself. *Sharing minds? Flying with her? She-*

"Amalia?" A hand landed on her shoulder. "What—"

With a single twist and grab, Amalia hurled Destrick's body into the royal chambers. He flew through the air, landing with the crash of splintered wood and shattered glass.

But what brought Amalia out of her anger-filled fugue was the cry as he flew away, the sound fading with distance.

"Wait!" Amalia fumbled with her feet, chasing after him with her hands outstretched. Marchen jogged ahead, barking several times as he bounded over the threshold. "Destrick!"

"Gods be *damned!*" His voice was pained, but whole. "What in Nome's name was that?"

Amalia reached him, her hands searching, landing on splinters of wood, leather armor, and dust before finding his face. "Are you all right? I thought…"

He grabbed her questing hand before it got to his eyes. "You hurled me across the room, Amalia." He coughed, groaning as he sat upright, pieces of detritus and debris falling off of him and onto the floor. "That shouldn't be possible. How did…" Destrick trailed off. "What gave you such strength?"

"I…" Fear burned through Amalia's veins, her heart - she felt the trembling beginning in her lips. *What a fool I am! Losing control like that! What if he figures it out? No one can know.*

Destrick brought himself to his feet; in his movements, Amalia could hear the creaking of leathers and the pattering of the last few shards of wood falling on the ground, then the sound of his tongue sliding over his lips before he spoke. "Princess, something has happened to you. I think you know what it is, but you're afraid to say it."

Amalia retreated, her arms coming up and hugging herself, a defensive posture; her mind raced, and her senses reeled from the overload of information. "Destrick, I…" She couldn't form the words, couldn't think of anything to say that wouldn't make it worse.

"Gorman should know. Have you spoken to him?" Again he approached closer, his proximity pressing in on Amalia's nerves. "Perhaps exposure to the dragon that…"

"Shut your mouth!" She advanced on him in one smooth motion, her face contorting in rage. "You have no idea what you speak of! Be silent rather than accusing others of heresy and black magic!"

Destrick rocked back, almost falling into a squatting position. "I didn't—"

"You do things and say things as if you know everything, as if you're completely in control, but you're not!" Amalia's throat began to burn, rubbed raw by her screeching, but her anger wouldn't let her stop. It was as if a dam had exploded, flooding her blood with fury that could only be expelled through her words. "You condescend, talk down to me as if I'm just some pet, some woeful creature that you need to take care of."

"That's not—"

"No! I hear it, in your voice, in the care you take with every step, every motion. You tiptoe around me. It is as if you think that, because I cannot see, I am blind to what you do, what you are." Her voice cracked, and her chest began to hitch in phantom tears. "I know what feelings you profess, Destrick. Have you forgotten? You admitted as much to me, that day."

"I have not forgotten." He stood up, coming back to his feet with only a slight groan. "I meant it entirely. And still do." A moment's hesitation. "But that doesn't change the fact that—"

Energy surged through Amalia's arm, and she spun around, planting her fist in the wall, feeling the stone give under her strength until her hand lay buried within it. "No! You don't!"

Then the strength left her, left her feeling desolate, empty. She slumped down the wall, burying her face in her arms, folding her legs up underneath her. "Just go, Destrick. Go."

The knight hesitated, and Amalia knew that he was looking at the new hole in the granite. "But—"

"Go, now. We can talk about this later." She brought her head up, the muscles in her face twitching, her voice clotted. "Leave me. Please."

"…As you wish, your Majesty." His leathers creaked as he bowed, backing toward the door without changing his facing. "I will see you tomorrow, for the coronation. I hope you sleep well."

The door closed behind him, the metal latch sliding into place. High Princess Amalia Therald held herself together for another six seconds, then broke down crying.

CHAPTER FIVE

"What is the matter with her?"

Destrick paced up and down the Royal Councilor's chambers, the luxurious furnishings and tapestries lost on his preoccupied mind. He scarcely managed to keep himself from knocking over Gorman's vases, filled with flowers every color of the rainbow, or the stacks of books and scrolls that filled in every available space.

"Should I allow you to continue? Or do you actually want me to answer the question this time?" The older man sipped his beer, holding the mug between his hands to warm it. "Because I'm quite enjoying watching you. It's rather soothing, like a metronome."

The knight-Commander stopped, turning toward Gorman, his cheeks flushed, jawline set. "The Princess just threw me out of her room, screamed at me, threw me into her bureau, and all you have are jokes?"

"Young man, I find that taking things too entirely seriously leads to a shorter life and much less happiness." He opened one wrinkled hand, stretched his fingers. "But, rest assured, if I were concerned that this was, in some way, detrimental to Amalia or Aetheria, I would be taking action already."

"I see." Destrick ran his hand through his hair, pulling his bangs back from his forehead and exhaling through his nose. "So you're saying that I'm exaggerating?"

"Perhaps, but I wouldn't expect that of you. You aren't that creative." Destrick's eyes widened, and Gorman chuckled. "What I mean, Destrick, is that I've never known you to lie to me. Else, I doubt you'd have been made Commander."

"Funny." Destrick sighed, then sat down facing the councilor. "It's just...one moment, I think that I understand her. She speaks like we're friends, and I see hope...and the next, something sends her into a fit. She hurls things – hurls me – or puts her fist in a wall. A *stone wall,* Gorman. It was madness." He shook his head, both palms on his eyes, massaging the tension from around his forehead.

"I'll say it again, Guard-Commander. That simply isn't possible. You didn't see what happened correctly." He shook his head. "No doubt flustered by being toppled by the young lady."

"Gorman. I saw what happened. I was there." Destrick exhaled through his nose, flaring his nostrils. "How is she doing these things? No one should be that strong. It reminds me of stories about…"

"Don't even say it, Destrick." Gorman's words left no room for argument. "Amalia is not dragon-tainted. They killed her father."

"I know. It sounds stupid. But…I don't know what else it could be." He turned his eyes to the councilor, hoping for some other explanation. "I don't know what to do."

Gorman took another drink, then put the mug down on the table beside him. He reached out, taking Destrick's hands in his own, and held the man's eye when he looked up. "I think you should set aside the strength for a moment. There are a thousand other possible explanations for that, and without having been there, I can't begin to postulate on which is correct. Instead, you need to think about why you're garnering these reactions from her."

Destrick narrowed his eyes. "I don't understand."

"And that's exactly the frustration that she's suffering from." Gorman released him, leaning back on his couch and brushing the hair from his eyes. "Consider what she's going through."

"I know. I was there when the physician examined her." Traces of irritation began to show around Destrick's eyes. "What does that have to do with anything?"

"I'm not talking about her exhaustion, although that may, certainly, have played a role." He brought up a hand and started ticking off points. "Tomorrow, she takes her father's place as High Monarch. At seventeen years old. She isn't ready, and, worse, she's intelligent enough to realize it. Still, she's terrified of letting anyone find out, so she puts on a front, a façade of confidence that she hopes will be convincing enough to let her get her bearings."

He shifted in his seat, his voice transmuting into the teacher's, the lecturer's. "Second, she isn't just taking her father's place in the kingdom. He's gone. And, while we all feel his loss, he was more than High King to Amalia, more than a friend or a mentor. He was her father, and the only parent she had left." The jovial attitude Gorman had worn since Destrick's arrival faded, and his gaze floated down, towards the floor. "And he was killed by the same thing that killed her mother."

"The dragon." Destrick breathed the words, remembering the scene – the sword fight between the Princess and King, the vicious attack by the small dragonling that caught him off guard, his screams as the creature tore him apart, bloody ribbons of flesh still on its claws. "I remember. And it was just after the two of them had fought. Maybe that's…"

He glanced toward Gorman again, the question on his lips, but the councilor shook his head. "Leave it, Commander. I don't know, and I recommend you not pry. These last few months, it's been difficult enough to keep that story from spreading past the soldiers and nobles that witnessed it."

"But what if it's a sign of something deeper?" All the pieces seemed to fit now, seemed to come together in Destrick's mind. "Perhaps the Princess has…a sickness. A disease of the mental faculties. And it goes along with her strength. A corruption."

Gorman frowned. "I don't think so." Despite his words, Destrick saw a flicker in his eyes. *Doubt?*

"Why?" Destrick stood up, resumed his pacing, almost knocking over a glass vase filled with tulips and daisies. "It all makes sense. The stories…they talk about dragon corruptions. Even if one hasn't sworn to them, sold themselves to them, just being around the beasts can drive one to madness."

A slow nod. "I've read the same books. Legends and stories from before you were born." He licked his lips, then shook his head. "No. Amalia hasn't been exposed to such a thing. I think you're reading too much into this, Destrick."

"But what if I'm not?" His voice grew louder, to the point of almost shouting. "What if we're about to put our kingdom in the hands of someone who isn't only unqualified, as you yourself said, but isn't capable of taming her mind?" He leveled a sharp gaze at Gorman. "If she's in a meeting with the other monarchs, and an off-the-cuff remark leads her to throw the *table* at one of them…"

Gorman stood as well. "Stop. I will not have you slandering Amalia. She is the greatest of us, worthy of following in her mother and father's footsteps."

Destrick folded his arms, shook his head. "She's *human*, Gorman. And that means that she's just as vulnerable, just as weak as any of us. I know that you've built this fantasy of her in your head. Hell, I had, too. She's strong, capable in so many ways." A half-smile crept up on him. "And she's beautiful, in the way she moves and in the passion that fires every action she takes."

Then the smile faltered, replaced by grim determination mixed with sadness. "But she isn't stable. She isn't acting rationally. She lashes out at those around her for the crime of speaking to her. How is this the ruler we need?"

"Even if I were to agree with you…and I *don't*." Gorman rubbed his temples. "Then there wouldn't be anything we could do about it anyway. Not before she took the throne."

"Then you're risking a popular uprising, when she starts making decisions based on whatever insanity is going through her mind." He got very close to Gorman's face. "I'm going to say it again. She *punched through a wall.* Right next to my head. Because I tried to question her, and she took it poorly."

Gorman didn't respond, so Destrick backed up, turned, and left the room, slamming the door behind him. The force of the impact tumbled over the vase, spilling water and flowers all over the floor.

The councilor picked up his feet, letting the liquid flow beneath him, lost in thought. *What if he's right?*

Gorman ran over Amalia's recent behavior, searching for patterns, looking for any indication that there might be an external cause, something that would lead to her being so erratic, so easily angered.

Apart from the stress, he couldn't find one. Frustrated, he breathed out, his mustache and beard fluttering from the force of it. Standing, Gorman grumbled as his feet hit the spilled water and scattered flowers.

"Damn it." He took a few steps, getting out of the puddle, then kicked out his feet to shake some of the water off of them. Then he went to the door, staring down the hall, toward the doorway that separated the royal area of the palace from the rest of it. *It should be easy enough. If he's right, then there will be evidence.*

"Amalia." The word tore at his heart, leaving a hollow ache in his chest. "I pray that he's wrong."

~~~

"Why won't he leave well enough alone?" Amalia choked the words out through sobs. "He always asks, always wants to know more, and digs into things he need not know!" She wrapped her arms around her folded legs, digging her fingernails into her palms. "I wish he…"

Marchen snuggled up to Amalia as her crying slowed. She wrapped one arm around the large dog, bringing him closer, taking comfort in the feel of his warmth and his fur pressed against her.

"Gods, I'm an idiot, Marchen." She shook her head, the muscles in her cheeks twisting her face into a vision of sadness. Now that the moment had passed, she felt completely different, confused rather than angry. "What ailment has befallen me of late? I am unable to control even the most basic outbursts of my temper."

The dog didn't answer, instead wagging his tail and burrowing in closer. Amalia's hand moved in practiced patterns, up to Marchen's head, then down his neck and back, petting him over and over as he calmed, then stilled.
~~~

She smiled as the dog's breathing followed suit, evening out to a rhythmic pattern.

"I wish I could sleep that easily." But that wasn't accurate – sleep hadn't been eluding Amalia. When the physician suggested it, she had wanted to deny the claim, but…

But the truth would have been more unbelievable than the idea. She relaxed against the wall, shifting her body to put pressure on different places. Fatigue rolled over her muscles, bringing with it an involuntary yawn. The cold of the stone was relaxing, soothing the hot blood that had been flowing just a few minutes prior.

Why was I so cruel to him? She shook her head, the memory bringing the echo of sadness and grief, the sorrow at the loss of her father and of how she had pushed Destrick away, back to the forefront of her mind. *He didn't deserve that. He doesn't know. He can't know.*

She settled in, Marchen's breathing a soft, soothing sound, lulling her to sleep. She felt the muscles in her neck relaxing, losing their ability to hold up her head. Her thoughts began to come apart, taffy on a warm day, the remnants dribbling down her consciousness on their way to oblivion.

Just for a few minutes. As she gave herself permission, she began to lose track of her limbs, her body. She felt wrapped in a warm blanket, the wool prickling her skin and trapping her heat within as her spirit, her consciousness, detached from her flesh. She allowed the heat to move from her skin into her core.

~~~

And she opened her eyes.

The luminescence glinted off the cave walls; crystal structures caught, reflected, and magnified the reddish hue so that it illuminated the entirety of the cavern. Water from one of several tide pools bounced the setting sun's light into the opening, mixing a different set of golds and oranges with the ruddy firelight of the dragons.

Below, two dragonlings fought for the remnants of a goat carcass while several of the older youths looked on. Tiny claws sparked on stone, the flashes of shadows thrown on the wall more terrifying than the actual creatures making them. Amalia laughed to herself, the sight warming her heart.

Welcome.

Glorianna's thought shook with amusement and pleasure, and Amalia's viewpoint shifted as the dragon stretched her claws, bending and flexing her spine like a housecat. *I knew that you wouldn't stay away.*
~~~

How could I? The High Princess enjoyed the feel of the moist cave wall under Glorianna's claws. *This is amazing. Wondrous.*

It is. Glorianna took several steps forward, coming out of the cave nook she had chosen for her latest nap, allowing her long neck to crane and examine her surroundings. The other dragons in the brood were waking as well from their afternoon slumber, spreading their wings and taking to the sky to gather food or enjoy the last of the sunlight. ***I'm very glad that you can still appreciate that.***

What do you mean?

Simply that it is obvious – and expected – that you are preoccupied with your* human *kingdom's concerns at the moment. The emphasis that Glorianna placed on the word "human" carried with it undertones of irritation, borderline condescension.

I seem to recall that you once thought a particular human was fascinating. Amalia called up the sense-memories of the day she met the dragon – the conversations, and discussions, the sharing of apples. *Or, at the least, worthy of your attention for a while.*

And if you'll recall as well, that particular human turned out to be more than she seemed. A rolling chuckle reverberated through the Link. ***So perhaps, even though***

I didn't know it at the time, it wasn't the human I found fascinating, but my sister.

Amalia let that go, choosing to focus instead on the wind, the smell of the sea…and, of course, the fading sunlight and brightening dragons. As the light from outside dimmed, their bodies grew more radiant, until the inside of the cave burned with their inner fire.

So beautiful.

I agree. Glorianna turned her head to the top of the cave and roared, the sound bouncing off the walls and reinforcing itself, so that it grew louder and louder before finally fading away.

As the last remnants of the sound vanished, the dragon threw herself from her perch, hurtling toward the floor of the cave and the tidepools that covered it. The ground approached rapidly, and Amalia's heart pounded faster as fear crept around the edges of her mind.

Wings! Please!

Glorianna laughed, then unfurled her wings; her downward momentum halted, and, with a single thrust, she went soaring through the mouth of the cave, coasting above the water until she broke free into the open air. Amalia joined in the laughter, the adrenaline and sheer joy of the sensations pulling it from her, unbidden.

Does it make you sad? The dragon went into a lazy spin, keeping her eyes fixed on the horizon while she rolled over once, twice, thrice, then straightened and pushed up higher into the sky. *That you need help to experience this?*

You've asked me this before, Glorianna.

But you never tell me the truth.

If you believe I'm lying to you, why do you keep asking?

Glorianna blew through her nose, then perched atop one of the many spires that circled the dragon's home. She turned to gaze upon the Queen's Roost, the space reserved for the Matriarch when she rested or wished to speak to her subjects. It lay empty, small pools of rainwater filling the dips worn in the stone by the knees and elbows of mighty Dragon Queens of ages past.

Because I think you believe what you're saying, but I do not. Glorianna paused, mulling over the situation. **I think you're lying to yourself.**

Amalia raised a mental finger. *A strong accusation.* Then she sighed. *Why do we need to argue? I just want to enjoy this.*

Because you're using my eyes, sister. To emphasize the point, Glorianna slammed her eyelids down; at once, everything went dark for Amalia, except for the slight red glow coming from the inside of the lids. **And I want you to be happy.**

Happy? I don't believe that. You killed my father, led my mother to her death – and I had barely made acquaintance with her! Anger boiled between the two parties of the Link.

Then why are you still here? Glorianna blinked, the shutter over her vision moving up, down, up, down. ***If I am truly as terrible as you say, why do you suffer my presence? You could easily blockade your mind, prevent me from speaking to you.*** She took off again, gliding through the air toward the Roost. ***But you don't. Why?***

Amalia didn't want to admit the truth, but as soon as she recognized it within her mind, Glorianna knew it as well.

That's what I thought. The Roost grew as they approached it, covering the distance more quickly than a zephyr on the wing. ***It's addictive for you, isn't it? Being able to see.***

*No. It's...*Amalia shook her head. *Enough. I don't want to talk about this anymore.*

As you wish. Glorianna spun again, thrusting forward to accelerate, coasting along the sea surface. She turned her neck to look downward, her eyes catching their reflection in the ocean. Amalia watched as well, and the sight took her breath away.

What do you wish to see today? She came to rest atop the spire overlooking the Roost, and her field of view panned across the horizon. ***The towers of your palace? Or the castle of King Catlin? Perhaps you'd like to dive through the waters of the sea, or fly until we encounter a pack of wolves and see their cubs?***

You've seen all those things, haven't you? A heaviness settled over Amalia's heart. *A lifetime of wonders, things that I've missed.*

There is always more to see. More to experience. The dragon took a deep breath, savoring the smell of the sea breeze. Her next thought dripped with remorse. ***Amalia, I am sorry that this was taken from you.***

Thank you. Amalia sighed. *But it was not your doing. These decisions were made and their consequences suffered long before we knew one another. I know that you wouldn't have wished this upon me.*

Still, I feel I must say it. Glorianna lowered her head; Amalia could see the cresting surf, dull white against the slate grey of the sea, and make out jumping dolphins leaping through the waves, chirping and squealing as they played. ***Because, despite our differences, the circumstances and the judgments levied upon each of us by the other, I truly wish the best for you.***

Part of Amalia wanted to believe that – and, indeed, she could see a perverse sense of logic behind much of what the young dragon had done – but another part of her was still too wounded to accept it. To that part,

Glorianna's words were platitudes, niceties mouthed to keep her from causing trouble.

Thank you. She turned away from the vision, allowing her sight to go dark again, pulling herself away from the stimuli surrounding the dragon. *But I need to go now.*

Of course. Glorianna's mind speech faded as Amalia's consciousness drifted back into her own body. **I look forward to seeing you again, sister.**

CHAPTER SIX

The palace gates opened wide, admitting a flood of morning sun that washed over Amalia, warmth tingling her skin. Her left hand gripped Marchen's leash, and the dog stayed sitting by her side as the loud cheer erupting from the crowd nearly knocked her over. She held on to her smile, raising her free hand and waving to the gathered audience.

"Let's go. Take me to Gorman."

Marchen hopped up and began to walk. At first, Amalia had to rein him in, keep him from rushing ahead and ruining her stately gait, but he got the message and trotted alongside her. She held her head high, shoulders back, keeping the smile pinned to her lips as she turned her face back and forth, panning the crowd. Beneath the cheers and well-wishes, Amalia made out several gasps as those closest to her saw the exact details of her disfigurement.

She ignored them.

Listen to all those people, Amalia. Glorianna's voice reverberated with pride and happiness. ***They are proud of you, happy for you.***

Yes. The overwhelming tide of approval worked its way into her muscles, easing the tension that resided there. Her forced smile became more natural, and the measured steps flowed more elegantly, more free. *My people. My country.*

A small corner of her heart bemoaned her missing father. She could imagine him, clapping along with the rest of the gathered nobles, taking the crown from his own brow and placing it on hers. The thought, the pseudo-memory, came to life with such vitality that she felt her throat close up.

"Papa! It's the Princess!"

Amalia paused at the last row of the crowd, turning to the voice. Raising one hand toward the center stage, she took two steps, to the row where the visiting dignitaries and nobility sat. Silence claimed the audience, spreading outward in a wave from the people who could see her through the hundreds gathered around them. Just before she reached the row of seats, Marchen stopped, letting her know to follow suit.

"Thomas?" Amalia smiled down, her practiced hearing and sense for heat picking out the locations of the nearest people. An overpowering smell of camphor rose from their clothes, and one of them shifted in his seat, back and forth, as she approached.

That must be him. "It's nice to meet you again."

At first, the boy didn't say anything. Then Amalia heard the muffled *thump* of an elbow against cloth, and he coughed. "Good…good morning, y'Majesty. It's nice to see you, too."

"Thomas!" His mother hissed at him, clopping him across the back of the head. "I told you—"

Amalia raised a hand. "Good lady, please." She smiled again, not letting herself flinch from the wave of intense camphor odor that hit her, riding on the wind from the mother's swat. "It is a common phrase. He meant no offense." Back to the boy. "Did you, Thomas?"

"No, y'Majesty. I didn't." She heard him swallow. "M'mum and da told me that I had to be good or I wouldn't get any supper, y'see. Said I had to mind my manners and be very polite t'ya."

No supper? The smile wavered. *For not knowing how to speak to a Queen? What nonsense is this?* Then an idea occurred to her, and she reached out, laying a hand on Thomas's shoulder. "Why don't you and your family join me for dinner? Today is a special day for me, and I would be honored if you would share it with me."

His parents stood up in their seats, the two of them babbling, their words intermixing such that it was impossible for Amalia to differentiate them, to understand what they were saying.

"Your Majesty—"

"We couldn't—"

"Don't want to be—"

"So many things—"

She held up her hand, and they went quiet. Putting on her best regal expression, she gestured for the two of them to sit, then refocused on the boy. "Would you like that, Thomas?"

Through her touch on his shoulder, she felt him glance at his parents, heard their hair stirring the air, their skin rubbing on their garments as they shook their heads. "That'd be real nice, y'Majesty. But, like my folks were saying, we've got work to do, and…"

"I see." Amalia smiled again, standing fully upright. "Then I wish all of you the best. I hope you enjoy the feast and celebration."

She turned and walked back to the main corridor, part of her attention still on the family behind her. Only Marchen's warning yip kept her from walking too far and crashing into a small orange tree.

Thank the gods for small favors. Feeling the weight of everyone's gaze, she squared her shoulders, nodding. *Gorman signals the buglers.*

From all corners of the plaza, trumpets sounded the call to attention. The sudden burst of sound quieted the last mutterings of conversation in the crowd, focusing everyone on the important matter about to happen. Amalia tried to ignore the weight of their gazes, the prickling feeling on the back of her neck that everyone was watching her, and instead concentrated on the next step.

Count to seven. One…two…three… Amalia felt sweat beading on her forehead, and her stomach knotted around her guts. She took a deep breath, then expelled it, keeping the count going. *Four…five…*

The trumpet sounds ceased, as one, and the players snapped to smart attention. The collective held their breath as Amalia counted off the final two beats in her head. Her heart pounded in her ears, and her tongue darted off to lick the sweat from her upper lip.

Twelve steps forward.

She kept her steps precise, long, her muscle memory working to maintain the pace. Only the occasional mumble broke the silence as she crossed the distance, her nervousness growing with every foot closer. Now she could make out the shifting and breathing of the ceremonial staff. The eleventh and twelfth step took her up a small flight of stairs, and a warm, wrinkled, familiar hand reached out and touched her wrist just as she finished the last.

She stopped, the nerves preventing her from smiling. *Thank you, Gorman.* A nod. *The scepter.*

She reached out with her right hand, and cool metal filled it. The royal scepter felt heavy in her grip, heavier than the gold, silver, bronze, and jewels warranted. Amalia's brow wrinkled as she hefted it, curious.

The Archprelate of Aetheria, representative of all the gods in the universe, stepped forward, sweeping his hands above his head. His heavy robes flapped in the wind, smelling of cinnamon and clove, and his powerful voice reached out of the small space and flowed over the crowd.

"Many question the wisdom of our gods in these times." His strong tones reverberated, resonating in his throat before he projected them outward, and took Amalia by surprise.

I always thought the Archprelate would be an old man, like Gorman, or older. She held her mien steady, but found herself hanging on his words, savoring the flavor of them.

"Aetheria has lost one of its greatest souls, and we mourn for him." He paused, a moment of silence for the deceased, and there was a ripple of skin sliding over skin and cloth over cloth as the crowd bowed their heads and held hands. "We mourn because we knew him, whether as our High King, as our leader, or as our friend. His death came far too soon, and he leaves behind a kingdom desolated by his departure."

Amalia mouthed the reply, which ran through the group in a low murmur: "May his life be a beacon in the darkness, and his soul reside in the Crystal Palace forever."

The Archprelate turned in place, to address the entirety of the encircling crowd. "Nome has taken our King to himself, and we rightfully grieve. But three months have passed, and he now sups with the gods, drinking their wine and beer, feasting on endless delicacies the likes of which we can scarcely imagine." Another pause, but no chorus responded to this one. "Paradise awaits us all when we leave this life and are brought into the loving arms of He Who Never Sleeps. Nome guides us to our eternal reward, watches over us, and protects us as we learn who and what we truly are."

He turned again, his footsteps loud on the wooden platform. Amalia kept her head down, and she added her own portion to the benediction, vocalized under her breath.

"I hope that you and Mother find each other there, somehow. Maybe in death you can understand one another at last."

The Archprelate let loose a laugh, shocking Amalia and, judging by the gasp that rippled through the nobles and assembled peasantry, everyone else as well. She brought her face up toward the chortling holy man, her mind spinning. *What is he doing? What does he think is so funny?*

"You are all wondering why I laugh." The words were broken up by those very sounds, interrupted by chuckling. "I remember something that High King Marcus once told me. He said that, when his time came, he would look down on his kingdom, his daughter, and he would weep his last tear before entering paradise." More shifting of the Archprelate's heavy robes, and he took a step toward Amalia, laying his hands on her shoulders. She bowed her head again, but her brow wrinkled. *Why is he touching me? This is not part of the protocols.*

"And look, all of you!" A gasp, uttered slightly off-time from a thousand different mouths, reached Amalia's ears, followed by several chairs shifting, moving back to free their occupants from incarceration. "Do you see? Marcus's last tear, shed for his family, for his people. He blesses us from Nome's realm, his eyes upon us as he enters the Crystal Palace!"

Loud murmuring and mumbling broke out, and more than a few of the gathered peasants erupted in outcry, praising Nome and the other gods. The Kings and Queens and other nobles managed to keep their reactions more tame and controlled, but Amalia could still hear whispers of discussion between them. For her part, she turned her face to the sky, wishing that she could see what everyone else was marveling at.

Wait! Her head whipped around. *Glorianna! Do you see it?*

Yes. The dragon's voice conveyed a sense of awe. ***Join me.***

Amalia did so, throwing her mind toward her sister's, their consciousnesses linking in an instant of effort. After a brief moment of vertigo, the world sprang into being. The azure sky filled their field of vision, a few white streaks of cotton dividing the vault into large segments.

And cutting through all that, a sword of fire pierced the heavens.

Amalia's throat caught as she watched, her mind unable to grasp the enormity of it. The sky burned like dry grass, crackling and flickering, an enormous arc of flame that coursed from one horizon to the other. She felt her heart drop and her breath freeze in her lungs as she struggled to comprehend what she saw.

Do...do you know what that is?

No. She felt the same fear, the same confusion, in Glorianna. What she saw made no sense; neither of them had any basis for understanding, any background that would help fit this event into the wider schema of the world.

Except for the obvious.

Is it...Is it Nome? Amalia breathed a silent version of her thought, clasping her hands together. *Could it be?*

Impossible. Glorianna shook her head, but kept the spectacle in view. ***Your gods don't exist. We don't accept them.***

Then what is *it?* Amalia pointed up at the streak of flame, which had begun to fade from the sky now, leaving only a thin remnant that guttered and died in seconds. *It has to be something from the gods!*

She felt something close on her upper arm, and the suddenness of the sensation startled her, making her recoil and stumble back two steps. It also broke the Link, throwing her against her will back into an unseeing mind. The sudden descent of darkness brought on a wave of vertigo, and Amalia put out a hand to steady herself.

"Your Majesty?" Everything else was quiet save Gorman's whispered voice. "Are you all right?"

As her senses adjusted to her consciousness's return, Amalia became aware that the benediction had stopped.

Oh, gods. How long have I been standing here like an idiot? She locked her muscles up, back into the proper positions, and Gorman let go of her arm. She gave him a quick nod, then brought her face forward again. She gripped the scepter, then bowed her head toward the Archprelate.

"Amalia Therald." She heard his steps as he approached, felt the air move and the weight of his nearness. "On your shoulders lies the weight of your ancestor's legacy. Francis the Uniter brought this continent together under one banner, and in so doing took responsibility for both the strong and the weak." Someone stepped up behind the Archprelate, and hard metal changed hands. "By the will of Junandar, Ruler of the Gods, it is done. As passed from Fendrin, to Marcus, the crown, and responsibility, of the High Kingdom of Aetheria comes to you. As Junandar rules over his brothers and sisters, you stand above the Kings and Queens of the land, guiding them and protecting them. The gods watch you now, and when you have need of them, they will come."

The metal settled over Amalia's brow, atop her hair, pressing into her scalp and temples, the gold reforged during the three-month mourning period to fit her. Along with the crown, the new Queen could feel the weight the Archprelate spoke of, the authority and power she now had over the lives of everyone in her kingdom – and even farther away. It felt like she was crossing a threshold, taking a step into a new place she had never been, never experienced, only heard vague stories about. Her breath fled her lungs in a ragged stutter as the Archprelate leaned in and kissed her on the forehead.

She'll be easy to control as long as I keep fluffing up her father. A deep feeling of smug contentment washed over Amalia as she saw herself through his eyes, an undeserved crown atop a blinded girl, scars gnarled and twisted where her eyes should be, an abomination before the gods. Then, for a moment, the image shifted to another woman, this one older, dark hair draped over bowed head, submissive. *Bitches like this always listen to their masters, when they're properly trained.*

Then it was over, and he stepped back, raising his arms and his voice. "Your Majesties and Highnesses, ladies and gentlemen, I present to you your High Queen!"

First the nobility and gentry, then the peasants, began to applaud. More and more hands clapped together, and Amalia could just make out the sounds of shuffling and seats moving as they rose to their feet. The applause rose, louder and louder, until the tide of the sound threatened to overwhelm the young Queen.

But her mind wasn't on that.

Did you hear what he was thinking? She threw the thought towards the dragons' isle, towards Glorianna. *The bastard thinks to find me easy to control.*

Who? The religious one? The Archprelate? Glorianna's reply carried none of the righteous anger that Amalia expected; instead, it was laced with confusion and concern. **What did he say? I must have been distracted.**

You didn't hear his thoughts, as I did? Her body moved on its own, up another small set of stairs. Marchen tugged at his leash to guide her. *I thought that everything I heard or smelled, you could as well.*

Amalia's shin bumped into something; reaching out her free right hand, she felt rich, polished wood, curling in ornate whorls and swirls. Her mind drew her back in memory, to the times when she sat on her father's lap and traced her fingers around the very same designs – so often that she had memorized them before she was seven.

The Throne of Aetheria. Despite having sat in the throne before, when her father was away or during certain state functions, it still held a mystique for her. More than the crown or the scepter, the throne felt like the true seat of power, the focal point for all the authority and responsibility of the kingdom. As she ran her hand over the wood grain, she shelved her concerns about the Archprelate.

Amalia? Are you—?

Not now. Amalia's fingers tingled, and her heart fluttered as she gripped the armrest. *We'll discuss this later.*

But—

With a brief exertion of will, Amalia cut her sister's connection to her mind. The Archprelate's poisonous thoughts ran through her consciousness once again, and she felt the low glow of the embers within her chest begin to rise, to heat her blood. Her fingertips pressed into the armrest, and she swung herself around, one smooth motion setting her into the seat.

"You look like you belong there, your Majesty." Gorman was the first to speak, standing at Amalia's left, his head three feet below hers. "May I present your vassal rulers."

More applause as the Kings, Queens, Princes, and Princesses lined up before the throne. Each approached, one after the other, and handed Amalia a small token. She thanked each one, allowing Gorman to take the item out of her hands before the next one approached.

"Where is King Joram? Or his family?" As the line drew to an end, she realized that he had been missing. "Did they not attend?"

Gorman sighed. *His hesitation is answer enough. He must not have wanted me to worry.* A sad smile crept across Amalia's face. *Truly a good man.*

"I apologize, your Majesty. I…I should have informed you earlier. King Joram—"

Amalia shook her head. "Don't concern yourself with it, Councilor. We shall have plenty of time to discuss this issue, and several others, I'm sure." She laughed, but the sound was raw. "I don't expect to get a full night's sleep for quite some time."

"Undoubtedly true, your Majesty." The Archprelate approached from the other side of the throne, and his approaching presence drew a rash of goosebumps from Amalia's skin. The former soothing quality of his being was gone, vanished into the ether, leaving instead a feeling of dread in the pit of Amalia's stomach. "There is much to talk about, now that the mourning period is over and control of the kingdom has passed on to you."

"But before we can speak to either of those concerns, we must address a larger one." Amalia allowed her fingers to curl around the ends of the armrests for a second longer before she used them as leverage to stand. Taking a deep breath, she projected her voice outward as far as she could, picking her words with care.

Now or it won't happen at all. Junandar, grant me strength.

"Good people of Aetheria. You and I, together, mourn for our lost High King. No one can replace him. I won't even try."

She cleared her throat; the silence stretched, thick and heavy. "But our kingdom survives. Its people – you – survive. We survived the Dragon War, together." She turned slightly to address the seated nobility. "Before that, the Kingdoms wrought lasting peace from conflict, ending the Expansion Wars five hundred years ago. Our lands have been safe so long that it can be hard to imagine a time when they were not."

Then she faced forward again. "But what of myself? I know the whispers, the worries that run among you." In the background, she heard Gorman gasp, and the crowd shifted, with hushed commentary reaching her ears, but she pressed on; her voice rose, straining at the confines of her throat as her blood began to pump hot in her veins. "Some, especially those who have not met me, have not had discourse with me, have not watched me on the field of battle or in discussions at court, believe that I am weak, crippled by my blindness." She made a slow revolution, her brow furrowed and hard, her breathing coming faster as she brought the hand holding the scepter up to touch her scars.

"These scars are the first wounds that I suffered for Aetheria." Nothing for a moment; Amalia took a breath to try to steady her emotions as the strangeness of her statement caused the murmurs to silence. *Don't lose control. This is what you wanted.* "Less than an hour old, and I lost my sight to a traitor. One of our own wished me dead, and it was only the will of our gods that my eyes were the only casualty."

She paused a moment, letting the new chorus of discussion fade. "Since that day, my father, your King, made sure that I would be able to succeed him when the time came. I learned to protect myself, learned ways to get around my lack of sight. Even my free time was an exercise in overcoming this disability, as I practiced horsemanship and archery. I can hit a man from a hundred yards, if he isn't running too quickly." The crowd let out a small laugh, but she didn't join them, allowing her scowl to silence them before moving on. Then she raised her scepter, holding it parallel to the ground in one hand. "He was killed by a dragon, after sl...slaying another in single combat."

My mother. The sadness threatened to engulf her again. *Stupid, foolish...*

It took a second for Amalia to realize that everyone was waiting for her to continue, and, for a moment, she was grateful for her lack of eyes, lack of tears. "And I know that some of you have been worried about a dragon resurgence. I can swear to you that it will not happen, and that I have put steps in place to deal with the problem."

As the demands for her to disclose the plan began to rise up, she put up a hand. "And I'm sure you understand that these steps cannot be disclosed, for fear that they could fail."

Gods, I'm playing into the prejudices.

"I don't tell you these things in some bid to impress you, or to hold you in awe of my prowess. I don't feel that my skills are deserving of praise, other than to acknowledge the effort that's gone into it." Her wrist pivoted, leveling the scepter at the crowd, panning around to encompass the entire gathering. "And I don't want you to feel sorry for me, either. Pity is something that I came to expect, and then to loathe, some time ago."

More whispers, murmurs, and shifting garments drove small needles into Amalia's ears. *I wish I could see them!* Her mind began to reach out, reach for Glorianna to share her eyes...but she pulled back, though the effort felt like tearing a tree's roots out. *No, Amalia. You have to be* here.

She shook her head, then thrust her chin out. "I want you to know that I haven't given up. As easy as it would have been to allow Father's position and wealth to take away my problems for me, I refused to let my troubles become your troubles. And this is how I pledge to lead you – as a ruler that provides for you, not one who takes from you. I want you to feel safe in the knowledge that I will defend this country from whatever may come. In prosperous times or troubled ones, my fate is tied to yours."

Putting her other hand on the scepter, she flipped it around so that the head faced her and the hilt toward the peasantry. "If I ever become unfit to lead you, I will hand this scepter and crown to another. You have my word."

The outcry now was no small murmuring of side conversations or whispered questions to a neighbor; it seemed that the whole gathering rose up at once, their voices competing with one another to be heard. The nobles were no exception, with several shouting for Amalia's attention or questioning what she had said. She could hear Gorman trying to calm everyone, and she winced.

Louder than I thought it would be. She frowned as the cacophony grew. The sounds of argument and disbelief began to mix with the shuffling of people as they moved about, milling in small groups. Guards began to shout for the peasants and merchants to settle themselves and sit down, but, if what Amalia could make out was any indication, they weren't prepared to listen. Indeed, scuffles were beginning to break out as opposing viewpoints clashed.

"Lies!" A voice from the left, warbling, arrogant. "The Queen wouldn't surrender her power. She's saying this to placate us, so we don't look too closely at her flaws while she takes the throne. And what about the dragons? Why haven't we marched out to slay them? It's a ploy, nothing more!"

Amalia's head whipped around to face her accuser, but before she had the chance to say anything, someone in the crowd did it for her.

"Shut it, ya lout!" Flesh and bone hit cloth, sending feet backpedaling and their owner toppling onto the grass. "Ya wouldn't know a straight-talker if she spit in your ear and rubbed her nose in it! The Queen's got the Uniter's blood in her, and that's good enough for me!"

The crowd continued to factionalize, with the opposing sides growing ever more vocal. More scuffles broke out, and Amalia could make out the mail armor of the Royal Guard as they assumed formations, ready to march in to restore order. Everything else began to disappear behind a cloud of madness, of competing sounds that fought for her attention. She shook her head, retreating into herself, hunching her shoulders and taking a step back.

I didn't think they'd...no. Amalia clenched a fist, forcing herself upright. *I did this. I need to stop it.*

Gripping the scepter again, she inhaled, filling her lungs with air. The scent of summer flowers and fruit trees – orange, lime, and elder – filled her nose.

"That's enough!"

The words burst from her lips like a thunderclap, detonating the air. In its wake there was no fighting, no violence; everyone went quiet, cowed by the Queen's shout.

I guess dragon blood comes in handy for more things than breaking doors or getting angry. She savored the feel of everyone's eyes on her; unlike before, when she walked into the clearing, she held no fear, no temerity. Instead, Amalia bristled with confidence, feeling the right of rulership in her heart and on her brow. She strode down the stairs, Marchen taking up his customary position on her flank, and stopped three steps away from the line of guards.

"This is how you honor our country?" She slammed the scepter to the ground, feeling the impact reverberate up the metal and into her hand. "By fighting amongst yourselves at your Queen's coronation? What happened to faith in our countrymen, our common goals?"

Amalia thrust the staff into the air. "You saw what the Archprelate saw. The sign from the gods, the tears of my father in the Crystal Palace. And here, less than an hour after witnessing a miracle, you sully yourselves with petty recriminations and accusations."

Then she took a step back, using the pointed end to scratch a line in the dirt. "Any who wishes to speak against me, may do so." A gasp swept across the crowd, and low murmurs that quickly stopped. "But I wish that he or she come here, that they may speak their recriminations to my face, and that I might answer them likewise."

More whispers and murmurs. The crowd surged like the tired sea, swaying and shifting without changing their location. Amalia raised her hands, beckoned them. "Is there none here that believes strongly enough in what their hearts tell them that they would face me with them? I have promised safety to you. I have no wish to harm any of you for speaking when I have invited you."

She waited. Still nothing. Amalia shook her head, her lip curling into a sneer. "If none amongst you has the courage, then—"

"Your Majesty."

The voice came from Amalia's right, and she nodded to herself, lips set in a tight line. *I wondered which of them it would be.* She ran over her rehearsed scenarios in her mind. *Peasantfolk, trustworthy; handle him well and the rest will fall in line.*

"Come forward." She could hear Gorman and King Catlin whispering behind her, and the sound both irritated and amused her. *Probably trying to figure out how to stop me before I dig myself in deeper. Don't trust me yet, not this far.* "Donnen Cooper, I believe you said your name was?"

"S'right, your Majesty." She heard the man's thick boots against the ground, knew everyone was staring between the two of them, holding their breath to see how this would go. He marched straight up to the line she'd drawn in the dirt and stopped.

"State your concern, Donnen. I would hear it from you, before I hear it from the mouths of others."

"Your Majesty…" She could hear the folding and unfolding of cloth, rumpling, clutching, fidgeting. "It's…it's about His Highness. Prince Harne."

The silence took on a new character; instead of the nervous tension and confusion that it had held, now danger spiced the quiet. Amalia felt the blood drain from her face, and her heart stuttered in her chest. *Oh. I didn't…damn.*

"Go on."

"Well, y'see…" Donnen shifted, uprooting small clumps of grass with his boots. "We…that is, some of us…we heard that…" A swallow. "That y'were the one that killed him."

The words dropped like the headsman's axe. While Amalia processed them, Gorman stepped forward, anger clear in his voice. "That's enough of this! Your Majesty, you don't have to subject yourself to—"

"Councilor." Amalia shook her head. "If I cannot answer a charge such as this before my own people, then what sort of Queen shall I be?"

Truth, but not all the truth. The line echoed as she remembered sitting beside her father after a court session had ended. *Tell people what they need to know, keep the rest for yourself.*

Then she stepped up to the line, across from Donnen. She heard his boots fumble as he stepped back, smelled the mix of nervous sweat and camphor. She drew in another breath, projected it outward with the same strength she had used to demand silence, turning her head slightly to avoid shouting in the peasant's face. "Let this be known: Prince Harne's death was tragic, and horrible. I mourn his loss, as does his father, King Joram. But regardless of what you may have heard, I had nothing to do with his death."

Then she turned back toward Donnen. "I was the victim of an assassination attempt." Another gasp from the crowd. "Someone had persuaded the servants to poison my bathwater. Only the intervention of my Councilor and Prince Harne ensured my survival."

She spread her free hand open wide. "To cause the wounds they found on Prince Harne, one would have needed a bladed instrument, razor sharp, and sufficient strength to rend through both skin and bone." Amalia's throat began to close as, against her will, she remembered the horrible screams and the sounds of his death, remembered the still-warm body she had stumbled over.

Like dragon's claws.

"Even had I such an instrument at the time – which I did not – I was still recovering from the attempt on my life. Poison does not leave the body quickly, especially not the sort I faced."

Amalia swept her hand towards Gorman, King Catlin. "I have many witnesses, trusted people, who can attest to what I suffered, and to the situation at the time. I did not kill Prince Harne."

For a count of twelve, no one spoke. Amalia held her tongue, waiting as the audience digested her account, weighed it against whatever rumors they had heard. *Joram's words reach far indeed.* She clenched her teeth to suppress the rising anger. *I must speak with my ambassador to…discuss…this.*

"S'enough for me, your Majesty." Donnen bowed, one knee scraping the ground. "I'm sorry for troublin' ya."

Amalia nodded, not trusting herself to speak in that moment. Thomas's voice rang out from a few feet away, carrying over the entire crowd. "See, Ma? I told you she wasn't bad!"

The innocence of children. The comment brought a smile, then a laugh, to the Queen, and the tension broke with such strength that she couldn't stop. The laughter doubled her over, gasping for air, and each time it began to subside the very thought of it sent her into another bout.

"I think…" She fought to her feet, heaving herself up on the scepter, leaning on it for support as the tremors shook her body again. "I think that it's time we took our leave." *Snicker.* "Thank you…thank you all so much for coming. May…" *Titter.* "May the gods be with you all."

"You heard the Queen!" Destrick clapped his hands. "Escort everyone out to the banquet hall. Keep them together!"

"Yes, Commander." The guards saluted, metal striking metal as their fists clanked against their mail-clad chests. As the guests shuffled out, discussion and banter bouncing between them, rubber on stone. Destrick hurried over to Amalia's side, leaning down next to her to bring his lips closer to her ear. She felt the warmth of his breath tingle down her back as he spoke.

"What were you doing?"

Yes, what were you doing?

The strident tone took her by surprise. The remaining laughter died, and she backed away from him. Not for the first time, she wished that she could see his face, see the way he was looking at her. Glorianna's thought-question also jabbed at her awareness, forcing her to divide her attention, preventing her from giving Destrick her full attention for a moment.

Just listen, then. She directed the thought-arrow at her sister. To Destrick, she stood upright, drawing herself into what she hoped was a distinguished mien.

"I was addressing a problem." To cover the defensiveness of her response, Amalia retreated back into her royal training. "Do you disapprove of my actions, Guard-Commander?"

"I…" Destrick took a step back, responding to her change in demeanor. "Simple concern for your well-being, Majesty. You were in very close proximity to the crowd several times. I was not sure my soldiers could have kept you safe, had someone attacked you."

"Didn't you have archers waiting, as I asked?"

"Yes, but…"

"And weren't they all disarmed, peace-bound, before they entered today?"

Destrick shuffled his feet. "Of course, your Majesty."

"And I was armed, even if only with a scepter." Amalia nodded, punctuating her statement. "So I feel any danger would have been—"

Before she could finish, Gorman intervened. "We…I hadn't expected you to so directly address the issues caused by your injury, your Majesty." He put his hand on a shoulder and let loose a slow, warm chuckle. "Although

I suppose I shouldn't have been surprised. It's exactly the way Elise would have done it."

"Then I take that as an indication that my…unexpected actions resulted in total and unqualified success." She raised her brow, turning toward him. "At the very least, it certainly gave them something to talk about. Although I didn't expect for it to come to blows between them."

"So this was planned?" Gorman's voice took on a different tone. "I *am* impressed, then. Though you could have informed me, took mercy on my aging heart."

So am I. Glorianna's approval rolled across the Link. ***Risky, of course, but better than wishing the problems away. You handled that masterfully, and you couldn't even hear their thoughts.***

Humans generally can't, if you recall.

"Your Majesty." The Archprelate's smooth tones interposed themselves between Amalia's thoughts. "I hope you do not find it too much of an imposition if I remain here for a day or two more? The accusations leveled at you are serious ones, and I would be remiss in my duties as Archprelate if I did not ensure that the roots were investigated."

She felt bile coat her tongue, disgusting and foul, but she swallowed it back down and mastered her expression as she turned toward him. "Of course. The emissary of the gods is always welcome. Gorman?"

"Yes, your Majesty?"

"Ensure that enough staff are made available to His Eminence to fulfill all of his needs." Then she turned away from the Archprelate back toward the palace, taking long steps that forced Marchen to quicken his pace to stay close. Without breaking stride, Amalia bent down to wrap her right hand around the leather leash, keeping hold of the scepter with the other. A pair of guards scrambled to pull the door open so she could pass through.

"Thank you, gentlemen." At the threshold, she turned back to the courtyard. "Destrick, join your soldiers at the Festival." She allowed herself a small smile. "And try to enjoy yourself. Gorman, please convene the Council. We have things to discuss."

"I will escort you to the Council Chambers once I have seen to His Eminence's accommodations and lodgings while he is our guest, if you don't mind, your Majesty."

Amalia's small smile grew into a full-fledged version. "Not at all. I'll get some refreshments and let Marchen relax." She leaned down a little toward her hound, detaching the leash. "Marchen. Play!"

At once he leapt to his feet and bounded out into the grounds, jumping and barking like a child set loose after a long period of enforced stillness. Gorman took a hurried step back, and Destrick forced himself to contain laughter.

Amalia reached out for the door, imagining the looks on their faces. *At least you can do that now.* She sighed. *But it's just not enough.*

~~~

"Gorman, I need to speak to you." The Archprelate leaned in to the Councilor's ear as Amalia stepped through the doors, breathing the words as the wind in the reeds. "It is vital."

"Yes?" *When powerful men speak thus, it never bodes well.* He turned and crossed his arms. "What is it, Eminence?"

Clad in the golden robes of his office, the Archprelate removed the gleaming coronet from his black-haired head and glanced around. "Is it safe here?"

Gorman arched an eyebrow. "As safe as anywhere, as long as we don't seem like we are hiding something." He waited a heartbeat. "*Are* we hiding something?"

The priest took the Councilor's forearm in his hand, pulling him out of the main lanes of foot traffic. "The man in the crowd brought up a point that I feel her Majesty has been ignoring for too long." His eyes seemed almost
~~~

black, even in the bright daylight, pupils wide and irises deep.

"The death of Prince Harne?" Gorman couldn't hide the shock in his voice. "Why would she—"

"No, not that. The *dragons.*" The Archprelate spoke the last word with the same reverence shown to offal and festering sores. "Why hasn't Aetheria moved against them yet? Called up the armies of the vassal kingdoms?"

"It's the period of mourning, your Eminence." Eyes narrowed, the Councilor leaned in toward the younger man. "A holy time. The succession just occurred."

The priest frowned, took a breath, met Gorman's eyes. "Yes. I understand why *Amalia* hasn't made a proclamation yet. It would be unseemly. But you could be organizing the other kings and queens on her behalf. Sending out scouting parties."

Gorman leaned back to a normal standing position. "Are you an expert on governance, your Eminence? Military tactics? I am both. Trust me when I say that the issue will be addressed as soon as it is proper and prudent to do so. The outer borders are watchful. There have been no further sightings since the High King's death."

"If she does nothing, then it will only fuel what others have been saying." The priest glanced away again. "You know what I'm talking about, don't you?"

A tremor ran down Gorman's back. "The rumors of dragon thralldom." He shook his head, caught his voice before he spoke too loudly. "I've told others and I will tell you. Amalia Therald is no dragon-thrall."

"I hope you're right, Councilor." The priest's eyes danced to the side, toward Gorman, then away. "For all your sakes'."

CHAPTER SEVEN

Destrick watched as Amalia passed through the door, not relaxing until she had gone through and closed it behind her.

Those other Councilors are in for more than they bargained for. The thought made Destrick smile, but he banished the expression before he turned to face the rest of the crowds. *All right then, Knight-Commander. Security and fun. I'm sure you can manage.*

"Knight-Lieutenant Corynn, reporting for duty." The voice came from Destrick's left, along with the slamming of metal on metal as she made her salute. "What orders, my lord?"

Turning his head, Destrick raised his eyebrows. "That didn't take you long, did it? Good. The Queen wants us on security detail, so divide up the squads and give each of them a section of the grounds."

"Should I set one on roving patrol, to keep an eye on the entrances and exits?" The Knight-Lieutenant released her formal stance, but her voice continued its respectful cant. "Or do you think that the sectors are sufficient?"

"Set someone on the entrances to the castle - that's where the Queen is - and another inside it. Rotate them out every hour or so; if they're so distracted by the Festival that they neglect their duties, they might as well not be there."

"I'm sure they'll appreciate the consideration, my lord." Corynn pressed her lips together. "Will you be attending the Festival yourself?"

"As the Queen has commanded." Destrick made a mock half-bow toward the castle. "But I shall be around, so if something happens, don't hesitate to find me."

"I think that we can manage the Festival without needing to summon the Knight-Commander's personal attention. We've managed it every year since…"

"Don't bring down misfortune," admonished Destrick. "But fine. Enjoy yourself too, Corynne. Just not too much."

The young woman's bright amber eyes twinkled. "I will endeavor to keep myself restrained, my lord." She saluted again, then made a small bow and ran off, down the slopes toward the Festival grounds.

Nodding, Destrick strode onto the grounds himself. Several people nodded or gave him partial salutes as he passed, acknowledging his presence; to each of these he saw, he returned the gesture, smiling. The music of the Festival warmed Destrick's heart, familiar and comforting - each year, the same themes and songs played, with minstrels challenging one another for the most poignant retelling of the country's legends or history. The sweet smell of wines and ales competed for his attention, and savory cakes and sweet meats beckoned him with their rich aromas. Before long, he found himself with an armful of prizes, delicious foods he rarely had the chance to sample.

Where do they hide it the rest of the year? he asked himself, though not for the first time. *Some of this has to come from the other nations; there's no way they make it here.* Taking a bite of a warm, flaky pastry filled with chopped ham and cheese sauce, Destrick almost rolled his eyes. *So good.*

"Have your fortune told, Knight-Commander?"

The sudden voice from behind him, a small child's, took the guard by surprise, but he recovered his composure quickly, before he lost any of his treasures. "I'm sorry, but I'd rather…"

"My name is Midra, Knight-Commander." The girl came around his side into Destrick's view. Her small frame held up a patched-together leather dress, and her unshod feet bore the scratches and scrapes of barefoot adventures in the brambles; indeed, her hair resembled those same brambles, with snarls and knots that would have taken the most skilled hairdresser in Aetheria hours to tease into compliance. "I'm Lady Astrid's personal soothsayer. And I'll tell your future for only three sovereigns."

"...All right." *Astrid must not pay her enough. Maybe she'll be able to buy some shoes if she does well today.* "Just let me put these things down…"

Destrick set his pastries and sweets down on the grass near the makeshift tent that Midra had set up - little more than a beaten tablecloth on a rope, tied down at the corners by scrap metal pins. "All right. Go ahead."

The girl brought out a small, beaten metal box from one of the corners of the tent, and, opening it, revealed a deck of cards wrapped in a handkerchief, blue as the sky. "Are you familiar with the cards, Lord Destrick?"

"How did…" He shook his head. *Stupid question.* "Not very; some friends used to play at them when we were children, but I never learned it."

"I will shuffle the deck, and then I will ask you to do the same." Small but nimble fingers unwrapped the cards, laying the handkerchief down on the grass; the sun worked its way through the blanket forming the roof of the tent, and sweat beaded on Destrick's face from the heat, forcing him to wipe his brow. "Don't overthink how your hands move. Just shuffle as long as it feels right, then let them go."

As the young girl handed him the cards, Destrick almost dropped them; they felt *heavy*, denser than they should have been. He began to shuffle, feeling the edges beneath his fingertips, sliding them across one another. His thoughts wandered, the heat made sweat drip into his ears, and the buzz of conversation outside merged into one giant mass…

"Now for the reading." Midra's voice startled the Knight-Commander, and he stared down at his own hands, now open as she extracted the cards from them. "Three cards, representing past, present, and future - a simple reading for a simple man," she added, giggling at her own joke.

Destrick laughed despite himself. "Your patter is very good, Midra. You know how to put someone at ease."

The young fortune-teller paused, leaning over and spreading her hands in a mock bow. "Why, thank you, milord. I will take your praise with me to Nome." Then she resumed her previous pose.

"The first card, then." With the air of a showman, Midra brandished the top card, laying it down with a flick of her small hand. "The Lovers Lie Slain."

The strangeness of that name drew Destrick's attention from his own inner musings; the card depicted two people, sitting completely covered by a blanket and locked in an embrace, but each held a dagger lodged in the other's back, their attacking arm visible, blood running in small rivulets from the blade.

"What does that mean?"

Midra raised her eyebrows. "Two people, who loved one another. Betrayal led them to battle rather than home, and they both died because of it." Then a small laugh escaped her lips. "But I cannot - *will* not - try to tell you what to think, Knight-Commander. I'm just here to entertain."

Before Destrick could respond, Midra drew the second card, laying it crosswise on top of the first; this one showed a man, a knight like himself, standing in profile with his head bowed - but behind him, back to back, a dark shadow in the shape of a man brandished a knife, ready to attack.

"Your present. The two-faced man. Easy to understand, harder to figure out who it is. Someone you know…" And here she paused, a small grin crooking one corner of her mouth. "Or you, perhaps, hides something. A deep secret, that if exposed could destroy everything they work for. The world sees one thing, but the mirror sees another."

"Not me." Destrick tried for courage and authority in his voice, but found only temerity, a feebleness he had not felt since childhood. "I don't keep secrets."

"Is that so? Remember, my lord, this is just for fun." The child flashed another smile. "The third…"

Destrick couldn't keep his eyes off of the girl's hand as it plucked the next card from the deck, as it brought it up to her eyes...the eyes that widened, the smile that vanished, pupils that danced from the card face to his own, then back.

"What is it?" The knight almost shouted at the girl, only his military discipline and training allowing him to restrain the sudden surge of fear that her attitude brought on. "What is the card?"

Without a word, she dropped it onto the other two, where it landed across them, at an angle so that the two below could still be seen. This card shone with a great dragon, a scaled monster that filled the entire card, but it differed from the stories and pictures that Destrick had seen before: this one had two heads.

And both lay severed at the dragon's feet, blood coating the ground.

"The dragon, twice-beheaded." Midra's voice shook. "A sign of calamity, of death and betrayal and sadness. This is your future, Lord Destrick." She took a breath and closed her eyes. "And I am sorry for it."

"Wait!" Destrick's own eyes devoured the card, memorizing every detail as if his life depended on it. "What's going to happen? You can't..."

Then he stopped, hearing his heart beating in his ears, something triggering in his brain that drained the fear like a plug. "Well done." He began to clap, his hands coming together once, twice, before stopping, a grin spreading across his face. "You played this very well. I'm impressed - I imagine you've practiced this often." Then he raised his eyebrows. "And you even kept telling me it was just for fun, and I still fell for it, didn't I?"

There was a few moments of pause, where Midra didn't respond, but then her eyes opened again and a sunny smile burst forth.

"Glad you liked it, my lord! Was it worth the coin? I hope so!"

"Worth it and more. I truly believed you, almost." He tossed another sovereign her way. "Keep at it, and you might become known yourself one day."

Midra took the coin, holding it to her chest in a closed hand. "And to you as well, Lord Destrick," she whispered as he left her makeshift tent. "Take care."

~~~
~~~

Greagor watched as Destrick exited the tent, raising one hand as he hailed. "Rusty. Can I talk to you for a second?"

The Knight-Commander stiffened, his back straightening as his muscles tensed. "Your lips still move, huntsman. What do you have to say?"

The foreigner twisted his lips into a mock scowl, shaking his head a few degrees to each side. "Do you win many arguments with that kind of attitude? The old saying, right? More flies with honey?"

"If you're the fly, I'd rather be the vinegar to ward you off." Destrick crossed his arms, then stepped back to let a small family pass by, the aroma of boiled meat and mead apparent. "What do you want? Make it quick."

"Fine." Greagor leaned back against a nearby oak. "The Queen hasn't been attending her training sessions. I thought that maybe you could persuade her that it's important enough for her to spend her time on."

Eyebrows rose. "You want *me* to tell Her Majesty that she should spend more time with *you*." Destrick blinked - once, twice - then let out a loud, hearty laugh. "Next you'll be telling me that I should promote you to my second-in-command."

"You could do worse. At least I'd keep you out of your rusty armor." Greagor held up both hands. "But this isn't about you, or me, or who Amalia spends her time with. It's about being prepared for attack."

Destrick stayed silent.

"I don't want Amalia to die any more than you do." Greagor pressed the point physically as well as with his voice, stepping forward. "I won't lie. You've taught her a lot about combat. But she's woefully unprepared for an ambush, for a multi-person threat. She focuses strongly on one target and switching can confuse her."

More silence from the Knight-Commander; from somewhere nearby, a small child began to cry as her parents ushered her away from a laughing jester, painted face contorted and teeth showing in a manic grin.

"No." Destrick straightened, shaking his head. "I think you have points worth considering, but my Queen decides on her own fate. If you can't convince her of the rightness of your position, I won't do it for you."

Without waiting for Greagor to respond, to make a counter-argument, Destrick stepped past him, scarcely missing bumping the other man's shoulder with his own. He glanced back, once, to see the huntsman's eyes burning holes in his back, barely-contained rage seething under the skin.

He didn't like that at all. So angry. A strange thought crossed his mind, unbidden and quickly discarded:

Almost like he wants to put his fist through the wall. Facing front again, he picked up his pace. *Almost.*

CHAPTER EIGHT

"Your Majesty, may I be the first to welcome you, in an official capacity, to the Lawgivers' Council."

Amalia nodded her head. "Thank you, Lord Jaydin. It is truly an honor to be here." Her fingers traced the marble carvings, the friezes that circled the room, low on the walls. "I've always enjoyed the smell of this building. Like a library, but richer, somehow. Older."

"Yes. Well…" Jaydin trailed off. "I suppose we should begin…at the beginning?"

Another nod, and Gorman echoed her assent. "Excellent. Lady Astrid, I think that we should start with an introduction to the trade situation?"

"Of course." Lady Astrid's voice was cultured and careful, her vowels clear, consonants precise. "As the center of power in Brandil, the vassal kingdoms provide us with one-quarter of the tariffs they collect on their trade goods. This is particularly profitable regarding trade with the Outer Kingdoms; most of our vassals maintain a fifteen percent tariff on their exports. Combining that with our direct trade surplus—"

Amalia made her way into the room; her hands landed on a large wooden chair, inlaid with deep carvings depicting dragons and battle.

Scenes from the Dragon War. The carvings held a new meaning for her now, and she found herself visualizing the scenes, the intense combat between man and dragon. It was almost like being there: the sound of steel on scale, the screams of dying humanity and the shrieks as blades and arrows sank into draconic flesh. Her fingers tightened against the wood as blood ran down the shafts of arrows and open claw wounds to mix on the ground, red with red.

Instinctively, the woman reached out her mind to her dragon-sister, as if sharing thoughts would ease the unease...but she felt nothing but a solid wall, a rebuff like she had scarcely experienced.

Why is she denying me? Her grip on the wooden arm tensed even further. *Have I—*

"Queen Amalia?"

She raised her head, smiled, nodded, trying her best to hide the tremors of her lips. "I'm glad to hear that our trade is going so well. I'm wondering, though, as to why you feel I need to know the exact amounts of the tariffs and taxes on each and every good we import and export."

Lady Astrid seemed startled; Amalia could hear the woman's neck turning amidst the folds of her gown as she glanced back and forth at the others in attendance. "Well…your Majesty, it's important for a ruler to be versed in everything that pertains to their kingdom."

"Your father held this ideal in high esteem, Amalia." Gorman spoke from his seat directly to her right. "That's one of the reasons he wanted you to have such a comprehensive curriculum."

"Oh, I'm aware." Amalia rested her royal scepter on the table, reaching up and adjusting the crown on her brow. *Heavier than it looks. No wonder he took it off whenever he could.* "Father spoke to me of it many times. And do you know what I gathered from his lessons, the words he used in private quarters?"

No one answered.

"He felt stretched thin, responsible for too many things." Amalia leaned forward, crossing her hands over the wood, turning her face to address everyone seated around the table. "He told me once that he didn't even understand why he paid so many highly-educated people when it was always him doing the work for you."

She shook her head. "That's not how it's going to work, now. I've spent a lot of time going over matters, and deciding which are worth my attention and which I can delegate. You were chosen for these tasks according to your skills, and you will use those skills to accomplish those tasks for the greater good of Aetheria." Then she shrugged. "If you don't remember how to do that, then I'm sure I could find a replacement for you."

Then Amalia smiled. "I hope that this arrangement is amenable to everyone. I would hate to have ruined anyone's chances for an early lunch."

Several people around the table shifted in their seats, as if a squirming insect were trapped beneath them, but they didn't dare get up.

"Excellent." She faced Gorman. "Is there anything that I actually *need* to know?"

"Well…" Gorman shuffled a few papers around; a large *thump* made those seated closest to him startle. "I thought so. We received a letter some few days ago. Ragna, one of the Outer Kingdoms, wants to speak to you about reestablishing diplomatic relations."

"Reestablishing?" The Queen pursed her lips. "I asked my father about them once. He said they were anathema, not to be talked about." She frowned, reaching out for her sister again, and again receiving the same result.

"Your predecessors cut off diplomatic contact with them."

Amalia tilted her head, forcing herself to refocus on the conversation. *You can ask her later. Just stay here for once.* "Why did we cut them off in the first place? Was there a specific reason?"

Another voice spoke up. "Your Majesty, this edict comes down to us from your ancestor's day. During the Dragon War, he called for aid from the Ragna people. Their King refused him, saying that his war was more than pointless, that it was an affront against the natural order."

What!?

"That…that is quite an interesting claim." Amalia folded her hands to still the sudden trembling that threatened to take them, but her feet, under the table, could not be controlled. "Do we know why my father did not reestablish relations himself?"

"He never spoke to me on the matter, your Majesty." Gorman tapped on the table with his stylus. "I knew of the original order, of course, but it never came up. This is the first time Ragna has contacted us since they were banished from the realm."

"When do they arrive?" Amalia's heart quickened, and her throat went dry. "I find myself eager to speak to them."

"Why?" The first speaker drew her attention again. "Forgive me, but I don't understand. They refused us aid. Let us fight the dragons alone when they could have sent in ships and men to assist. Why would you entertain the idea of rebuilding the bridges that they so clearly wanted burned?"

Amalia took a second to formulate her answer before speaking. Her nails scratched on the wooden table, nervous hands finding a sliver to pick and pull at. "Burning bridges doesn't mean that they can never be rebuilt. As I said, I have...dealt with...the dragon problem for now, and I don't anticipate any resurgence of issues."

How prescient.

Grimacing, Amalia shook off Glorianna's snide comment, but a wash of relief fell over her as the connection came through, and she could hear the difference in her own speech. "Besides, I doubt highly that the Ragnan ruler is the same as when the refusal was made. They have made an overture of friendship; we will honor them with an audience, to discuss the opportunity, at least."

More murmurs and grumbles from the assembled Council. Amalia kept her face stately and stern, but her heart grinned like an idiot's. *They didn't expect me to take charge this quickly, I imagine. More the fools they.*

Then the excitement crept back in. *And Ragna knows something about dragons that we don't. Perhaps the path to peace lies therein.*

"Anything else?"

No one spoke this time.

"Very well." Amalia stood, stepping to the side of her seat and reclaiming the scepter. "I shall return to my quarters. If anything needs my personal attention, please don't hesitate to let me know."

She turned, feeling her dress sweep out behind her as the lavender fragrance filled her nose, then marched back out of the room. Marchen guided her to the right so she didn't collide with the wall.

I need to become more familiar with this room. She allowed her fingers to brush against the doorframe as she passed through it. *I don't like having to rely on him.*

Amalia heard the door close behind her as she entered the hallway, turning left toward the royal suite. Her steps quickened as she got back onto more familiar territory, and soon she was almost running back to her room, her mind already preparing the Link, anticipating the mental fusion.

"Your Majesty?"

Destrick's voice brought her up short. By her mental map, he was standing in one of the connected corridors, probably leaning against a wall by the sound of it. She took a second to breathe and compose herself before turning toward him, willing herself to not appear angry.

"Yes?"

The Knight-Commander stepped toward her, pausing several feet away to bow. "Queen Amalia, I thought I would take this opportunity to discuss the status of your guardsmen. They are due for an inspection, and I would be most honored if you would attend."

"I see." She pursed her lips. "You know that I would be of little help in inspecting troops. Why do you need me?"

Not like that, Amalia; you're being too short with him, making it too obvious.

"I won't lie." Another step closer. She could hear the breath moving in and out of his lungs, smell the sweat and musk that followed him around. "I heard what you said at your coronation. I know that we had everything prepared, as you said, and that you were probably in little danger there, but..."

The tension thickened; Amalia waited for him to continue, but he didn't. She heard him swallow, imagined him clenching his fists and tightening his lips as he tried to think of what to say.

Then she couldn't wait anymore.

"Yes?" She beckoned his response with a circular hand motion. "Please, Destrick. I want to hear what you have to say."

A little more fidgeting. "I'm concerned, your Majesty. Amalia. I'm worried that you've opened the gates for your enemies to come and find you."

Her brow wrinkled, and she turned her face away for a second before refocusing on him. "I don't understand."

"Walk with me, if you don't mind." He took a step down the hall, then paused. "Please, Amalia."

He's really worried. She caught up to him in three quick movements, and the two resumed their walk. "All right, Destrick. What is it?"

"You were very brave there, Majesty. I admit that I was surprised when you decided to speak on that particular subject. Most would have saved that for when they were more firmly entrenched in their office."

A buzzing sounded in Amalia's ear, like a bee or wasp caught within. She shook her head and brought her hand up, but there was nothing there to make the sound. "I wanted to head it off before it became a problem. I don't want my citizens whispering behind my back every time I see them."

"Laudable, but dangerous." Destrick hurried ahead, pushing open one of the castle's double-doors, then waiting for his Queen. "You already know that King

Joram's vendetta against you hasn't died down in the least. The question from that farmer showed that his words are reaching even as far as here." He cleared his throat. "And that is what has me worried."

"You think Joram would make an attempt on my life?" Amalia shook her head, but her hand gripped the leash more tightly. "Absurd. He wouldn't dare."

"Amalia. You *can't* afford to be this naïve." They made the last turn toward the royal suite; a soft nudge on the shin guided Amalia to the side of the hall in time to avoid a collision. The other person bowed, shifting a heavy weight in her hands, accompanied by the sound of water pit-pattering onto the stone floor.

"Excuse me, Majesty."

"Of course." She waited until the washerwoman was far enough away before continuing. "What do you mean, naïve?"

Destrick's teeth ground together. "Gods, Amalia. He thinks you killed his son. The only thing that's keeping him from declaring open rebellion is the strength of the Aetherian army, and our allies. But you just offered an open invitation for anyone, any of them, to start doubting and questioning you."

Amalia stopped, her hand on the door to the royal chambers. "That doesn't make sense."

"That's because you're living in a world where nothing can touch you, Amalia." Destrick lowered his voice and came up behind her. "You live inside your own mind, a dream, almost. You can't see the glances people give each other when you're talking, or the fear in their eyes. Do you remember what King Joram accused you of, how he said you killed Prince Harne?"

"Of course I do." Amalia's voice trembled as she relived that day – the weakness brought on by the paralytic poison, the sound of Harne's death, the warm blood on the floor, on her hands and feet…and the realization that Glorianna had done it. "It's a hard thing to forget. He claimed I had used unholy powers, that I was a dragon-thrall."

"And you just poured more fuel on that fire, your Majesty." He reached around and took Amalia's hand, bringing her around to face him as he held it in his. "Don't you see? You laid out for everyone in that audience exactly what you could do. They haven't watched you as you spent hours and hours training yourself for those skills, seen you as you take the precautions and steps that you use to familiarize yourself with a new room." He sighed. "They haven't walked beside you while you leaned on them and asked them to describe what there was to be seen."

"Have I imposed on you, my Lord?" Amalia's pride throbbed in her chest, and she turned away. "I never intended—"

"Will you *stop!*" Destrick forced her back around again. "This isn't about your damned eyes! It's about the fact that people want to kill you because they're afraid of you!"

Amalia could feel Destrick's breath on her face, feel the tension in his hand as he held hers. Her lips quivered, and her heart throbbed in her chest, a slow-beating drum. "What about you?" The words passed like a breath in the wind, almost inaudible even to her ears. "Do you fear me, Destrick?" Her tongue passed over her teeth, the air moving over her skin taking away the nascent drops of sweat that formed there. "Am I a monster to you as well?"

"I'm still trying to decide that." The Knight-Commander sighed, his fist landing against the stone above them - not angrily, but not softly either. "Some of the things you do, Amalia...they frighten me. Frighten everyone. And if someone like me, someone who has cared for you, bled for you, for years, can be frightened so...what of the others? Those you addressed, the ones who haven't grown with you as I have? How can you expect them to understand?"

"I can't." Amalia didn't change her position, part of her reveling in their closeness. "But I don't ask for understanding from everyone. What if it were true?" A pause, two heartbeats. "What if I were a dragon-thrall, or an assassin? A murderer? Would it change who I am - the girl you laughed with, the woman you trained? Your Queen?" She leaned just a bit closer. "Would it change anything?"

In reply, Destrick pressed his mouth against Amalia's, lips moving, hungry. The kiss hurt, filled with pent-up longing and desire, and she returned it with just as much force. Each brush of skin against skin, each touch of tongue to tongue sent tremors of heat through her body. At first, the newness of it all consumed the entirety of her attention as her mind processed what her heightened senses were sending it – the throbbing in her belly, the tingling in her lips, the sudden change in Destrick's smell and her own—that her hands were frozen in place, clutching the scepter and Destrick, clenching tighter and tighter with every second until they ached.

Then, after an eternity that lasted but for the space of two heartbeats, Destrick pulled away, leaving Amalia desolate, alone. Her body and heart cried out, and for a moment, she didn't know where he was. Her own breathing and low cries of fear and separation.

And she never more cursed her blindness than that moment.

"Destrick? Don't…please don't leave." Amalia swallowed down her rising hysteria, reaching out with her left hand, fingers splayed.

Then she let out a shuddering breath as her fingers touched leather, heaving up and down in slow, deep waves. "I'm…I'm sorry, your Majesty. I overstepped my bounds."

Amalia's mind burned, twisting and turning on itself. Conflicting emotions ran through her, the alternating fear, desire, worry, and happiness thundering down her nerves like runaway carriages and paralyzing her. Her fingers slipped off of Destrick's chest as he turned and ran, his footsteps pounding the stone faster and faster, until the distant sound of a door closing rang down the hallway.

Amalia slumped down to the ground, letting the scepter slide from her limp, still-aching fingers, and allowed herself to cry…as best she could.

~~~

Amalia?

Glorianna paced back and forth on the Roost, circumnavigating the rock. The sounds of crashing waves did little to calm her nerves, and the other dragons picked up on it. They stretched and flexed, and the younger ones dove into the water, coming up with mouthfuls of fish.
~~~

What is it, Matriarch? Whaur, the dark red drake who had appointed himself as her consort and protector, coasted in to land next to her. *How can I help you?*

Leave me alone. Glorianna turned her back on him, closing her eyes as she sought to make contact with her half-sister. ***I have no time for your concerns.***

...Yes. Whaur flapped his wings, the wind stirring the dust on the rock, and coasted into the air.

Glorianna didn't notice.

Where is she? Fear and worry crept into the draconic group mind, leaking from her own. ***This isn't like her, to shut me out. She went over the last interaction they had had. I didn't think she was in any immediate danger. Why won't she answer me? Is she simply being petty?***

The dragoness raised her head, roaring her frustration to the open air. "Damn it, Amalia! Why do you always have to be so inconsiderate?"

Then, after a few more seconds of grumbling to herself, she took off, spreading her wings and rising on the updrafts as she set her course for Aetheria.

~~~

Amalia floated on the ocean's surface, bobbing up and down in the waves of the sea. Every breath came easy, filled with the tangy, salty smell of fish and kelp, and the
~~~

breeze that blew across her face and caressed her skin made her smile.

"I wish I could do this all the time." She took another breath through her nose, relishing the smell. "Perhaps I should have taken up a career as a sailor, rather than studying courtly procedures and law."

A few droplets splashed into her face, making her muscles twitch. "I doubt that you would have been truly happy with a life of such luxury, my dear."

She shook her head, rolling it to one side until her cheek dipped into the surface of the ocean, then the other. "But what if I could have been? Father, what if I am better suited to something other than governance?"

Marcus laughed, and the rich, warm sound calmed her further. "We are the choices that we make, and the ones that are made for us." A hand touched her forehead, began to stroke her hair. "The gods have their reasons for our suffering and our joys. We must trust in them."

Amalia's breathing hitched at the physical contact; Marcus's skin felt cold, colder than it should have been given the water temperature. Her hands paddled to keep her afloat.

"Then why did you kill Mother?" The hand on her forehead stilled. "How was that in the gods' plan?"

"I…" He trailed off, started again. "The two of you were getting too close. I was afraid that you would go to her, rather than stay with me." He came up next to her, floating beside her. "And may the great Mother forgive me, but I would do the same again."

"What?" The answer echoed in Amalia's ears, breaking her concentration and causing her to choke on seawater. Forcing herself back to the surface, she spat it out, coughing.

It doesn't taste right. The sea was warm, rich, and, instead of salt, it smelled of iron and copper. But before Amalia could process this, before she could begin to work something out in her mind, Marcus's hands were on her. He grabbed the sides of her head, squeezing, pressing in with his thumbs where her eyes should have been.

"And you're doing it to me, anyway, aren't you?" He pushed her down, into the ocean. "You can hide it from everyone, but not from me, Amalia. Not from your father."

She fought against his iron strength, but she couldn't break free. It was all she could do to keep her mouth and nose above water; the skin where his thumbs pushed inward began to split, to bleed. She could feel the droplets running down her cheeks, unholy simulacra of tears.

"Da! What…?"

"Dragons and dragons and dragons!" He pushed harder, and Amalia went under for a second before she regained the surface. "Better that you die a thousand times than be drawn in with them, throw away your life for their madness!"

His thumbs dug into her scars, sending streaks of searing pain through her body. She screamed, thrashing in the water, but her strength failed her. She reached up and clawed at his face, but she might as well have been attacking stone for all the effect it had. Deeper and deeper went his thumbnails, sharp as knives, sharp as bone.

Then they pulled back, the sudden decrease in pain leaving Amalia gasping. She pulled herself back to the surface, fighting for breath. The smell around her intensified, putrescence and rot mixing with the brine and metal.

"Open your eyes!" Her father's voice came from everywhere. "Open them and see what happens in the world you're looking to build."

And she did. From the holes in her face, the holes put there by her father's hands, she peered out.

The ocean was gone. The boat was gone.

In their place, a sea of blood, thick, red, clots floating on the surface. Vultures swept in to land on what first appeared to be floating debris, but a second glance revealed the debris to be corpses, rent from stem to stern, torn apart by massive, sharp blades. Entrails dangled from the lacerations, drifting in the blood-sea, while the birds pecked and tore at the bodies.

Amalia gasped as the nearest vulture dipped its neck, tearing the eye of its ride out and swallowing it down. Against her will, she glanced at the body's face.

Destrick. She shook her head, her vision clouding, wavering at the edges. *Gods, please. No. No.*

In an attempt to tear herself away from the sight, she turned her face upward, toward the sky. A strange, phosphorescent red light gleamed from several places behind the clouds, giving the heavens a mottled, angry appearance.

Then the clouds moved, and they weren't clouds anymore. They were a rain of blood, pouring down over her face, flooding her open mouth, the new holes dug into her scars. Amalia recoiled, screaming, flailing...

Nothing.

She heard nothing but the sounds of her own despair and fear, felt nothing but terror and pain and death. She couldn't hear herself crying out, couldn't hear the maidservant calling out to her, couldn't hear the pitcher drop and splash its contents onto the ground.

CHAPTER NINE

"I understand your concerns." Gorman blinked the sleep out of his eyes, rubbed them with his thumb and forefinger, and watched as Queen Amalia thrashed on her bed, her sheets tangling in her legs for the fourth time since he'd arrived. He rose from his seat, then took them in his hands, unwrapping them from her limbs and replacing them over her body. Marchen whimpered as he put his hand on her forehead, and she flinched away, screaming again. "She isn't ill. At least not in the traditional sense. She has no fever, no symptoms of poisoning or infection." He crossed his arms. "But madness? From a nightmare?"

Gorman shook his head, then turned toward the young maiden, standing and twisting her skirts in her hands. "Dearest Elsa, have you never awoken from a dream to find yourself covered in sweat, caught in your own bedclothes and blankets?" He nodded, turning back to the Queen, not giving her a chance to respond. "I know I have."

Elsa ran a hand through her short hair, wiping sweat from her brow; her lips trembled and her tongue flickered out as she searched for the words to answer. "Of course I have, Councilor. But this…" She waved her hand over Amalia's prone form. "I've never seen it like this. Look."

Gorman followed where the woman's index finger indicated; one of the bedposts was splintered, a wound like a sledgehammer or maul gouged into the wood. His eyes narrowed, and he traced over it with his finger, musing. "Another assassin, perhaps?"

"I don't think so, my lord." Elsa glanced back and forth between the Queen and Councilor. "Her hand."

It didn't take long for him to understand what she was talking about; Amalia's right hand dripped blood onto the red silk sheets from a series of thin cuts upon the knuckles. He took her hand in his, flinching when she groaned and turned over, trying to pull away from him. Splinters of wood had dug into the wounds.

"Gods help us. I must be more tired than I thought; I didn't even see it." He stared at the injuries for a moment, then up at the bedpost. "How did she do that?" Gorman's eyes flicked back and forth, his mind racing. *It's like what Destrick was saying. Where is she getting this strength?*

He stood straight, then strode toward the other side of the room, gazing down at the floor until he came to where there were still fragments of glass that had escaped cleaning; his eyes came up, hesitant, afraid.

To see the small crater in the wall, just as he knew, he *knew,* it would be there. His heart caught, and he saw everything around that mark swim in his vision.

It can't be. Not her. Please, Junandar, not her. He rubbed the bridge of his nose with his right thumb and forefinger. *Is this my fault? Did I show her the way to damnation?*

"I don't know, my Lord." Elsa twisted the rag she held in her hands, eyes flicking from one side to the other. "But it's got me frightened."

Gorman took a second to bring his emotions under control, to compose his face into the mein of the caring counselor. "All right." He came back to the bed and, as carefully as possible, Gorman placed Amalia's hand on her chest. He began to pace around the room, his eyes dancing, unseeing, as his thoughts collided with one another. "So tell me the whole thing. From the beginning, when you found her."

Given a clear directive, the worry passed from Elsa's face. She nodded, wiping her brow and licking her lips, then took a deep breath. "The Queen started crying just outside the chambers, Councilor. I heard her 'cause I was in here working on tidying up, and so I went out to check and see what was goin' on."

Gorman frowned. "What made her start crying? Do you know?"

"Well…" Elsa shuffled her feet, twisting the rag some more. "I…I think I heard the Queen out there arguing with Lord Destrick."

"The Guard-Commander?" That brought him up short, and he narrowed his eyes when she nodded. "Are you certain?"

"Can't be certain." She gave a small, apologetic smile. "But I'm pretty sure, my Lord. Sounded like him. I've heard him many times before."

"But it *could* have been someone else?" She nodded, slow. "I see. Did you catch what the argument was about?"

"No, my Lord." A shrug and a sorrowful head-shake. "Just the voices. Then it went quiet for a few moments, then Her Majesty was bawling her…" She caught herself, her hand going to her mouth. "Gods, I'm sorry, my Lord. I swear I didn't mean to offend, I just…"

Gorman waved her off. "Just...what happened when you found her?"

"Yes. Um…" Amalia shifted in the bed again, and let out another scream; her feet pedaled, kicking the sheets from her and leaving her in bedclothes alone. Marchen whimpered again, then jumped up into the bed, laying down next to her with his muzzle on her chest.

Almost at once, she calmed down, one arm going over his neck.

"Go on." Gorman's teeth ground against his words. "Please."

"Right! Yes." Elsa snapped back to the Councilor, whose weary eyes bored into hers, awaiting an answer. "I helped her up and got her ready for bed. She didn't say much, moved just enough to let me get her dress off of her. Her hound was more lively than she was, truth be told." She ran a hand through her hair, her voice catching. "Do you think she's going to be all right, my Lord?"

"I do." Gorman stepped over to the bed again. Amalia's sleep seemed deeper, her breath coming more easily. "The Queen has been under an unprecedented amount of stress as of late. Bad dreams come with that." He turned back; his eyes had moistened, and his face stretched with worry. "I had several myself in the first few weeks after King Marcus's death. A dragon, cutting him down. I couldn't believe it." He glanced back at Amalia, speaking more slowly, one hand going to his mouth and scratching at his lips. "Frightened me. Terrified me."

"Maybe." The maiden nodded, not taking her eyes off the Queen, whose brow wrinkled again. She braced herself for the scream…but it didn't come, and Amalia relaxed back into the bed. "I hope that's all it is."

"As do I." Gorman grimaced. *I truly hope Amalia chose a trustworthy lady-in-waiting for herself.* He put a hand on the woman's shoulder. "Can you watch over her for me, Elsa? I'll have a messenger stationed at the door so you can get in touch with me if anything changes." He turned her to face him, holding her shoulders and looking into her eyes. "Anything at all. I don't want you to go anywhere. Just stay here until I get back, and notify the messenger to come get me. Can you do that?"

"Of course, my Lord." Elsa held his eyes, straightening tall and folding her arms over her chest. "My Queen's wellbeing is paramount. Caring for her is why I'm here."

Gorman smiled, clapping her on the shoulder. "That's right." Then he glanced past her to the sleeping woman on the bed, and his smile faded, transforming into a small downturn of the lips. "And it wouldn't hurt if you prayed for her."

"My Lord?"

"Just as a precaution." He let her go and turned, walking out the door, mumbling to himself. "It can't hurt to try."

~~~
~~~

The sun rose into the sky, its rays casting long shadows over the land; trees, buildings, and early risers all took on the golden glow of the dawn, and the dark gave way to the first hints of blue. As the brightness grew, the assembled guards could clearly make out the circles under their commander's eyes, the firm set of his jaw, and the utter lack of anything resembling a smile. A few glances passed between them, filled with curiosity, nervousness, and confusion.

"We have a new Queen." Destrick projected his voice over the entirety of the courtyard, the surrounding stone walls echoing it back to their ears. The sound drowned out the rustling of the leaves and the burbling of the waters in the marble fountain behind the formation of soldiers; his brows tensed, tying themselves into tight configurations and bunching into mountains on his forehead. "And, thus far, we all have a piss-poor track record of keeping her safe."

A few of the guards, especially newer recruits, winced, and one or two mumbled amongst themselves. Destrick whirled around, his eyes blazing blue death, and their mouths clapped shut.

"Do you disagree? Let's tally it up." He brought up his hand. "We allowed her to go out on her own, where she almost drowned, and where, as I understand Councilor

Gorman, she encountered a whelp dragonling." He paused a moment to let that settle in. "We allowed an assassin to get into her rooms less than four months ago. We allowed her to ride out on her own, to face a battlefield with dragons. *Dragons.*" He swiped his hand through the air like a knife. "A guard force of any competence would have been able to stop her, or, failing that, would have ridden with her to protect her."

"But, Commander..." Everyone else locked into attention as the speaker dissented. "We didn't know she was leaving. I mean, not until she was already gone."

"Thank you, Trin." Destrick nodded. "And that's our first point, the first weakness that we need to address." He pointed out at the formation, sweeping his hand around to encompass all of them. "How in the great Mother's name did Amalia get out of this palace without the gate guards sending a message to the rest?" He strode to one side of the group, facing the two men at the corner. "Well?"

"My Lord Commander." The man on the corner saluted, bringing his closed fist to his chest. "The Princess—"

"Queen."

A moment's hesitation. "Yes. The Queen demanded to be let through the gates, but her father had left strict orders that—"

"I'm not asking for a *summary*." Destrick raised his hand, cutting off the other man's words. His teeth ground together, and only his military training kept him from laying into his troops. As it was, he knew that his words were harsh, but he found himself unable to restrain them. "We went over this already."

Confused looks passed between the two gate guards. "Then…I'm sorry, my Lord, but…"

He sighed, and that sound carried with it hours of fuming and frustration. "You didn't tell anyone. *That's* the problem."

"No, that's not true!" The second guardsman shook his head. "We sent out immediate notification to the towers. But by the time they heard, she had already passed them and was gone."

Destrick frowned. "So we can't even keep someone in the *palace* when we're told to?" He shook his head, his voice gaining in volume. "Pathetic. Pathetic!"

Then he swirled his extended finger in a circle. "I want all of you in full gear and back here at seventh bell. We have a lot of deficiencies that need covered, and I won't have you being responsible for something happening to *my* Queen."

No one moved.

"Are you waiting for chocolate? Go! Go!"

And they went, each rank breaking and hustling out of the courtyard. Each sound they made, each step that reached Destrick's ears, only irritated him more. His muscles bunched together and he brought one hand up to his mouth, sinking his teeth into his own knuckle. *We can't fail her again. We can't.*

"You don't normally raise your voice so, my Lord." Gorman stepped into the courtyard from the stairwell that led to the upper balcony. "Most of your training sessions are, if I may say so, rather fun to watch." The older man shook his head as he finished his approach, scratching at his beard. "This one was not."

"They're idiots." Destrick released his knuckle, only peripherally aware of the throbbing pain that had set in. "They think that all it takes to protect someone is to watch the doors and switch places when the bell sounds." He shook his head. "They have no sense for preemptive action, for watching for betrayal and deception before it happens."

"I see." Gorman stepped past him, his back to the Knight-Commander, watching as the last remnants of the guard scurried away. "And how do you plan to remedy this? Why haven't you addressed it before?"

"I thought I had." He kicked at the ground, his fist tight, his words violent. "But then Amalia decides to give that gods-be-damned speech yesterday and…"

He trailed off, punctuating his anger with another kick, this time to a nearby apple tree. The metal of his boot clanged into the wood, gouging a large section out of it.

"Is that what your fight last night was about?" Gorman stepped around to keep the young man's face in view, putting his hands behind his back. "Elsa told me that she heard you two arguing about something. Outside the royal suite?"

"Ahh…" Destrick's face flushed red, and he averted his eyes from Gorman. "Something…something like that. She didn't understand."

"I think that there's more to this than you're telling me. And I think I know what." Gorman scowled. "So I'm going to ask you this once, Guard-Commander, and I want you to look in my eyes when you answer."

Destrick brought his face up toward the older man. Gorman's lined visage seemed the face of Death itself, all joviality and cheer gone. It sent a chill up his spine, but he fought not to show it.

I've never seen him like that before. He looks like he's about to kill me. Destrick set his jaw. *Not surprising.*

"Are you ready?"

Destrick nodded, not taking his eyes from Gorman's. "Yes, Councilor."

"Fine, then. Lord Destrick, did you attempt to force yourself on Queen Amalia last night?"

"I…" He shuddered; his mind replayed the scene, the anger flying between the two of them, the nearness of her lips, the smell she had that drove him mad...

And I must have been mad! He ran his hand through his hair. *What was I thinking?*

"You haven't answered me." Gorman's voice took on a more sinister note; he leaned forward, almost growling. "And I'm running out of patience."

Destrick took a breath. "I don't know."

The response took Gorman by surprise; his eyes widened, and he backed up a step. "You…you don't *know?*" Then the anger returned. "I'm not in the mood for games."

"No. You misunderstand." Destrick put both palms up. "It's…we were arguing, as you said. I was angry that she had taken yesterday's speech and made herself more enemies with it, and I wanted to let her know that I thought she was endangering herself."

Gorman crossed his arms over his chest, but the scowl didn't leave, and neither did the sharpness in his eyes. "Go on."

Destrick straightened, assuming an almost military posture, the junior officer reporting to his commander. "It happened so fast. One second, I'm yelling at her, the next she's…she's kissing me." He softened his stance slightly, making a half-turn towards the Councilor. "I broke it off as soon as I realized exactly what was happening, Gorman. I swear it, upon Junandar and the rest. I left immediately."

Gorman's eyes searched his face; Destrick could feel them, burning into his, hunting for any indication that he was lying.

"I see." The anger slowly dissipated, and Gorman's posture relaxed…somewhat. He brought his arms back down to a neutral position, and his eyes lost some of their fervor. "That would be why Elsa found her crying, then." He shook his head. "I shan't have you as a traitor, which pleases me; instead, I'll need to cuff you for the fool that you are and for hurting someone dear to me."

"What?" Destrick's eyes narrowed, his brow tightened, and he stepped closer to Gorman. "Say that again, Counselor?"

"You're an idiot." In less than the time it took Destrick to process the insult, Gorman's hand flew out and slapped him across the face. The force of it knocked him to one side, making him stumble. "An absolute idiot. Do you know nothing of human emotion?"

Shocked, Destrick couldn't think of anything to say. His eyes watered from the sharp pain in his cheek, and he rubbed it with the tips of his fingers.

"A young woman gives you an inviting look from across the room." Gorman leaned against a nearby trunk, steepling his fingers under his nose. "The two of you talk for a while, get to know one another. Maybe this takes a single night, or several. But you grow comfortable with each other. Perhaps you make a pass at her, and she rejects you…but that doesn't end your relationship. You remain friends." He spread his hands wide. "And, one day, she leans into you, pressing herself to you, her lips to yours. You've already made the fact that you're enamored with her known, even if you'd given up hope on anything happening." He crossed his arms again. "Then you run. You don't even discuss what happened, just leave her." The anger in his voice rose again, making his words strident, harsh, forced through his teeth. "You leave her in the hallway, confused, with no experience to guide her and no one else to talk to."

Gorman raised his hand again, and Destrick closed his eyes and steeled his spine, waiting for another blow…but it didn't come. When he glanced up, the older man had dropped his arm, shaking his head.

Destrick exhaled, turning his head to the side, staring at the grass. "You're making it sound simpler than it is." He rubbed his cheek again, with the back of his hand. The skin had reddened, and he knew he'd have a bruise there soon. "She's the High Queen. There are channels. Procedures. I can't just…" He shook his head. "The Queen can't just have a dalliance with a Baronet Guard

Commander. I'm hardly noble; it would be a scandal. Give everyone more ammunition to attack her with." He met Gorman's stony glare. "I will *not* be the reason that Amalia falls…no matter what I might personally feel for her."

"So it's altruism. Protect her by separating from her. Is that the plan?" Gorman laughed, stepping away before turning around. A light breeze stirred the summer leaves, bringing one of them fluttering down between the two men. "She's young. Even younger than you…although, at the moment, I'm hard-pressed to believe it, based on how you're acting."

That stung Destrick worse than the blow to the face; his eyes widened, and his mouth slackened for a moment as his brain fought for what to say.

"Young people do stupid things. It's a well-known fact." Gorman faced away from him again, staring up to the sky, almost musing. "And maybe this is a stupid thing that she did. Maybe there isn't anything to it, and you'll end up breaking it off with one another."

Then he turned and jabbed his finger toward Destrick's face. "But just leaving her like that? No. Cowardice of the highest level. Behavior more worthy of a frightened vermin than a nobleman, a highborn." The disgust in his voice dripped down over Destrick's ears, coating him in its slime. "If that's the kind of courage you bring to the battlefield, it's a wonder that the Outer Kingdoms haven't taken our palace already."

Without another word, Gorman strode out of the north exit of the courtyard, his feet heavy against the flagstone path. He muttered incomprehensible words to himself, the grumbles fading as he increased his distance from the crestfallen knight.

Destrick watched him leave, his emotions in turmoil. His pride ached, and his first instinct was angry indignation. *Who does he think I am? Calling me a coward!* He fumed, breathing hard, standing, every motion containing more violence than necessary. *Junandar's ass!*

He maintained his frustration and anger for long enough to get out of the courtyard himself, through the southern exit. Servants and visitors made way for him, but he didn't notice; all of his attention focused inward, replaying the Councilor's words, his condescending tone, the anger in his face.

As if I don't know how to handle a relationship with a woman. A new burst of energy fired his limbs, and he shoved the next door open hard enough to smack it against the wall. *When's the last time* he *had occasion?*

He brushed past a courtier passing through the hallway, his ears not registering the man's indignant cry. The sound of his boots clomping, metal ringing, and heart throbbing filled his senses, drowning out everything around him and making way for his own angry thoughts. *And how does he know what she would want, anyway?*

When his boiling, rambling mind turned to Amalia…the anger stopped, simmering away like a pot taken off the fire. He sighed, turning to the wall and leaning his forehead against the cold stone. "How would I know what she wants, unless I ask her?" He turned around, now resting the back of his head on the wall, and closed his eyes.

"I'm an idiot."

~~~

Greagor watched the interplay between the elderly Councilor and the young Commander, lounging on a window ledge, smiling to himself.

"Nice one, Rusty." He swung his legs over the lip of the ledge, letting them hang over the courtyard. The two men below him ended their conversation, Gorman striding with his long steps out one entrance and Destrick storming out the other. "Sounds like you had your shot."

He turned and stood in the hallway, yawning and licking his lips, bending his back behind him and lacing his hands together to give himself a better stretch. As one of the multitude of servants passed him by, giving him a
~~~

curved up, questioning eyebrow, he nodded and touched one hand to his forehead.

The servant gathered his hands to himself and ran off, scurrying like a discovered cockroach. Greagor laughed and strode down the hall in the other direction, toward the center of the castle.

Toward the royal suites.

"No telling how much time I have." He mumbled to himself as he moved, the words almost lost in the sound of his footfalls and breathing. "Should be enough. But no chances."

He picked up his pace, transitioning into a low jog, Windows and bricks passed through his awareness as his speed increased, and he found his heart matching it.

Pushing open the next door and wincing at the slight creak it made on its iron hinges, Greagor peeked his head through the opening and glanced up and down the hallway.

Almost there.

A few seconds more found him in front of the royal chambers. Two guards stood their watch in front of the ornately-carved double doors, and a young woman of no more than fourteen summers, dressed in a peasant's dress and bearing no shoes on her feet sat beside, playing Jacks, apparently unnoticed.

Greagor watched as the ball bounced and the youth made his grab at the small metal figures. The sunlight dancing off the jacks mesmerized him for a second, and he knelt down beside the girl, who glanced up at the sudden realization of his presence.

"Is something wrong?" She spoke with articulation that belied her age. "I do hope that I'm not in your way."

He grinned. "No, not in my way." His eyes touched her face for a moment, then hurried away with a strange, uncomfortable feeling in his stomach. "Having trouble with five?"

The youth nodded, her eyes boring in on Greagor's face. "Perhaps. Too many things to keep up in the air. My family always says I'm trying to do too many things, anyway."

"Of course." Greagor raised an eyebrow, then picked up one of the jacks, running his finger along the smooth metal surface. *It almost looks like silver in this light.* "Do you mind if I try? I used to be quite the player, back when I was your age."

"If you wish." The young girl scooted to the side, making room for Greagor to take her spot. "I look forward to seeing what you accomplish."

Greagor smiled at the comment. "This old man has seen things you wouldn't believe, young lady." Then he tipped her a wink. "Now let's see if the gods favor me or not, hmm?"

He turned back toward the game field, tossing the jack into play. His eyes danced over each piece, memorizing their positions and converting them into muscle memory.

"All right, then." He put his hand out toward his audience, and the youth dropped the rubber ball into his palm. "Here goes."

He tossed the sphere into the air, high, its arc almost reaching the ceiling. As soon as it left his grip, his hand moved, fingers plucking the metal jacks and bringing them into his palm. One, two…he grabbed each one after another, his movements precise, quick.

The tenth found its way into his hand, and, in the same motion, he extended his arm and caught the descending ball. After a second to make sure everything was seated in his hand, he glanced up at the youth.

"Brav-o, sir." The girl clapped, shaking her head. "Don't know if I've ever seen anyone hit the full week without even letting the ball hit the ground first. Damned fine."

"Practice makes everything." Greagor held out his hand, dropping the jacks and ball into the young lady's hand. "You keep at it."

"*You* shouldn't." She pocketed the jacks. "But you will."

As the tiny pieces disappeared into the girl's pocket, Greagor's mind shook off the strange fog that had eclipsed it. His head came up, turning left then right. *Damn. Got distracted.* He stood, keeping his eyes away from the youth and striding toward the door.

"Sorry, my lord." The nearest guard, a grizzled, middle-aged figure whose neck and jaw still showed the muscle he had trained to acquire, shook his head and tightened his grip on his halberd. "Councilor's orders. No one's to enter unless absolutely necessary."

Greagor grinned, spreading his hands wide. "Is that you, Henri?"

The guard blinked, then smiled back. "Greagor? Where've you been?" He reached out with one hand and clapped the huntsman on the back. "And when did you get here?"

"First arrived just before the…" Greagor trailed off and gestured with his chin to the door behind Henri. "And then I took off for most of the mourning." He sighed but still retained his smile. "You know I've never done well with grieving folk."

"True enough." Henri tapped his comrade's shoulder with the haft of his weapon. "Cyl? Did I ever tell you about the time this damned fool got us into a fight at the Rusted Wagon?"

"No." Cyl scowled at the both of them. "And I don't care to hear it. We have a job to do, Henri. You shouldn't be jabbering at the mouth."

"Oh, hush your face." Henri dismissed Cyl with a wave of his hand, then turned back to fully face Greagor. "But, it's been, what, fifteen years? A little longer?"

Greagor nodded, leaning back against the stone wall opposite the door. "A little longer, I think. You had just gotten into the service."

"That's right!" Henri's eyes turned up, staring through the ceiling, before he came back to the present and refocused on his old friend. "The gods have been kind to you, though. If it weren't for the different clothes and the beard you've grown out, I'd peg you as the same age you were then."

Greagor rubbed the stubble. "Hardly grown out, Henri. Just haven't taken care of it in a few days." Then he raised a hand. "Anyway. I'd really like to get in there with the Queen. The King - may he rest eternal in Nome's palace - hired me some time ago to watch after her and see to her personal security."

The guard made a point of checking down one side of the hallway, then the other. "Yeah. Well, Queen's not doing so well, if I may say so. Had a damned fight with Lord Destrick; sent one of the maids runnin', screaming for Lord Gorman. Had his hands all over her, is what I heard." He made a sour face. "Don't know why he'd be interested, personally. What with her face all—"

"That's enough." Greagor put up a finger to cut his friend off. "We don't want to be talking about our Queen that way." Then he chuckled. "Besides, not everyone is as shallow as you are, always looking for the nicest set of lips and curves in a room."

"Man's got to have hobbies. That's all." He glanced back behind him to the closed door. "And I'm not saying that she's going to be a bad queen, or anything. It's just that she's frightening to look at."

"Imagine how she must feel about it."

Henri raised an eyebrow. "It isn't like she has to look herself in the mirror. She doesn't have to deal with what she's inflicting on the rest of us."

"Ouch." Greagor put a hand over his heart, then glanced back down the hallway. "I'd love to debate this with you right now, but I need to check on the Queen. Councilor Gorman wanted me to make sure that she's still doing all right."

"Oh. Of course." Henri stepped back and gripped the door handle, but Cyl put his hand on the door.

"The Councilor instructed us not to let anyone in, Henri." He glared at Greagor, his dark brown eyes lancing into the huntsman's blue ones. "He didn't say anything about making exceptions."

Greagor didn't flinch from the other man's scrutiny. "You're right, of course." He held Cyl's eyes, boring into them with his own. "But you'll let me in, because you should."

Henri shook his head. "It's no good. Cyl's a real stickler for…"

He trailed off when he saw his companion's face. Cyl's hard-set lines and furrowed brow had gone smooth, and his eyes blank. He blinked, slow, the lids sliding over his eyes like a curtain before retreating.

"It should be fine." He nodded, still keeping his eyes locked to Greagor. "Go on in. Let him through, Henri."

Greagor pivoted his head as he walked toward the door, maintaining the gaze the whole way. "Henri? The door, please?"

Henri crossed his arms, grinning. "It's been a long time since I've seen this trick." He scanned Cyl up and down. "Damned if he isn't completely out. Didn't you promise to show me how to do this one day?"

"Never mind." Greagor reached out and took hold of the door himself. "I can do it. Have a good lunch, Cyl. I'm sure that it'll be delicious."

"Yes." Cyl nodded again. "My girl made sure that I had strawberries today."

Henri chuckled as Greagor slipped through the entrance, then turned back to face the hallway. When the door clicked closed, the other guard blinked once, twice, thrice, then shook his head, looking up at Henri with bleary eyes. "Where did he go?"

Henri just shrugged.

~~~

Elsa's head snapped up when Greagor entered the room. "What's wrong? Is something—"

He shook his head, raising one hand. "No, no. Everything's fine. Councilor Gorman just asked me to look in on the Queen, make sure everything's all right." He walked past the antechamber, stepping around a large floor table to reach the sleeping area.

As he crossed the threshold, he felt his breath catch in his chest.

Amalia lay sprawled on cushions of crimson and gold. Taffeta curtains of the same color framed her body, covered only by a thin sheet. Her hound rested beside her, his nose in her neck and her arm draped over him.

"You shouldn't be in here, you know." Elsa peered around him, trying to get through the doorway. "She isn't decent. She kept getting tangled up in her dress while thrashing around the bed, so I had to get her out of it."
~~~

Greagor couldn't take his eyes off the sleeping Queen. They traced her outline in the sheets, caressing her skin through the fabric. "Did she wake?"

"No." Elsa made it through the man-shaped blockade and reached out, pulling the curtains closed and breaking Greagor's near-trance. "Slept through the whole thing. Had to convince the mutt that I wasn't about to hurt her, though. He's protective of her."

"I know." Greagor grinned, his eyes flicking once more to the curtains before focusing on the maid. "She's told me stories."

"So what'd you say you were in here for, again?" Elsa crossed her arms, unintimidated despite their differences in height. "Did you say the Councilor sent you?"

"Yes." He nodded, then sat in a nearby chair. The cushions felt pleasant on his back, firm enough to support but much more comfortable than solid wood. "He just wanted me to check in. See if anything's changed."

"He was in here himself just a quarter-bell ago." She peered at him, not relaxing. The sound of footsteps outside caught Greagor's ear. Heavy footsteps.

They won't let him in, will they? He turned his head, slightly, toward the main door. *But he might be able to order them to. Damn.*

Then he turned his attention back to the curtain. He could *feel* Amalia behind them, knew the turmoil that she was in. *It wasn't supposed to take this long. No time left, if that's Rusty out there. Wake up!*

He threw the thought at her, projecting his will like a bullet. The taffeta jerked, and a small sound of surprise burst out from them. Elsa dropped her suspicious pose and ran over to the bed, opening the curtains just enough to look between them.

"Your Majesty? Are you all right?"

"…Elsa?" Amalia's voice, slurred and thick with sleep fog, reached Greagor's ear. "Is that you?"

"It is, your Majesty." She reached in and put her hand on the Queen's forehead. "You don't feel warm."

"I was dreaming." Amalia turned over, jostling Marchen out of his spot; he barked once, then hopped down from the bed, trotting over to the foot-end and sitting down. "It was…it was horrible…"

"I'm sure it was, your Majesty." Greagor spoke up, keeping his voice low enough to avoid startling her. "I came in to check on you, and found you well attended by your woman, here."

Elsa glanced back at him, eyes icy daggers, but Amalia moved again, the feathered mattress bulging in several places. "Greagor? Elsa, move, please. I need to see him."

"But…" Leaning in, Elsa narrowed her eyes. "You can't see, your Majesty."

"I...That's not what I meant." Amalia shook her head, twice.

Elsa turned back into the bedspace. "But, your Majesty, I don't..."

"Now, if you please." Her words, still sleepy, nonetheless held the tone of one used to command. "Thank you."

The lady-in-waiting bowed her head, stepping away from the gap in the taffeta.

CHAPTER TEN

The silk tickled Amalia's bare skin as she shifted under the sheets; as Greagor approached, she became very conscious of her nudity, how little separated the two of them. One hand came up and clutched the sheets to her chest as his aroma flooded the space – that mixture of cinnamon and ocean salt that set her head spinning every time she was close to it.

I wonder what he looks like. Maybe I can ask Glorianna to... Her hand twitched on the sheet as she imagined running her fingers over his face, tracing the outline of his nose, his lips. Then she shook her head. *What is wrong with you?*

"Did I offend you already, your Majesty?" His voice, full of familiar joviality, felt like warm honey poured into her ear. "I've only just arrived."

"Of course not." She smiled. "You'll have to forgive my current state of dress, Greagor. I…I haven't been well, apparently."

"So I've heard." He leaned in, closing the distance between them. "But don't worry. I don't mind."

Amalia's cheeks flushed at the innuendo.

"Anyway, I was just here to check on some of the rumors that I had heard." He licked his lips and put one hand on the bed. The sheets tugged at Amalia's hand, just a fraction, and the feathers bent under his weight. "Some of the guards are saying that Lord Destrick tried something that he shouldn't have."

The mention of Destrick's name brought the events of the previous night back into Amalia's consciousness, an avalanche of emotion and confusion. She turned her head away, throat closing up. All symptoms of arousal vanished, replaced by a heavy, lead weight in her chest.

"No." The word came out in a whisper, scarcely audible to her own ears. "He didn't do anything."

"Glad to hear it." Knuckles cracked, *pops* coming one after another. "I was starting to worry that I was going to have to have it out with Rusty on the field of honor."

Amalia shook her head again. "Nothing like that. We just had a…a misunderstanding." She swallowed, then faced the huntsman again. "If you don't mind, Greagor, I need to get dressed and find out what has transpired during my absence."

"I'm sure that Gorman has everything taken care of." He reached out and put a hand on hers. "There's no rush."

Amalia began to pull her hand from his, but paused, wrinkling her brow.

"I can't hear you."

"Do I need to speak up?" He chuckled. "I don't think that's a problem."

"No. Never mind." *Damn. I almost gave myself away.* "And I truly think it best if I attend to matters myself, Greagor. Thank you for your visit."

A moment of silence passed between them. "As you command, your Majesty." He stood up. "I'm glad you're feeling better. I'll see you later."

Then, without another word, he spun on the heel of his leather boot and strode toward the door. Amalia heard the *creak* as it opened…then the collision as he ran into something large and metallic.

"Damn it, Henri! Why were you standing right in the middle of the doorway?"

"So sorry." The guard laughed. "Maybe you should've had your eyes forward when you stepped out. Would've stopped you from hitting me, I'd wager."

The door shut, leaving only muffled voices on the other side. Amalia let out a breath, her muscles relaxing, her head dropping back onto the soft bed.

How long have I been asleep? Her lips narrowed as she thought…and shuddered. *And that dream. When will I stop having that dream?*

Just the memory of her nightmare sent her trembling again. She rubbed her upper arms, letting the sheet drop to her waist. The sudden cold air made her skin dimple with goosebumps.

Glorianna? She reached out with her mind, trying to find her sister, to share the dream with her...but there was nothing. *Sister? Have I angered you?*

Marchen let out a low whine, the sound drawing her out of her introspection. She reached out her hand to scratch the top of the dog's head.

"Elsa? Are you there?"

The young woman came to the opening in the curtains. "Yes, your Majesty?"

"How long have I been asleep?" Amalia stretched, gripping her left elbow with her right hand. "I feel like I've been in bed for a week."

"No, your Majesty. Only about two hours or so. Long enough to get the Councilor and myself into a panic." Elsa allowed a laugh, but Amalia could hear the tinge of nervousness and worry that it hid. "But I'm so glad to see you doing better."

"Help me. I feel like I've been presenting a poor image for a new Queen." Amalia leaned forward, massaging her temples. "What's something that I could do, something that a Queen should do? I need some sort of distraction from my own thoughts, but I'm at a loss."

"Well, your Majesty." The Queen could hear Elsa's foot tapping against the stone floor as the woman considered. "That's an interesting question. I suppose a surprise inspection of the guards might be something you could do. I know my mother accompanied yours on more than one occasion to one of those."

"A guard inspection. That sounds perfectly mundane. Thank you." She turned and planted her feet on the bed. "Can you pick out something appropriate?"

"At once." Elsa hurried over to the chests of drawers, opening and closing lids as she shuffled through the piles of clothing. Amalia stood up, scrunching her feet on the stone floor, enjoying the scratching sensation.

Marchen panted at her side, nudging her thigh with his head. She reached out, scratched behind his ears a moment, then pushed him away as she walked to where Elsa was laying out garments.

"I think this will do just right, your Majesty." Elsa turned and presented the Queen with undergarments. "It's a loose-fitting gown that will help you move. Not one of the fancy formal ones for court."

"That should be fine then. Thank you." Amalia began dressing herself, slipping the clothes on over her skin, enjoying the feel of the fabric. The smell of lavender washed over her face, easing her tension and bringing an involuntary smile. She turned her head from one side to the other. "Where's my sword?"

"Hmm?"

"My weapon." Amalia rifled through her memory, hunting. "I don't remember where I left it."

"Oh, it's not your fault, your Majesty. I moved it." A soft sound of something passing through the air. "It's by your bedside, near the head of your bed, leaning against the wall. I thought it'd be easier for you to find there."

She grimaced. "Don't move my things, Elsa. I have to remember where I put them or else I lose track."

"Oh." She turned to face the Queen. "I'm sorry, your Majesty. It was just on the floor near the washroom and I thought—"

"No harm done." Amalia reached out, taking hold of the dress Elsa held. The lavender caressed her senses again, relaxing her muscles and drawing out a deep breath. "Thank you."

"My pleasure, Queen Amalia." Elsa turned back to the clothes, refolding and placing them back into the lavender-scented chests. "My pleasure."

~~~

Amalia burst through the wooden doors, startling the guards. Her left hand clutched Marchen's leash, while her right gripped her sheathed blade. After taking a moment to listen and get her bearings – the warmth of the hall told her it was about 8th bell, maybe 9th, and the nearest footfalls were two doors distant – she turned to the right, heading toward the barracks.

In the back of her mind, she felt a gnawing, as if she'd forgotten something important. Her gait slowed as she puzzled over it, trying to piece together exactly what was going on.

"Your Majesty!" Gorman's near-frantic voice caught her off guard. "Are you well? You have been in...distress...for some time." He cleared his throat and his voice fought itself back to a semblance of normalcy. "It is...Good to see you about."

She smiled, embracing the old man. "Good morning, Gorman. I'm sorry for the trouble I caused."

"No need to be sorry...but, if you could, avoid doing it again." He walked up beside her, threading his arm
~~~

through hers. Marchen obliged by taking several steps forward, clearing space for him to stand. "It gives us all great distress when you are indisposed for so long."

"I know." Amalia sighed, nodding, as they began to walk. "I promise that it isn't as terrible as it may seem. Fatigue, in the main, and stress, to which I shall soon become accustomed, no doubt."

Gorman patted her hand. "Delegation, Amalia. No ruler of anything more than the smallest borough can be expected to handle everything themselves." They took four more steps. "Where are you headed?"

"Destrick suggested that I inspect the guards." She turned a half-smile in the Councilor's direction. "I thought that it was a good idea."

"Ah. Destrick." She could feel his body tense, hear the change in the timbre of his voice. "Amalia—"

She sighed. "No, Gorman. He didn't force himself on me." At the silence, she continued. "I heard the same rumor from Greagor, when he came to check in on me. He didn't do anything wrong." She shook her head. "If anything, I did."

"I'm glad to hear that, your Majesty. A lot of people have heard those rumors already, and it shall be good to set them to bed." He took a breath. "But that's actually not what I wanted to say."

She paused, turning in place to face him. "Oh?"

"Yes." He cleared his throat. "The delegation from Ragna sent word that they are arriving within the week. Their messenger is currently enjoying breakfast in the Great Hall."

"Ah." She nodded, and they resumed their trip. A couple of courtiers passed them in the opposite direction, bowing and murmuring greetings to the Councilor and Queen, who returned the gestures in acknowledgment. "I imagine that some people are rather irritated by that?"

"Some. Many are curious. He hasn't caused any trouble, just been enjoying our hospitality so far." He laughed.

"Then why are you nervous?" Amalia tightened her grip on his arm. "I can feel the tension in your muscles, Gorman. You only get like this when you're hiding something from me."

Two seconds of hesitation. "Count it to simple worry, Amalia." He squeeed her hand. "There haven't been diplomatic relations with the Outer Kingdoms for the last thirty or so years. I know almost nothing about them."

"Then I look forward to meeting them. And their messenger." She gave him a wicked smile. "But let's allow him to enjoy himself a little while longer. I wouldn't want him to think we were begging for his approval."

"A fine tactic." They stepped out of the palace proper, and Amalia felt the sunlight playing on her hair and her face, warming her with small fingers of light that she couldn't see.

At least, I can't see them like this…

"How many times have you been to the barracks?"

It took Amalia a moment before she realized what he was asking. "Not enough. I have to be very careful on the path, so as not to lose my way or my footing."

"Then it's fortunate that I came along when I did." Then he paused, reaching down and patting Marchen's head. "Not that you would have had a problem getting her there, would you?"

The dog responded with a happy bark, hopping up and down in place.

"What's the sky like today, Gorman?" Amalia turned her face upward, soaking in the sunlight. "Is it likely to stay sunny like this all day?"

"No, unfortunately." Gorman shook his head. "The augurs say that the skies will darken with rain by the evening. Can you smell it?"

Amalia took a deep breath through her nose, then nodded. "Yes. The air is quite moist from the west. I expect the storm will be intense." She patted his hand. "Perhaps you can let the townsfolk know, that they might bring in their clothes and goods?"

"A very kind gesture. I'll make sure that it is done as soon as I leave you." The two walked on for some time in silence; Amalia kept track of her footfalls and orientation, reinforcing the mental map that she kept in her mind.

"You didn't sleep well last night, did you?"

The question caught the Queen off guard. "I…No, I don't suppose that I did. My dreams were…unpleasant."

"Dreams of your father?" His voice was thick with concern, compassion.

Amalia hesitated, then sighed, nodding for him to continue.

"I have them too, from time to time. I can only imagine what it must be like for you, having been there when he died."

That's not the worst of it, my friend. Not by a long shot. Rather than vocalizing her thoughts, she kept them to herself, choosing to listen instead.

"But I've had to keep busy in the aftermath. So many nobles to contain, people to take care of." He chuckled, throwing one hand to the side like he was showering confetti over a parade. "It helps distract me from the grief."

"I'm sure it does." The words tasted bitter in Amalia's mouth, cocoa beans without sugar. "I only hope that it does the same for me as well."

Gorman tapped Amalia's wrist with two fingers. "We've arrived. The door is right in front of you, a single wooden door with a handle on the right."

"Thank you." Amalia reached out and gripped the handle. The door swung open on well-oiled hinges, the speed startling her for a moment. Gorman pulled his arm free, then stepped into the barracks in front of her.

"All salute!" Three different voices echoed the cry as the Councilor entered the room. Boots thumped on floor and various objects – metal, wood, cloth – skittered across the beds and counters. Amalia covered her mouth, trying to suppress the smile that came to mind as she imagined the guards in scrambling disarray, trying to stow whatever it was they had been doing when Gorman walked in.

"Her Majesty, High Queen Amalia Therald."

Such ceremony. She arranged herself in a regal pose – head straight, chin out, Marchen tight to her side – and stepped in. The intakes of breath informed her that there were four guards present, scattered throughout the fifteen-bed barracks. The room smelled of sweat, oil, and steel, and was warmer than the outside air, even though the full sun of the day was filtered out by the walls; only a few windows allowed thin, weak rays to touch Amalia's skin.

"Senior officer, identify yourself and step forward."

The voice of a young woman surprised Amalia, coming from the left, three or four paces away. "Majesty! Knight-Lieutenant Corynn. Second-in-command to Knight Commander Destrick."

I didn't realize that Destrick's lieutenant was a woman. Amalia's stomach twisted, sending creeping tendrils of anxiety along her veins, gnawing at her insides...and the sensation surprised her, forcing her to take a split-second to reorient herself.

"Knight-Lieutenant. What's the status of the guard?"

"Commander Destrick has asked for all guardsman to report to training, your Majesty." Her words came across crisp and clean, military precision evident in each syllable.

Amalia tilted her head, turning toward Corynn. "To what purpose?"

"Well..." The Lieutenant faltered a moment, then recovered. "The Commander is dissatisfied with our performance of late, especially as it concerns protecting the royal person."

"Meaning me?"

"Yes, your Majesty."

"Hmm." Amalia stepped through the barracks, allowing Marchen's gentle tugs to keep her from tripping on or colliding with anything. "Is he worried about me? Does he think something is going to happen?"

Corynn cleared her throat. "He hasn't made that information known to me."

"I see." The Queen stopped in front of one of the other soldiers, hearing his breath catch when she turned to face him. "What's your name?"

"I…I'm Saren, your Majesty. Saren Borchester."

"Good morning, Saren." She bowed her head to him for a moment. "What do you think of being a guardsman?"

"It's…" He hesitated, and Amalia heard his feet shift weight back, then forth, as he considered his answer.

"Please." Amalia reached out, put a hand on the youth's shoulder. "Speak freely, if you would. I'm not here to catch you loafing about, or whatever it is that Destrick does." She smiled. "I just want to know something about my people."

Saren nodded, swallowing hard. "Well…It's much better than what my family has had before."

"Oh? What do they do?"

Saren's voice came across weak, feeble, embarrassed. "My father's just a farmer, your Majesty. Grows wheat and corn some thirty-six miles west of here." He sighed. "Doesn't even own his own land. Or not most of it, anyway. Has to lease it from Baron Greene."

"Listen to me, Saren." Amalia put her hand under his chin, bringing it up so he would look into her face. She felt his muscles tense, but he suppressed his instinctive flinching.

She ignored the twinge of pain in her own heart that the almost-wince caused.

"Your family does a great thing for Aetheria. They feed people." She shook her head. "Without farmers like him, we would not be independent. We would be vassals to someone much more powerful, someone that could produce foodstuffs to provide for their craftsmen, their armies, and their nobility." She turned and pointed outward, toward the castle. "Do you think that, for one second, we could survive here without grain and corn? Our people use it in a thousand different ways every day, Saren. *Our people.*"

She released him and backed off a few steps. "Don't look down on those who have chosen a life of service through work rather than through laying down their lives. Both are a form of sacrifice, and both are necessary if we are to remain free."

"I…"

"Thank you for allowing me to visit." Amalia turned back toward Lieutenant Corynn, bowing from the waist. "I am pleased by what I found here. Do make sure you aren't late to Destrick's training session."

"I shan't be late, your Majesty. And neither will those in my command."

Amalia nodded, then flicked the leash. Marchen moved at once, pulling her toward the exit, guiding her out through the door. She hit the cool air like a wall, taking a deep breath of grass and fragrant cherry.

"I'd say that was well done." Gorman clapped her on her shoulder as the door shut behind him. "I'm not quite sure they know what to make of you."

Amalia turned a beaming smile on him. "That was a very enjoyable experience. I hope that my arrival didn't disrupt them *too* much."

"My dear, that's the point of a surprise inspection." Gorman took his customary place at her side, and the two began walking again. "It's supposed to keep the soldiers on their toes by reminding them that you could show up at any time."

And maybe it will help them respect me a little more, to see me and speak with me in person.

"Would you like to meet the messenger from Ragna now?" She felt his body shift as he glanced up to the sky. "I think that the good weather should hold up for that long."

"Excellent." Amalia turned and pressed her lips to Gorman's cheek. He stopped, the sudden change in momentum making her stumble.

"What was that for?"

"Just a minor expression of royal gratitude." She grinned. "I hope you don't disapprove."

"Nothing of the sort, your Majesty." He squeezed her hand. "*I* just hope you realize that I'm far too old for you, and that it wouldn't be appropriate."

He said it in his matter-of-fact, proper tone, but the juxtaposition between the tone and the words made Amalia break into laughter. She doubled over, her breath coming in great heaves only to be expelled by the next bout.

"You know, your Majesty, it's rather rude of you to be laughing at a member of your Council, even *if* he's saying things that make no sense."

"I'll keep that in mind." Another round of chuckling. "What would I do without you?"

"Gods willing, you won't have to find out for some years yet." Then he unlaced his arm, wrapped it around her shoulders, and pulled her in for a hug. "But I think you'll find yourself more than capable when the time comes."

Amalia bowed her head. The strange nagging feeling emerged again, at the back of her brain. She reached out to her draconic sister, stretching her mind to make contact. *Glorianna? Is that you?*

No further response came, just that constant gnawing.

"Amalia? Is something wrong?"

She shook her head, smiled, relaced her arm. "No, Gorman. Just thinking about how fast things have changed." Before he could reply, she took another step and straightened her posture. "I believe that the Great Hall is this way."

"Right you are, your Majesty."

CHAPTER ELEVEN

The doors to the Great Hall opened as the Queen and Councilor stepped through. Their feet clacked on the wood, almost in unison, and Amalia heard a chair scrape across the floor as the person standing swallowed down the last mouthful of his food. By the smell wafting across the room, veal, corn, and apples were the order of the day, and Amalia found her mouth watering and her stomach rumbling.

I completely forgot to eat. She shook her head. *What a damned fool.*

"Lord Don of Ragna, may I present to you Her Majesty, High Queen Amalia Therald, the Sword of Junandar."

The foreign messenger approached, his steps slow, close together. When he spoke, his voice came from a point a foot higher than Amalia's head, and she reacted by bringing her face up toward the sound. Her nose filled with the scent of dried flowers and spice, although she couldn't place the exact variety.

"The tales told in the Outer Kingdoms pale in comparison to the reality, your Majesty." Don's words flooded her ears like a viscous syrup, his accent strange, his consonants stronger, vowels weaker. "Your kingdom is truly an example of everything we all aspire to…and you a reflection of its glory."

"Thank you, Lord Don." She breathed in, and again the aroma of food tickled her nose and stirred her stomach. "I hope you don't mind if I join you for your meal. Business of court has kept me from eating until now, and this is a perfect opportunity for us to speak."

"I agree, your Majesty." The chair slid again, and the man's bottom thumped against it as he sat down. "I must say, your cuisine is excellent, although lacking somewhat in depth. Perhaps some of my native peppers would go well with it. Especially the giantra."

Amalia disentangled herself from Gorman's arm, making her way to the opposite side of the table. As she moved, Gorman hurried across the room until he reached the server's entrance. "The Queen is hungry. Prepare her another plate of what you made for our guest."

"As you wish, Councilor."

Amalia reached her seat, larger by half than the others, and propped her sword on the side. *Why does everything royal have to tower over everything else? It seems so ostentatious and unnecessary. A few jewels or some gold on it would have done enough.* As she sat, her arms stretched out to lay on the armrests. *This must make me look so small.*

She took a breath, ready to speak; the scent of the ambassador's dish crept into her nose again, underlaid with…a spicy aroma she could not place, but one that made her nostrils flare and tingle. *I can't tell if that's a pleasant smell or not. Very strange.*

"So, Lord Don."

"You're the High Queen of Aetheria." He laughed, then filled his mouth with bread, dipping it in the meat juice from his veal. "You should just call me Don. I'm not 7your lord."

She inclined her head. "Very kind. Don, then. What brings you to Aetheria?"

In response, the ambassador let out a loud burp, then smacked his lips. "I truly must compliment your chef. And perhaps steal him away."

"I think you'd be hard-pressed to convince them." Amalia laced her fingers and tapped her thumbs together. "But I'm sure you're not here to seduce my culinary staff to Ragna."

An undertone of irritation crept into his voice. "I didn't realize that Aetherians had forgotten how to hold pleasant conversation."

Amalia smiled. "Oh, we haven't. It's just that we also prefer our pleasant conversation forthright and open, not dancing around each other like sparring partners in a fencing match."

"In Ragna, I suppose I would liken it to foreplay between lovers. Carefully caressing each other's egos until the right moment to begin." The grin on his face came clearly through his speech. "Speaking of fencing…" Don took several gulps of his lager, then slammed his mug onto the table, making it shake under Amalia's elbows. "Word has it that you're pretty handy with that blade you're carrying around. Now how does a blind woman, if you'll pardon the asking, learn to defend herself with a sword?"

Gorman tensed up, hissing as he took a breath, but Amalia raised her hand. "Practice. Many hours of intense practice, coupled with scars and scrapes and bruises." She tapped her index fingers, then brought one up to her hair, pulling it aside from her neck. "Do you see this? This was the worst injury I received during training. I was seven or eight years old at the time, and stumbled over my own feet while the master ran me through basic avoidance drills." She let the hair drop. "I fell right across the tip of his blade. Didn't think I could bleed so much and not die."

"Amazing." Don raised his cup again. "I salute you, your Majesty, for overcoming such adversity and prospering. You truly are an inspiration to many who hear your story. In Ragna, the noble halls are filled with whispers and suppositions, centering around your seemingly-supernatural abilities."

Amalia shook her head, laughing slightly. "Those words are very kind. But, and I regret that I must press this, you still have not explained why, after all these years, your kingdom wishes to renew relations with ours." She paused, drumming on the top of the table; from the far side of the room, the serving door opened, ushering in the arrival of three servants carrying the Queen's meal on porcelain plates. "I admit to being interested when I heard of your arrival, but your refusal to speak plainly on the manner is convincing me otherwise."

"As you wish." Again, there was no mistaking the grumbling in his voice; apparently, citizens of Ragna enjoyed their idle chatter too much for Amalia's liking. "Before High King Francis unified Brandil, Ragna enjoyed a very lucrative trade agreement with Aetheria. Your country's fruit and produce are exceptional; in fact, some of the farming families in Ragna and the other

Kingdoms have wondered what must be in your soil to produce such results."

"There's no secret, I'm afraid." Amalia shrugged, picking up a crust of bread and dipping it into her meat. "Noble Haphapshem blessed this land, causing all the green things to grow all year, except the winter."

"I do believe I've heard that legend as well." A slight squeal as Don put knife to meat, cutting his veal into small pieces. "But we were hoping that there might be a more conventional method we could use in order to avoid having to appeal directly to the Green Lord." Then he put a chunk into his mouth. "By the gods, this is fine. So smooth it almost melts on my tongue; it feels like it's caressing the inside of my mouth." He swallowed, then chased it with a gulp of beer. "I swear, if I don't get anything else from you on this visit, even if you condemn my country and sentence me to death for treason or what have you, I will get this recipe from you and deliver it to my homeland."

Amalia's cheeks stretched as her grin grew. "We can discuss that after we've decided if I'm going to hang you for treason, Lord Don." She cleared her throat, holding up a hand. "I'm interested in exactly what Ragna has to offer in exchange for Aetherian produce. You'll forgive me, I hope, but I am not well-versed in your nation's culture or history."

"We are a small country, but we have wealth in the form of jade and spices." He brushed his hands off on the towel beside him, the fluffy cotton brushing against his fingers. "Some of which aren't found anywhere else that we've ever seen. I brought some samples for you to try, if you're interested in seeing what they're like, but…" He took another bite, thumping the table with his free hand. "I swear, add some giantra and maybe taurisian to this and you wouldn't be able to keep people away."

"I'll take that under consideration. Have some of your people give your samples to my cooks; they'll examine them and see what can be done."

"That sounds like a fair arrangement." Don burped again, more quietly this time, then picked up the ear of corn to his right. "King Crelm asked me to convey his condolences on your father's untimely passing. We understood him to have been a great leader, worthy of the respect of both his people and others."

Amalia nodded, her throat closing, swallowing to force the passageway to stay open. "Our kingdom is certainly worse for the loss. I can only hope to carry on his legacy, and the legacy of my ancestors, in such a way that they are pleased with my work."

"Speaking of legacies…" Don tapped on the edge of his glass with his knife, and a servant scurried over to refill it. The sound of beer spilling into the mug reminded the Queen how thirsty she was, and she motioned to have the same. "Is it true that he was slain by a dragon?"

The cessation of movement from the other side of the table told Amalia that Don was watching her, examining her face, her hands. For a brief moment, she considered lying to him.

But what good would that do? A sigh. *It's not like others didn't see.*

"Yes. That is accurate." Amalia sipped at the warm broth, allowing it to flow down her throat like molten silk. "A full wing of dragons made to attack, and he met them in the field. Challenged their leader to one-on-one combat." She breathed slowly, hoping that Don would take the difficulty she was having as evidence of grief for her father – which it was – and not as hiding the fact that the dragon leader was her mother.

"That was very brave of King Marcus, to face such a challenging foe as a dragon." Don tapped the hilt of his carving knife against the table, *knock, knock, knock.* "But I had thought that the Red Clan had been driven to extinction during your Dragon War. Do you have any idea how they resurfaced?"

"The…The Red Clan?" Amalia shook her head, and she heard Gorman take a step toward the table. "I'm afraid I don't understand."

"Oh, you probably have another name for it, I imagine." Don laughed, scooting his chair back and smacking his lips as he began picking at his teeth. "But some time ago, we - that is, our ancestors - decided that the color differentiation was the simplest way to classify them into groups."

"You mean…" The implications were staggering; Amalia couldn't believe what she was hearing. "That there are different kinds of dragons?"

"Of course there are." Honest surprise. "You didn't know that? Just in Ragna we have Yellow, Black, and Green clans. There are others, in other kingdoms." He leaned forward again, his chair creaking, then the table under the weight of his elbows. "I'm surprised that your father didn't tell you this."

"As am I." She shook her head, turning to the side. Her hand came down and beckoned Marchen up, grunting as the huge dog landed in her lap. Her right hand stroked his fur, head to tail, as she thought. "Gorman?"

"Your Majesty, if anyone knew of other dragons in the world, then it was the most tightly-kept secret I've ever encountered. I didn't know, and, although I can't say for sure what was in your father's mind, I would have been very surprised to learn that he knew." Then the older man put his hands on the table. "Assuming that Lord Don is accurate in his assessments, of course."

"You doubt whether or not I know if giant flying creatures can be found in *my* homeland?" Don laughed, pounding the table with his hand. "They can, although they're fairly rare. Skirmishes between themselves keep their numbers down, but they're useful beasts of burden as well." Another laugh. "Still, our lands hold more than many others - a blessing for us, or we'd be at a disadvantage ourselves, being so small and unable to field a large military."

"You…" Amalia shuddered, making the hound in her lap jump down. "You use them to fight one another?"

Don laughed again, and took another three gulps of beer. "This is very nice. The flavor is warm and flows through the throat." Another sip. "And no, we don't. At least, we haven't had to for some time. The Great War was several generations ago…and the devastation led us to decide that we had better things to do with our time." Then he rapped on the table. "But I suppose I should be thanking the gods, as Ragna was formed out of the treaties signed to end that war. We're almost as young as your High Monarchy."

Amalia tried to smile. "This is…this is very interesting, Lord Don. And I thank you for the information." Her mind raced, trying to weigh the implications of this new data, to parse out how - or if - it changed anything. "You have given me much to think about, and…" Her words failed her, leaving her brow furrowed and her lips moving without sound. Then she stood, pushing the large chair behind her, almost forgetting to grab hold of her sword again before it clattered to the ground. "But I have many things to attend to. I hope that you find your lodgings acceptable, and I look forward to speaking with you again."

Don followed suit, hurrying to stand, clattering his plate and scraping the feet of his chair against the floor. "And I you, your Majesty. Thank you for the hospitality. I'll make sure that your chefs have access to those spices as soon as possible."

Amalia gave the foreigner a shallow bow, then turned and extended her right arm. Gorman stepped up and took it in his own. The two left the Great Hall in silence.

But Amalia's mind was *not* silent.

Glorianna! She lifted her mind's voice, calling out with all her strength. She felt for the link between her and her sister, sending out her thoughts upon the thin tendril that connected them.

But it wasn't there. It felt as if her thoughts were echoing in the darkness, fading with distance.

Amalia's stomach sank, her heart pounded in her chest, sour bile welled up in her throat as she stopped walking.

"That was…interesting." Gorman patted her hand, turning toward her. "I thought that…"

Then he trailed off as he saw Amalia's face, reaching out and putting hands on both her shoulders. "Amalia, what's wrong? You look like someone just died."

"No. Nothing like that. I…," She coughed, more to distract from the situation than from any real physical need. "The discussion about the dragons…it reminded me rather strongly of Father's death. I did my best to hold it in while in front of Lord Don, but…"

"Say no more, your Majesty." Gorman gave her a quick hug. "I understand entirely. If you need to take some time to rest, you—"

"What sort of ruler will the people perceive me as if I continually run back to my rooms to hide?" She set her lips. "No. I will overcome this. Worry not."

Gorman sighed, then nodded. "As you wish. I just hope you aren't taking too much onto yourself already."

Amalia's brain burned with her impatience; he didn't know, *couldn't* know, and so she had to get away from him in order to investigate. "Can you make contact with the other Councilors? I'm curious as to what they'll think of our meeting with Lord Don."

He cocked his head, scratched at his beard. Amalia smiled to herself. *It's shorter than yesterday. He must have trimmed it.*

"Are you sure? It's no trouble for me to stay with you."

"To be honest…I'm feeling cramped. I'm not used to being so tightly watched and regimented, Gorman. Not even when I was the Princess Regent." Another sigh, this one long and filled with frustration. "I just…I wish to have some time to myself, exploring, wandering the grounds or the village. Just as I used to."

Before Gorman could protest, she raised her blade. "I have my weapon. I have my whistle, and my Marchen. No one will come near enough to harm me."

"Very well." She could hear the rebellion in his words, feel his muscles tense, the exhalation through his nose like a bull confronted with an insurmountable wall. "But I hope that you will be back before the 7th evening bell. Supper will be served, and Lord Don is expected to be in attendance, along with the other councilors, the vassal rulers, and any other nobles who wish to attend. It would be very bad form if you were not present."

"I will make it back in time for that, Gorman. I promise." She leaned in and embraced him again. "Thank you for understanding."

He chuckled. "I'm not sure I do, your Majesty. But I understand where the impulses come from. Both your mother and father were people of passion, disinclined to sit still while there were things that needed doing."

"I suppose that's the way of it." They separated, and Amalia turned, flicking Marchen's leash to remind him to attend her. "I will return soon."

She stepped away, walking toward one of the nearby doors, her keen ears tracking her companion until she heard him enter one across the way, leading to the western side of the castle. When that door slammed closed, she stopped, her free hand reaching out to the arm of a resting bench, crumpling to the seat as if all the strength in her limbs had been pulled out of her with a pair of forceps.

Glorianna? Now, without the mental focus needed to keep walking, to keep track of where her feet were and where objects and pitfalls lay, she threw everything she had at the Link, digging into her own mind, a sapper set to destroy whatever walls stood in her way. Her awareness of her surroundings faded, dissolving into the mental mists that enveloped her whenever she joined the Link.

And there *was* something in her way.

In her mind, Amalia perceived it as a smooth obstruction, a wall made of marble or glass. It was cold to the touch, almost cold enough to burn, and it stretched for as far as she could sense. The air around her baked with heat, dry, sucking the moisture from her throat with every breath.

And her sister was on the other side.

Glorianna! She called out, but her voice rebounded from the wall back to her, echoes in a place of shadow and memory. She slammed her fist into the wall, but might as well have been striking a mountain for all the impact she had.

...amalia...

The voice was faint, distant, like a child calling from the bottom of a cliff underneath a waterfall, but Amalia caught it. She pressed herself against the wall, her fingers seeking any sort of purchase in the strange stone, her ear seeking any further hint of the voice or any other presence.

Glorianna? She called out to her sister as she tried to get through the wall; it felt almost pliable, as if her fingertips could sink just a fraction of an inch into the surface. Sweat from her exertions broke out across her face.

"Amalia?"

She turned. "Glorianna?"

All at once, the feeling of the grass, the air on her face, and Marchen's warm body returned. She breathed in, cool moisture rushing through her nose and mouth. *How did I get outside?* Her fingers dug into the dirt, granules under her nails. *I wasn't outside before!*

A servant's voice. Male. Someone she didn't know personally. "Your Majesty? Is everything all right? Should I fetch the Councilor, or—"

"No, no. I'm all right." Amalia pushed herself up, her muscles and voice trembling. Her hands ached where they had hit the mental wall, and she rubbed one with the fingers of the other. "I just wanted to relax, and I suppose I must have dozed off."

"I'm glad you're all right." The servant took a step back. "May the gods keep you safe."

"And you as well."

Amalia bowed her head as he left. *What is going on here?* Then she resumed walking. *This doesn't make any sense.* Her pores opened, and she could smell her own sweat streaming from her face and body. Nervousness forced her into a run, her hands coming up just in time to push open the first door. *Why now? Did I make her angry? Is she intentionally shutting me out?*

Windows filled with sunlight and breeze whipped by her as she hurried down the hallway toward the royal suite. *And how did I get out there? Did I walk, by myself? Did Marchen lead me? And why there?*

Her footsteps echoed off the stone walls.

No, something's wrong. Something has to *be wrong.* She shook her head, moving so fast now that Marchen had to jog to keep up. *But what could do something like that?*

She rounded a corner, so deep in her thoughts that she didn't hear the person on the other side of it, colliding with them so hard that it knocked them both off their feet.

"Gods damn it!" Amalia shouted in surprise as she hit the ground. "Who is that?"

"My apologies, your Majesty."

Destrick?

"What are you doing here?" She got up and brushed herself off while Marchen took a position between the two of them.

"I came to see if you were in your rooms, before I went out to instruct my troops." Something was different about his voice – it was less confident; he hesitated between his syllables as if searching through his mind for the right word. "I...I think we need to discuss what happened yesterday." He rubbed the back of his neck. "I believe there may have been a misunderstanding."

The shock of falling and colliding with Destrick had momentarily swept her concerns from her mind, but now they came back, full force, and so it took her a moment to realize exactly what he was talking about. "I'm sorry?"

"You're going to make me say it, aren't you?" He laughed, nervous, and his voice stuttered. "As you wish.

I want to talk about the kiss. I acted like a complete, bumbling fool."

The memory returned, and Amalia felt her face flush. "Oh. Destrick, this isn't really—"

"No, it is." He swallowed, shifted from foot to foot. "I made an absolute ass of myself, Amalia. I did. When you kissed me, I..." He laughed, scratched his neck again, breathed in. "There's so much that went through my mind that it's hard to describe it all."

The back of Amalia's brain itched, nagging at her, calling her. *What is that? What does that have to do with what's going on? Anything?*

"As you know, I've been...attracted to you...for some time." Destrick started to pace, making a tight circle in front of the Queen. "I've grown up alongside you, seen you grow from the lovely young lady into the full bloom of womanhood. At the same time, you've proven yourself amazing in so many ways. Learning to overcome your blindness..."

Then he sucked in air through his teeth. "Damn it. That's not the way I wanted to say that. I want you to know that...that I think you're a magnificent person." He let that hang in the air. "And that had to go against the fact that, now, you're the High Queen. And I'm supposed to be the one protecting you, keeping you safe from harm."

His voice faded from Amalia's ears, replaced by a buzzing, the whine of bees on flowers, with low thuds underlying the sound. She cocked her head, pursed her lips. *What...?*

"Queen Amalia...oh. Hello, Rusty."

Greagor's words cut through the fog, drilling straight into the core of Amalia's brain. She whipped her head around to face the newcomer as he stepped into range. Destrick stopped mid-word, turning as well, his toes curling in his leather boots.

"Huntsman. To what do we owe the pleasure?" Destrick stepped forward, angling to interpose himself between Greagor and Amalia. "I wasn't aware that you had a meeting with Her Majesty scheduled."

"Do I need to schedule?" He met Destrick halfway, his height towering over the other man. "I think that's a matter for the Queen herself to decide. Don't you?"

Amalia raised both hands. "Not this again. I've told both of you before. If this is how you are going to act every time the two of you are in my presence, then I'll exile one and execute the other, and I won't tell you which is which."

Destrick dropped back. "My apologies, Majesty. I just—"

"Amalia." Greagor moved to fill the gap that Destrick left, now standing directly before her. "I need to speak to you about your visitor, and about…" He paused. "…Your *friend.*"

"What are you talking about? The ambassador from Ragna?" Destrick laughed. "Just because you're from the neighboring kingdom doesn't mean that the Queen needs your advice on diplomacy." He put a hand on the larger man's shoulder. "Stick to the forests and let the nobility handle these things."

Amalia scarcely heard him; her entire being focused on the last two words that Greagor had spoken. *He remembers? How is this possible?* Then she shook her head again. *I can find out. I must.*

"Destrick, the huntsman needs to speak to me. Can we continue our conversation another time?"

Greagor snickered, and Destrick stood there, silent for several seconds. "I…of course, your Majesty." He bowed, a sharp, snapping movement of a few inches. "Greagor."

Then he about-faced, marching down the hall in military fashion, his steps fading into Amalia's eternal darkness. When he was far enough, Amalia took hold of Greagor's hand.

"How do you know something's wrong with her?" Her words spilled from her lips at a mile a minute, coming as fast as she could think of them, and faster. "What *do* you know? How do you remember?"

"Please, your Majesty. In here." He pushed open the door to her suite, holding it open to allow her to pass through. Marchen gave a questioning whine, and she flicked the leash.

"Go on in. Chair."

He responded with a bark, then trotted through the doorway into the antechamber. The smell of lavender and cinnamon wafted through the room from the everburning censers, sending an immediate wave of calm and serenity down her spine. The sensation made her shudder, and she suppressed a moan of pleasure.

Her feet followed Marchen's lead, and when his nails scratched on wood, she put out her hand onto a cushioned chair, turning and settling herself in the seat. Taking another breath filled with delicious aroma, she laced her hands together, settled them in her lap, and faced Greagor.

"Go on. Explain yourself."

The huntsman took his own seat, swinging the chair around and dropping into it. His feet touched hers, boots caressing boots, and he leaned in close enough for her to feel his body heat. "Amalia. You're going to have to take some of what I say here on faith. Can you do that?"

"That depends on what it is." Her frown deepened. "Only a fool promises belief without hearing what the matter is."

"My homeland, Hecval, is the most powerful of the Outer Kingdoms." He leaned back a moment. "Gods, how long has it been? When I left, their lands stretched for as far as I could see from atop Mount Virn, from the Sil to the Gagnis." Then he sighed and came forward again.

Amalia nodded, moistening her lips. "I've heard some of this, although not as much as I would have liked to know before today." Her face hardened. "But that doesn't explain—"

"Please." He chewed at his bottom lip, and Amalia could almost *feel* his teeth scraping the skin and flesh. "The royal families of the Outer Kingdoms…they have a secret, Amalia. A secret that they keep from everyone, including their own subjects. No one would understand, you see. They might revolt, out of fear, rise up." He took her hand. "So you have to understand how important it was to keep this secret, and how you'll have to do the same. I'm betraying my country, and all the Outer Kingdoms, telling you this."

"Telling me *what?*" Amalia wrenched her hand from his, ignoring the frisson that passed through her at his touch, with only a fleeting

(Again? Why can't I hear his mind?)

thought passing through her awareness. "You haven't told me *anything,* Greagor, and I'm losing patience with you."

The heat baking off him seemed to double; Amalia felt sweat break out on her hands and arms, her legs under her gown. The next breath she took was dry, arid; it felt like breathing in a desert, the very air drawing her moisture out.

Then it passed, before she could more than register the event.

"All right." Greagor stood up, went around to the other side of the chair. Marchen's head tracked his movements, the hound watching the man. "The royal family of Hecval, and Ragna, and all the rest…they're all dragon-born."

A chill engulfed Amalia's heart, stopping it cold in her chest. She put a hand up to her mouth, half-gasping. "What do you mean?"

"They're the offspring of dragons. Or descended from them, at any rate." He ran his hands through his hair, continuing to pace back and forth. "It's what makes them so strong, so wise. They're raised from birth to use their heritage to their advantage. They can read minds, talk to one another over long distances. All sorts of things."

By the gods. Amalia turned her face down, to conceal whatever might be crossing it from Greagor's prying eyes. *Is it possible?*

"If that's true, how have they kept it hidden for so long? Surely someone must know."

Greagor laughed, but the humor in it grated on her ears. "I know. A few close friends know, of course. Some of the nobles. In small doses, the knowledge serves to discourage dissent." Another laugh. "I mean, who's going to publicly argue with someone that they know can snap them in half?" Then, more seriously; "But it's impressed on us how important it is to keep it from the peasantry, the common folk. Because even a half-dragon, even a *family* of them, isn't going to be powerful enough to stave off thousands of angry men and women with scythes and torches."

"…No. I imagine not." Amalia caught herself holding her breath, and let it out in a great rush.

"You've been avoiding me, these last three months. After your father's death, after that dragon killed him. After you fought him for killing your mother."

The change in topic brought the Queen's head back up, and her brow knotted as she leaned closer, pointing her finger at his chest. "How do you remember that? Glorianna told me that no one should remember." Then the full understanding of what his remembrance meant struck her between the eyes. "And…and that means you know. About me, too." She heard his leather and cloth fold as he nodded, but kept speaking. "That's why you told me about them. Because I'm the same as they are."

"That's right. I wouldn't have expected less from a dragon-born." He took her hand again, sitting across from her, and this time she didn't pull away. "Your mother, Elise, was the leader of the Red, and you are her daughter." He chewed on his bottom lip again. "And, if I'm not mistaken, so was the one who killed Marcus. Your half-sister?"

Without fully intending to, the answer came in a whisper. "Yes."

"And now you can't hear from her. You've lost the ability to speak, mind-to-mind." When Amalia turned her face to his, questioning, he patted her hand. "I've noticed how distracted you've been lately. Your attention has been drawn to something else, and it's worrying you. Either your sister is very angry with you or she's gone. I didn't know which until I learned that Don had arrived in Aetheria."

"What do you mean?"

"Don is a dragon-born himself, but his blood is weak. Tenth or eleventh generation, if I remember rightly. But he's utterly loyal to the crown, to his country. And he'll do whatever it takes to advance their place in the political arena…or the military one."

"He told me that the Outer Kingdoms used dragons as mounts, as troops. Is that true?"

Greagor shook his head. "Once it was true. We haven't done that for hundreds of years, and for most people it's just a legend, like griffons or mermaids. Most of our people haven't seen a dragon, just like yours hadn't until your War. But we don't fear them, exactly, like your people do – they're more a force of nature, or the will of the gods: something to be endured, perhaps channeled, than fought against."

"So what does this have to do with Don? You make it sound as if he has an ulterior motive for coming here."

"Put it together, Amalia. Think." He started counting off points on his fingers, skin pressing against skin. "You lose contact with the Mind Link that you share with your sister. At the same time, a stranger from another land appears. If this were a war, what would be your conclusion?"

Amalia sat back in her chair, thinking. "If this were a war, and a diplomat came to engage me while my allies lost contact..." Her head jerked up. "A distraction, a diversion. Something for me to focus on while they destroyed my war assets."

He reached out and clapped her on the shoulder; as he neared, that intoxicating mixture of aromas found its way into her nose again, making her dizzy. "Exactly! So what would..."

But he didn't have time to finish. "He said that they thought the Red Clan was extinct. Breeding with them, producing more dragon-born, would make his family stronger. They could contest the larger nations of the Outer Kingdoms, maybe usurp their positions, their lands."

"And that's why I told you, Queen Amalia." Greagor pulled up on her hands as he stood, and she followed suit. "Because I knew that you wouldn't let this happen. It isn't about me, or you; it's about the threat he poses to both of our lands. Mine, because Hecval would be his first target if he were to accomplish this. Yours, because it's your sister, your family, that he's going to destroy in order to make it happen."

"Why should I trust you?" Amalia separated from him, stepping around to put the chair between the two. "This story…it's fantastic! How is it that I've never heard about it before? That there isn't a single book in the library, or old scholar, or any other indication that the Outer Kingdoms are filled with dragon-spawn?" She cut the air with her hand, and Marchen responded to her rising temper, jumping up into her vacated chair and growling. "Ridiculous! My ancestors *came* from the Outer Kingdoms; do you really think that this sort of insanity would have disappeared in the space of four or five generations?"

Greagor's voice was patient, a little condescending, and it rankled Amalia's nerves further. "It's understandable that you aren't going to take my word for granted. But think about it – the coincidental timing. Don's interest in you, personally. I'm told that, sometimes, dragon born can sense one another, sniff each other out like wolves." He paused, made to step forward, then retreated under the force of Marchen's scrutiny. "Did *you* notice anything like that, when you met him? Some sort of smell you couldn't place, or maybe a different, unfamiliar, sensation?"

Amalia began to shake her head, but then she stopped. Her recall brought forth the memory of sitting down in front of the ambassador, ready to begin formal discourse. She had taken a breath, enjoyed the smell of the veal, potatoes…

And that strange spice. *At least, that's what I thought it was. But what if it was something else?*

"You did. I'm not surprised." He cleared his throat. "If I may say so, your Majesty, the strength and prowess you've inherited from your dragon blood go far beyond anything I've ever seen."

She swung her face full onto him, and he nodded. "When you crumpled Destrick's armor in your hand, when we were arguing. That's when I first knew for sure. Then I heard about how you lifted that bar to leave the castle." He took a step around the chair, changing his angle relative to the Queen and her guardian. "I watched you fight your father. I know how hard that was for you, but I wish you could have seen yourself, Amalia. If he had been any other man, if you hadn't been holding yourself back…you would have destroyed him."

The corner of her mouth twitched, but the pride she felt was hollow, distant. "Then how was it you defeated me, in our spar? I've never known someone to move so fast. Even my masters did not."

"Who do you think trained *me?*" He laughed, and another shiver ran down her spine; the sound seemed to fill in the hollows in her soul, driving out concerns, confusion. "I've endured hours at the hands of dragon-born instructors, training me to kill their enemies, should they need killing." Greagor clapped his hands together. "A very challenging career choice, I know, but I was serving my nation."

"That's how you came into our service. Now I understand." Things were piecing themselves together, the tapestry unveiling itself for the first time. "Your rulers wanted you here in case there was a dragon-born that posed a threat."

Then her blood ran cold, and she felt her muscles lock in place. "Are you…you tried to kill me, didn't you? At the Spring Festival, last year." Her voice quivered, and her mind plotted the quickest course to the sword blade lying propped against the wall. "Poison in the bath."

"No, no." He took another step, but Marchen's growls intensified. "I had nothing to do with that. Except for Lord Don, if he knows – and he might not, his dragon blood is thin, weak – no one in the Outer Kingdoms knows about you. I had come for the Dragon Festival. Nothing more. And when your father put out word for someone to train you in combating dragons…well, how could I refuse? It was a well-paying position that didn't involve killing someone."

Amalia's honed senses searched for the telltale indicators of a lie, a falsehood, but she found none. *It sounds too coincidental to be true, though.*

Then she reached out, wrapping her hand around the rim of a metal bowl on top of the vanity. After a moment, she exerted her strength – her *real* strength – and, in less than a second, felt it folding under her grip, the steel crumpling into a small ball. It took less effort than crunching twigs between her fingers as a child.

A low whistle escaped Greagor's lips.

"Let's say I choose to believe you. At least some of what you say, at any rate." Amalia took a deep breath, steeling herself against the intoxicating smell that Greagor carried with him. "Then that means that Lord Don, and Ragna, have effectively declared war against

Aetheria. Except that the people don't know that." She ground her teeth together, tension in her jaw, in her upper back. "And I can't get them involved. It's as you said earlier; they wouldn't understand. They'd rebel."

Greagor didn't reply, but Amalia could hear the whisper of skin passing over more skin as he rubbed his hands together.

"Then I'll have to take care of it myself."

"That would be very unwise." Greagor moved behind her, putting his hands on her shoulders. The scent intensified, an aphrodisiac of the highest order. Amalia's mind began to fuzz, to fade out, her awareness transferring from cognitive to sensual, cataloguing each tingle, each rush of heat. It was only by supreme effort that she forced herself to focus on the conversation at hand, rather than being lulled by his smell, the deep rumble of his voice. "First, it would be dangerous. But I know that alone wouldn't stop you. More importantly, what will it look like if you go off by yourself, to the other members of government? To your people?"

Amalia shook her head. "I can't ask my friends to take this risk with me, unknowing. You're the only one that I would expect to come, but you have no reason to."

He pressed in closer, and the Queen bathed in his body heat, intense through the leather jerkin and gown. "Are you sure?"

For three seconds, Amalia was unable to formulate a reply. Then she swallowed, rallying her wits. "But…but even if you did come with me, who else could I trust with the secret? Who wouldn't abandon me at the first sign of what I am?"

"I can't tell you that. But I don't think we have a lot of time." He stepped away, heading forward to the wall, pushing past the curtains to stare out the window. "Especially not if Don has figured out who you are."

"I see." Amalia bowed her head, trying to make herself think. *Gorman would be loyal until the end, but I need him here. And he's too old to come on any sort of journey.* She thrust her hands into her hair. *And Destrick…no. I can't. He'd think I was a monster if he knew.* She bit her lower lip, almost smiling. *But maybe he wouldn't. Maybe…*

Then: *What am I doing? Gods, I'm acting like I have no sense at all!*

"Greagor! Can you follow Lord Don? Watch him, see if he's communicating with anyone?" Now that she'd decided on a course of action, her words came more quickly, more confidently. "While you're doing that, I will prepare for a journey to the Dragon Isle, where Glorianna should be." Then her face turned dour, dark. "And if she's not there, we'll hunt down the bastards that took her."

"At your command." Greagor bowed, then turned and hurried out the door. The sudden silence of the room pressed in on Amalia, whose knees went weak, jelly, and she collapsed to the ground. Marchen pressed himself against her, his paws on her leg, licking at her face.

She laughed, petting him behind the neck and eliciting a *thump-thump-thump* as his foot thumped against the ground.

"No, I'm all right, Marchen. Just…let me get my bearings again." She reached out, fingers grazing the side of the chair before she got a proper grip and used it to haul herself back up. Now that Greagor was gone, her mind began to clear, the fog unwrapping its tendrils from her senses. The small sounds and smells of the room came back to her, recreating the space.

"Gods." She passed her hand over her face, her lips; her skin tingled as she ran her fingertips over it. "Perhaps I *shouldn't* bring him after all."

CHAPTER TWELVE

Destrick waited outside the Queen's chambers, just out of sight of the door. He leaned against the wall, his eyes closed, his attention focused on the sounds coming from the hallway.

And on the twisting disquiet churning in his gut.

He's like a wildcat, stalking her. The look on Greagor's face as he approached filled his mind's eye, making his muscles tense again. *Sizing her up for a meal. I half-expected him to lick his lips and sink his teeth into her right there.*

His fist balled up, and only years of discipline and training kept him from bursting into the room and throttling the huntsman. Instead, he contented himself with slamming the heel of his hand against the wall, the pain that shot up his arm a perverse stand-in for beating the other man senseless.

"He wouldn't swagger so much if he met me on the field of honor." Destrick imagined himself squaring off against the other man, his opponent's swordplay woefully outmatched by his own. Moving in practiced forms, he disarmed Greagor, knocking his sword to the ground and holding his to the other man's throat. He watched the shame in Greagor's eyes, the utter defeat, and his fantasy stirred up pride in his chest as if the event had already happened.

He was so immersed in his imaginings that he almost missed the sound of the door closing. Peeking around the corner, his eyes narrowed as he watched Greagor turn back towards it, grinning.

Destrick wanted nothing more than to smack that grin from his lips with the hilt of his blade…or with his own bare fist. Greagor kissed his own fingertips, pressing them against the door to Amalia's chambers.

Rage burned in Destrick's chest. He took a step into the hallway, half-ready to run down and begin pummeling the huntsman, propriety and consequences be damned.

Then Greagor turned, nodded to a passing servant, and jogged out of the hall toward the main area of the castle. As soon as he was out of sight, Destrick came around the corner, his strides long as he headed to the royal suite, his armor scraping and banging against itself. As the door loomed larger in his sight, he swallowed down his nervousness, forcing his muscles to keep moving, forcing his inner narrative to be silent before it could change his mind.

Before his nerve could fail him, he burst into the Queen's room. As the door slammed against the wall, his eyes delved into the room, looking for Amalia. He just had time to register the wrecking ball of fur heading his way before it slammed into him, knocking him off his feet. The full hundred pounds of angry hound stood on his chest as he lay prone, growling in his face, drool and spittle landing on his skin.

"Marchen! Down!" The dog backed away, its hackles raised but its growling stopped. "I'm sure that the guard Commander has a damned good reason for bursting into my room without requesting entrance."

Destrick raised his head, but he couldn't see her yet; her voice came from deeper within the room. "Damn. I'd forgotten how much of a wallop he packs."

"It's been a long time since Marchen had occasion to protect me from you, Destrick." There was no trace of amusement in her voice; instead, her words felt chilly, like glass left out overnight in winter. Now that the heat of his own self-induced rage had been snuffed by a midair tackle, he felt chagrined, foolish.

"I…" He sought for something to say that would justify his intrusion. "I thought that the huntsman—"

"He has a name." Amalia shuffled around her room; he heard fabric *flump* to the ground, followed by lids opening, knocking against the wall. "Why is it that neither of you wants to use the other's name?"

"Greagor, then." Destrick got to his feet, trying not to wince at the bruises that he could already feel, and that he knew would soon be visible. "I saw him when he left your chamber. By the look on his face, I…" He gathered himself, stuck out his chest. "I feared that he had done something to you, taken advantage of you."

"And why would you think that? Am I so easily taken advantage of? I seem to recall your attempt to do so did not end well." Her head popped out from behind the doorframe, her black hair streaming almost to the floor, one bare shoulder exposed to his view. "So perhaps you need to reexamine your perspective, *my Lord*, on whether or not I am my own person or some sort of chattel that you seek to protect."

Why does she always take my intentions this way? New anger rose in the young man, heat rising to his face and arms like a bakery. "I am your guard-Commander, your Majesty. What other responsibility have I, if not to safeguard your person against miscreants and deceivers?"

"My guard-Commander." Amalia nodded, then slipped back behind the door. The sound of moving things resumed, with metal clanging on metal, then being muffled by cloth and leather. "That you are. And it's why I will expect you to keep order here while I am gone."

The word shocked Destrick out of his anger. "Gone? Where are you going?"

"That is no concern of yours at this time." He heard boots hit the ground hard, then Amalia reappeared, in a leather dress and leggings, festooned with belts, pouches, and knives. She hurried across the room, taking hold of her sword, then slipped the scabbard over her head with the hilt on the right side. Marchen circled around, taking his place next to her, and she ducked down, tucking the leash into the special pocket on his collar. "But I'm setting you in charge of making sure things are taken care of. Inform Gorman of the situation at once, and ensure that everyone is aware of what to do in the event I do not return."

A million questions spun through Destrick's mind, all fighting for expression by his tongue and lips, but only one managed to escape.

"...Do you plan to return?"

~~~

"Of course I do." The words were out before Amalia considered the question. "Why wouldn't I?"
~~~

Destrick coughed. "I…" Then he sighed. "It was just a question, your Majesty. Are you sure you don't wish to tell me where you're going? I know that Gorman will be worried over it." A low, sad laugh. "He'll probably ask me twelve or fourteen times before he believes that I don't know."

She joined in the laugh, mimicking its somber tone. "I wish I could." She stepped past him, pausing for a moment to allow him to move out of her way, then continuing. "But do make sure that your guardsmen are ready for anything that could happen in my absence."

"You have but to ask, your Majesty." His leather shifted and cloth folded in on itself as he bowed at the waist. "I hope to see you again soon. May Junandar keep you safe."

Amalia returned the bow, then swept off to the right. Her leather breeches hugged her legs. Marchen jogged alongside, the clack of his nails comforting to her, soothing her nerves.

Sanctimonious bastard. When she knew she had escaped the guard-Commander's sight, Amalia's stride lengthened, and she began to run in rhythm to her angry heartbeat. Her blood pumped in her ears and her veins, and she channeled that anger in her movements. *He thinks he owns me? Watching me, waiting for other people to leave? How is it his business who I'm speaking to?* Her thoughts came fast, as fast as her heartbeat, catalyzed by anger and fear and —

Then she stopped cold, a shudder running through her. She half-turned back, part of her mind expecting Destrick to come chasing after her, calling through the castle for the servants and guards to stop her. *Was he listening? Does he know?*

The thought paralyzed her. She was caught in between two actions – run back and question him or keep going on her mission to find Glorianna.

Then she shook her head. "No one will believe him, even if he says something." She exhaled through her nose, then carried on, resuming her run toward the palace stable.

Get Vivienne, head east. Uncertainty slowed her gait. *East? Yes, east.* She picked up speed again. *Get there before…whatever. It's not far.*

Left, then right; the smell of baking bread and stews streamed out of the kitchen on one side; chit-chat and footsteps from the nearby servants' dining area. Nervousness ran in her veins and trickled out her forehead as she opened one of the side doors and exited out into the mid-morning sunlight.

"All right, Marchen." Amalia knelt down and took the leash in her hand. "Horses."

He gave his answering bark, then tugged on his leash. Amalia followed his lead, her muscles responding automatically to the small bumps and uneven surfaces that she ran over, shifting her weight to prevent twisting an ankle or falling on her face. Before she realized it, Marchen had stopped his flight and was clawing at a wooden wall or door.

"Queen Amalia?" One of the stablehands, a young adolescent named Brill whose voice gave painful evidence of his ongoing puberty, scrambled to his feet. "Do you need something?"

"I need Vivienne saddled and ready to go, and an emergency pack of provisions for a long trip." She folded her arms. "And hurry. Time is critical."

"At…at once, your Majesty." Brill threw open the doors and yelled inside. "Hey! The Queen's goin' out on a trip! Run and get some saddlebags and food for 'er!"

Four other young folk leapt up from their makeshift resting places in the comfortable hay, dashing past the two at the door, the wind from their passing throwing the mixture of sweet hay and sweat into Amalia's face, making her grimace.

"Vivienne's been waiting for you, I think." Brill took hold of Amalia's wrist, pausing as she nodded her acceptance, then led her into the stables. "She's been antsy all day, like something's stuck in her hoof and she needs to stomp it out."

Amalia tipped the young man a gentle smile. "I haven't been able to take her out as much as I used to, with the succession preparations. I'm sure she's just feeling cooped up. A nice, long journey will remedy that, I think."

"I agree, your Majesty." He led her to the back of the building; the smell of horseflesh, warm and musky, filled the air, and the body heat of the many animals contrasted strongly with the brisk air outside. Several sets of hooves thudded against the straw-covered floor, and a whinny from three stalls down completed the ensemble. "A horse needs to spend sometime around her favorite person, be loved on, petted. Especially a horse like Vivienne."

"Oh?" Amalia stepped forward, putting one hand on the door of the stall and reaching out with the other; warmth filled it, soft, short fur, pliable skin, and the bony skull beneath. Her thumb felt moist, warm air, and she pulled it away as the horse whipped her head from side to side.

"That's a royal horse, it is." Brill stepped up next to her, shuffling in his pocket or pouch for something, then reaching out and taking Amalia's hand before wrapping her fingers around the hard, smooth surface of an apple.

"The breeding, the color, the temper…I haven't ever seen one like it before. Not even Lorne."

At the sound of his name, the stallion in the last stall trumped, coming up on his hind legs and kicking the air. Twice he stomped the gate of his enclosure, and Amalia could hear the bending of chains, the squealing of wood as it splintered under his power. He snorted, tossing his head from side to side, his whipcord mane slashing through the air like the edge of a knife.

Amalia broke away from Vivienne, trailing her fingers down the equine's nose before disengaging, and moved over to Lorne. The other horse paced up and down his spacious stall, his mighty muscles driving his hooves into the hay with small thuds. Each step was followed by an exhalation, and Amalia had the sudden impression that her father was in that stall, angry, stomping to and fro as he wrestled with some problem.

"He's been like that for weeks. We take him out when we can, but we're terrified he's going to just…just up and run away." Brill sighed, tapping his foot on the ground. "Took three of us to stop him last time. That was a week and a half ago, I think. Haven't brought him out since."

Amalia reached out her hand; the horse put his muzzle into it, smooth velvet to the touch. It was the same as Vivienne had done, but this action was more powerful, filled with barely restrained violence. The Queen breathed out, focusing herself on the stallion.

"He's sad." She felt her throat close up as the equine's emotions stole over her mind, blurring the line between the two. "He misses Father almost as much as I do. And he's angry."

"What?" Brill came up next to Lorne's head. The stallions had stopped his restless shifting, and Amalia cradled his head in her hands, now pressing her forehead to his, lost in the swirling tides of the horse's memory and emotions. "I know that he's been acting up lately, but you're talking like you know what's going on in his mind."

"He's angry that you're not letting him see Father." Amalia sighed. "I know. I wish I could see him, too. But it's not Brill's fault that he doesn't come anymore. Brill's just trying to take care of you, make sure you're happy and healthy. Understand?"

The horse pawed at the ground, his hoof sending particles of straw and dirt into the air. He shook his head again, and Brill took a step back, putting a cautioning hand on Amalia's elbow. "Your Majesty, I'd be careful near him. Francine got herself a nasty gash across the chest when she tried to go in there…"

He trailed off as the horse settled, his violence subsiding from explosive anger to grudging resentment, then quiescence. Amalia felt the tension in the animal's muscles still, relax, and come back down to earth as she stepped away.

"You're a horse whisperer or something, your Majesty." The awe in Brill's voice was apparent. "I've never seen anyone talk a horse down like that, especially not Lorne. Almost like magic, it was."

Magic. A shiver ran up her spine. *Magic only comes from dragons. That's what they'll say.*

"Not magic. Just understanding." Amalia exhaled, the breath carrying with it the anger and frustration she had drawn from Lorne's mind, the pent-up emotions that the beast couldn't understand or deal with. "I know what he's going through, the grief and loss. He can't understand that Father is never coming back to him."

Then she turned to Brill. "When I'm gone, let him go."

"He's a royal stallion!" The youth's shock ran in his voice and in his sudden movement forward. "What if a commoner caught him, bred him? He's worth more than his weight in gold!" Then he gripped the wood separating him from the proud creature. "What if he's hunted down by wolves, or poachers, or…"

Amalia bowed her head, reflecting on what she had felt from Lorne's mind during their connection. Above even the anger and frustration, one emotion prevailed. She turned back to the horse, stretching out her hand to touch his face one more time.

"Then he's yours." She nodded, feeling Lorne's assent, then took Brill's hand and brought him to the horse's muzzle. "By royal decree, the stallion, Lorne, is now your companion. Care for him, and he will care for you."

"But…" When Amalia removed her hand, Brill did not. "I'm not royalty. Just a stablehand. Why…?"

"Can you prepare Vivienne, now? I find myself anxious to depart." Amalia turned back toward her own mount. "Hurry, if you would."

"Um, yes. Yes, your Majesty." Brill leapt into action, racing around the stable like a beaver shoring up his home. Within minutes, he had the mare saddled and ready, just in time for the others to return with their bags filled with foodstuffs and supplies.

"Thank you all." Amalia hoisted herself up onto the saddle, reaching forward to smooth Vivienne's mane. "Take care of the rest of them while I'm gone."

"We will, your Majesty." Brill had to clear his throat to speak clearly. "May the gods go with you."

"May they go with us all." Her ears and other senses focused and ready, the High Queen nudged Vivienne forward, out of the barn. Marchen followed the horse, keeping pace with its ambling gait as it made its way into the sunlight.

Greagor's voice came from up high, almost like a deity issuing a proclamation. "So how were you planning to get there from here?"

Pride drew a smile from her lips as she pulled the horse around. "As long as Erasminos lights the way, I should be able to manage, at least until we are close enough to the coast." Then she stroked Vivienne's mane, leaning forward to reach the top of the horse's head. "From there, Marchen and walking will do the job."

"I'm tempted to hold you to that, just to watch it happen." Her ears picked up a low whistling through the air, then a thump and roll as he hit the ground, springing back up a few feet from her. "But I think it best we move now. Don has been sitting in his rooms since I left you, and I counted seventeen letters sent out and three received."

"All on the same day?" *He must have been busy. How many people are involved in this, that he would be receiving correspondence from them in one day?* "That's unusual, isn't it?"

"I wouldn't know in general, your Majesty." Greagor came up to Vivienne's side, and the first faint vapors of his presence began to percolate through Amalia's awareness. "But Don *is* an ambassador. Even if he weren't up to something suspect and untoward, I would expect him to have many people to speak to."

"Perhaps, but this isn't the time for it." She pointed up, toward the sun. "Most ambassadors and liaisons that I have met saved their letter-writing for the end of the day, when their duties were done and they could consolidate all they'd said and learned into writing." She shook her head. "For him to be engaging in such correspondence this early in the day tells me that he has important messages to be sent, messages that cannot wait."

"Then we should intercept them!" The sudden urgency in Greagor's voice startled Vivienne, and Amalia had to tighten her grip on the reins as the horse threatened to shy away. "If we stop his letters, then whomever he's speaking with won't receive that intelligence."

Amalia shook her head again. "Tempting, but no. If we're wrong, then we've violated the sanctity of an ambassador. War, or at the least another freezing of relations." Then she allowed herself a half-smile. "And while I'd like to, I can't hang everything on your assurances, Greagor. I'm not that naïve."

Not anymore, at any rate.

Several seconds' pause as Greagor turned, taking three steps back toward the castle, then rejoining her. "I see your point, even if I don't like it. All right."

"So how were *you* planning to get there?" She swiveled her head like an owl searching for food or predators. "I don't hear your horse anywhere around, and I don't expect that you want to run the whole way."

"I thought that I'd have to be sharing a horse with you." He let that hang for a moment. "It worked out well enough for us last time, and I didn't realize that you wouldn't need anyone to look out for you on the way."

The silence stretched, the sounds of the environment fading into the background of Amalia's awareness as her heartbeat picked up. She remembered the feel of her body crushed against his as the horse moved them back and forth against one another, bathing in that smell, feeling his warmth against her. It was intoxicating, distracting.

Arousing.

"No." She shook her head, repeating the word when it came out shaky. "No. Ask the stablemasters for another horse. They have several strong geldings that they can provide you for the trip." She clicked her tongue, and Vivienne began moving forward at an amble, leaving him behind. "I'd hurry if I were you. You'll have to catch up, and Vivienne is in no way slow."

She turned to face forward, the sound of Greagor's laughter reaching her ears, and nudged her mare into a fast trot. Her body moved up and down in rhythm with the horse, and the wind helped clear her mind.

You know nothing about him. She breathed out, hard, and her thoughts sped up as the horse did the same. *He's just a huntsman, here to help kill dragons. Or you.* She leaned farther forward, feeling Vivienne speed up into a full gallop. *Get your mind into the field where it belongs.*

"Slow down, Amalia!" Greagor's voice carried across the open space. "I can't catch up!"

You can't afford to be thinking with your loins and not your brain. The horse's hoofbeats sped up, leaving the huntsman farther behind as she raced against him in both her thoughts and reality. *He doesn't care about you. Not like that. Probably just sees you as some sort of game, conquest to be had and tell everyone about later. Disgusting. Pathetic.*

Vivienne's breathing began to grow heavy. Only years of training and practice allowed the meaning of that to activate Amalia's muscles. She reined in her mount, slipping off Vivienne's back as soon as the pace was slow enough. A loud bark from Marchen, followed by a howl, reminded her that she had left her dog far behind in her haste, and shame rolled over her, overpowering the roil of thoughts she had been fighting.

"I'm sorry, Vivienne." She rubbed the horse's flank, massaging the muscles. Amalia could hear the deep gasping breaths, could feel the lather escaping from the horse's lips as she tried to regain her strength after the sprint. Along with Vivienne's breathing, she could make out the clip-clop of Greagor's approach, almost matching beats with Marchen's own footfalls.

She found herself fearing and anticipating his arrival in equal parts. Her emotions warred with one another as she rested against Vivienne's side. *How is he getting under my skin so easily? I've never been enthralled by someone like this before.*

"Queen Amalia? What happened?" Greagor dismounted, coming down several feet from her. "Did your horse spook?"

Marchen caught up, panting, the last few steps dragging. He slumped to the ground, breath moving in and out while the rest of his body stayed still. Concern rising in her breast, Amalia dashed over to his side, stumbling in her haste.

"Are you all right?" She ran her hands through his fur, bringing her face close to his, feeling the warm air from his panting mouth. "I forgot you were back there, Marchen. I'm so sorry!" She hugged him close.

"He'll be all right, I imagine. He's a tough old boy." Greagor approached, grass bending under his feet. He spat into the field before kneeling down next to them. "But why did you take off like that? I imagined that perhaps your horse had seen a snake, or something similar."

"Nay." She shook her head, not raising it, speaking into Marchen's fur. "I simply…I was caught up in the exhilaration of the ride, and in my concern for my sister, and I failed to take proper notice of how quickly I was moving." The fuzzy feeling crept into the edges of her mind, laced with musk and sweat. The open air seemed to diffuse it, but it was there.

"You almost ran your horse into the ground." The huntsman went around her to the still-panting Vivienne. "I'll admit that I'm impressed by her speed. Few mares that I've seen could match it."

"I'm sure she appreciates your compliments." Amalia tried her best to keep her breaths shallow, thin. Marchen began to show signs of life again, moving under her hands and licking her skin, but Amalia's senses focused on Greagor's fingers, running through Vivienne's fur. It was almost as if those fingers ran through her own hair, sending tingles through her scalp and down her spine, shivers that ran to her core. "But I think it best if we do not press her so again, despite what she may be capable of."

"Of course." Greagor laughed, patting the mare on the flank before turning back toward Amalia. "So about how far is this island?"

"It takes Glorianna about three hours to fly it, from what I can remember. It's up the coast to the north, about a half-mile off of the mainland." She ran her hand over her forehead, grimacing at the texture of her scars, then brushed her hair out of her face. "And she flies about four times as fast as Vivienne can go at a gallop."

The huntsman gave a low whistle. "Damn. That's exceptional. The Red are powerful beasts, aren't they?"

Almost despite herself, Amalia leaned closer. "Do other dragons not move this quickly?"

"Not that I've heard of. Fastest is about half that." Greagor scratched at his chin, then tapped his foot on the ground. "It's going to take a while before your horse is ready to go at anything faster than a walk. Why don't you lead her, and we'll put a few miles between the city and us before anyone notices you're gone and sends the guards after you?"

"I think that's wise." She slipped past him, her path taking her within inches. He towered over her, her head only coming up to his chin, and an inadvertent breath overwhelmed her with his scent.

And people think that I'm *tall.* She paused in his shadow, her body frozen in place, muscles quivering. Being near him felt painfully arousing, shunting blood from her brain to her core, making her feel light-headed, oxygen-deprived, woozy. She put out a hand, and it landed on his chest, sending electrical sparks through her muscles. Her fingers lingered there, running over the shape of his carved musculature, the strength hidden under his garments.

He didn't stop her, but neither did he do anything to encourage it. She thought she heard his breath hitch, and part of her thrilled at the idea that, just maybe, she was affecting him in the same way he was her.

The fogginess wound its tendrils deep in her mind; her external senses dulled, occupying themselves with her own feelings; only her sense of smell seemed heightened; she found herself able to smell her own arousal as well as his, mixing with the flowers and grasses as she crept closer, one small step, with her other hand joining the one on his chest.

"What is it about you?" The words susurrated from her lips without her direct will, separated from her mind. "How is it that you keep driving me to distraction so easily?"

What am I doing? The remnants of Amalia's self-control, of her introspection, shouted at her from within a deepening cavern. *Is this really happening?*

His deep voice purred, rumbling in his chest, making vibrations that Amalia could feel through her fingertips. "Maybe there's more to me than you realize."

"Maybe." She took another small step forward; now her forearms were pressed against Greagor, folded against her body. "You're very warm. And your smell…"

She took an exaggerated breath in, a devilish smile creeping across her lips. "I could drown in it."

"That sounds just fine to me." Greagor wrapped both his arms around her and pulled her head up toward his, lancing her mouth with his tongue, thrusting it into her. She responded immediately, pulling on him, trying to draw him into her, closer and closer. Her clothes felt heavy, constricting, and every second of their embrace sent alternating jolts of hot and cold through her veins. Her skin ignited, sheets of flame pouring down her body, and her lips ached with the pressure of their kiss.

Fire burned. Amalia's rational self writhed in the flames, unable to form a coherent thought for the agony of lust searing her flesh. Her arms pulled down, bringing both of them to the ground as they broke their kiss for the first time. She barely noticed the impact of her hip and arm on the grassy dirt, consumed by the need to touch, caress, kiss, hold…

What about Destrick?

The impulse broke through the haze of desire wrapped around her brain. She pulled away, her breathing hard, intense, rolling onto her other side and curling up into a ball. The emotions and urges in her body frightened her, and she rubbed her upper arms as she fought to get them under control.

"What's wrong?" Greagor laid a hand on her shoulder. "Get back over here. We weren't done."

"No." She shook her head. "We are. Move away from me, please, Greagor." She shuddered again, her arousal cresting like a wave, begging for her to return, to satisfy the beast in her belly. The man behind her trailed his hand down her arm, caressing her skin through her sleeve, the touch making her whimper under her breath.

"I don't think you mean that." He crept closer to her, pressing himself in behind her; Amalia could feel the thick hardness of him through both sets of clothes, and her hips moved in response, her body crying out for him to take her, to fill her with his lust.

"I said we're done!" She rolled again, bringing her feet under her, stumbling; her back collided with a tree, sending a spear of agony through her shoulder muscles. Crying out, she went down to one knee. "Leave me be, huntsman!"

At the sharpness of her outcry, Marchen leapt to her defense, placing himself between Greagor and his mistress, beginning his warning sequence of barks to warn the man off.

Then he went silent. No whimper, no whine, just…nothing.

Before she could get her bearings, a blow struck Amalia across the face, sending her staggering to her right. Her hand came out to catch her before she hit the ground, while the other rose up to ward off any other blows. Her heartbeat thudded so loudly in her ears that she couldn't make out any exact sounds in her environment; all of her practice and training seemed to have fled her. She fumbled, thrashing around in the darkness, the pain in her cheek distracting, stabbing into her nerves.

"You don't get to tell *me* no." Greagor stepped toward her, bringing his boot up. She heard it coming just in time to catch most of it with her upper arm, but the toe struck her ribs, driving the air from her lungs and sending her back to the ground proper. "That's not the way this goes, no matter what bloodline you're from."

Her mind couldn't process what was happening; it felt like a dream, an illusion gone wrong. She struggled for breath, getting her arm back under her, putting some distance between her face and the ground.

Then Greagor was on her, pressing her down with his weight. His hands scrabbled at her gown, nails piercing cloth and tearing it, exposing skin to the prick of grass and cool breeze. His fingers dug into her skin, bruising flesh as he pinned her down.

"I told you that those class distinctions didn't amount to anything, didn't I?" His breath was hot on her back; he wrenched one arm behind her, forcing her wrist up. Pain shot through her shoulder, making her cry out.

"Damn you!" She shouted into the dirt, kicking ineffectually, fighting to get purchase on the ground beneath her. "Sniveling cur! You should be put down like the rabid dog you are!"

He laughed, panting with his exertions. "I don't think you'll be saying that in a few moments, Majesty." He spat the last word, his contempt oozing over the syllables. "In fact, I don't think you'll be saying anything coherent at all."

The fog in her brain persisted, confusing her attempts to formulate a plan of action. The fear and anger in her blood was stifled by a blanket of conflicting lusts and desires. Fantasies of sexual consummation clamored for her attention.

Despite the abrogation of her body and her will…part of her wanted him to take her. Wanted him to succeed, to plant himself within her. To make her grow full and heavy with his offspring. She could *see* it in her mind's eye as if it had already happened, as if it were a certainty, foretold and predestined.

She closed her fist. Dirt dug its way under her nails. Her will fought against her body, but it was losing the battle. Each second weakened her ability to resist, brought her closer to complete submission.

She exhaled, her muscles relaxing.

Greagor took the opportunity, slipping his hand around her body and under the front of her dress, caressing her breast. His strong, rough fingers worked her flesh, alternating between hard squeezing and gentle massages. The calluses on his fingers pressed against her nipple, sending sharp daggers of mixed pleasure and pain to different parts of her body, and she moaned, arching her back, lifting her hips off the ground.

"No!" She screamed, pebbles scratching her cheek. Her voice seemed to be the only thing still under the control of her conscious mind; her body had turned traitor, moistening itself to receive her assailant. She felt locked away within her own skin, trapped by some force that she couldn't comprehend, couldn't battle.

"Where's the high and mighty rhetoric now, Amalia?" He pinched her nipple again, and again she responded, surges of lust sweeping over her mind. She arched herself even more, pressing her chest into his accommodating grip, almost dizzy with the pleasure of it. "Where's the High Queen, the commander of everything she surveys? When did she become a bitch in heat, begging to be taken?"

His other hand released her arm, and the ceasing of pain in her shoulder allowed her senses to focus solely on the desire building in her loins. His now-free fingers danced along the side of her body, navigating their way south, toward her core, toward the center of that desire.

And she wanted him there. Yes, she wanted to feel his fingers penetrate her, feel them dance along her nerves until she couldn't stand it anymore. What would it be like? How would it compare to her own attentions? These questions demanded an answer, and Amalia's traitorous body was ready to find out.

And still, her mind was trapped, screaming, fighting. She could feel his actions, feel the touches and caresses that were working such sorcery upon her flesh, but a part of her remained untouched, protected, above the base sensations. It reminded her of the Link, when she spoke with Glorianna.

The Link! As she thought it, she separated from her body's experience, and her thoughts lit up with dragon fire, illuminating the prison she found herself in. In her imagination, she stood in a small room layered with brick. They fit together like puzzle pieces, each perfectly nestled within the other.

And the whole thing smelled of the same intoxicating musk that Greagor carried with him. But here, in this space, divorced from her humors, she found it repulsive rather than compelling; the intensity of it threatened to make her gag, and she had to swallow down her bile.

Clenching her fist, she flung it at the brick, hammering at the wall with all the strength in her arm. Over and over she pounded against the barrier; shards of masonry stabbed into her hand, drawing blood that rained down over her fingers. Each blow sent shockwaves up her shoulder, and she felt each in the recesses of her mind as the energy spent taxed her reserves. Fatigue and exhaustion blossomed, and the blows came more slowly.

How far? She hit again; this time, the impact barely registered, her hands were so numb. *How long until—*

Then it happened; Greagor's hands danced over her pubis, skimming over her folds before thrusting into her. The sensation pulled her out of her mental space, and she screamed again, shrieking this time as she bent her head back. The sound echoed off the trees, coming back to her in triplicate.

"You like that, don't you?" His words reverberated in her head, like a slightly off-center chorus. "You've been wanting me since we met. It's been driving you crazy." He pistoned his fingers in and out, stroking the inside of her walls, his other hand rough on her breast. The dual stimulation threatened to blank out Amalia's last bastion of conscious thought, to submerge her entirely within it.

Wrapping his legs around hers, Greagor pulled to one side, rolling over so that he was no longer atop her, but lay beside, lifting Amalia's face from the dirt. He pulled her to him, burying his face in her neck as he continued to violate her.

"I've been wanting you, too." He whispered it into her ear, and the whispers bounced in her mind as if it were an echo chamber, hollow, devoid of thought. "Every night, having to bide my time, waiting for the right chance, waiting for you to be ready…and it took so long!" He thrust forward with the exclamation, drawing from her a sound halfway between a moan and a scream. She could feel him, even harder now, against her. "It wasn't supposed to take so long!"

Amalia curled in on herself. Pleasure tugged at her, pulled at her, pushed at her; she fought to keep her mind above it, but she felt it lapping at her cheeks, at her mouth.

BUT NOW WE'LL BE TOGETHER, BOUND IN THIS FOREVER.

She froze.

You didn't say that out loud.

No response, but she knew what she had heard. And, in that instant, she felt the dragon fire in her soul, clear for the first time since he had caught up with her, and she thrust herself into it, immolating her mind. It burned, but it was *her* fire, it was *her* will, and with this last thing, this one thing that was *hers* and no one else's, she fought against the paralysis that bound her.

In one motion, Amalia bent at the waist, bringing her free elbow up as hard as she could. It connected with her rapist's temple, smacking his head against the ground. With a grunt of pain, he loosened his grip on her, and she took that chance to roll over, pulling herself free from him and bounding to her feet. She wavered for a moment, then steadied, bringing all her senses to bear, pushing aside the pain in her muscles, the air on skin where her garments were torn. She honed in on Greagor's breathing, and Vivienne's; taking two steps to the side, she reached out and put a hand on the horse's saddle. In the next moment, she had located and drawn her blade, leveling it at the man on the ground.

"You are a monster." Her voice trembled with emotion, thick with anger and revulsion. "There is no room in this world for such as you. I do everyone a service by destroying you."

She heard him plant his feet, stand up. "And yet you haven't done it. Instead you talk, trying to reassure yourself." He hissed his words, sibilant and subtle, as he began to walk to the side. "You couldn't beat me before. Why do you think you can do it now?"

The memory of their sparring match flashed across her awareness, this time laced with fear. She shook her head and brought her sword up into her fighting posture. "I know not how you invade my thoughts, but it ends now."

Amalia stepped forward, swinging her weapon at his torso; she heard Greagor dodge away, rolling into the dirt, and she pursued him. Her shredded pants hindered her movements, catching on her feet and knees, and she cursed under her breath.

With a sharp cry, Greagor counterattacked, his weapon coming down hard, his strength overpowering. Amalia turned it aside, then brought the hilt of her weapon onto the back of his neck, staggering him. She swept the weapon to her left, and her lips tightened as she felt the blade touch, felt the unmistakable sensation of parting cloth and flesh.

She resumed her stance. "The first point goes to me, I think."

"I'd say different." He laughed. "And so would you, about two minutes ago. Go ahead. Scream my name again. Tell me who won the first point."

She did scream, but in anger rather than passion. Her legs pumped as she pushed herself into an all-out assault, each strike backed by the full might of the dragon she was born from. She no longer thought, only acted, spinning and swinging her weapon as if it were an extension of her own body. Anticipating his sidestep, she altered the trajectory of her blade mid-swing, bringing it around in a sharp arc to where she predicted he would be.

Her steel met his, and she pressed into his guard with all the strength remaining in her. Her feet dug into the grass, uprooting it as she fought to make forward progress. Both combatants' muscle tension ran through the blades, making the metal squeal in protest.

He brought his face in closer to the deadlock, close enough that Amalia could feel his breath on her scars. His will battered at hers, pushing her in her mind just as his muscles did in the physical, but she was mistress of herself now. Her rage formed a steel bastion, an impregnable fortress, as she hammered away at his own defenses with her weapon. In the back of her thoughts, she marveled at his strength, his agility, as he dodged and parried each attack.

But his ability to defend was growing weaker, and she could feel it. She smelled his blood, the same blood that coated the tip of her blade, and it drove her frenzy to new heights. She abandoned defense entirely, lunging and thrusting with her steel. She could no longer think, no longer plan; each attack drew from the years of practice and from her own natural ability.

She held nothing back. It was exhilarating, as she poured the violation, the disgust, the revulsion from her body into her arms. Detached from it all, she allowed herself to be swallowed by the one urge – revenge. Death.

Murder.

Amalia brought up her weapon, swinging it over her head as Greagor hit the ground. She felt the tremors on the ground as the huntsman's blade struck the dirt. Screaming in triumph, she brought the steel down where she knew he was, where he *had* to be, bracing herself for the impact of her sword on his bones.

Instead, a sharp blow from the side knocked her down, sent her sprawling across the grass. She rolled over three times, then came back up in a crouch, snarling. Her rage redirected toward the interloper, the interferer, whatever it was that stood between herself and her prey; the fire within burned hot, hotter with each breath.

Whoever-or whatever-had stopped her was speaking; sounds came from its direction, but she couldn't process whatever it was saying. She shook her head, then lunged forward again, all her senses keyed toward the newcomer.

Her first blow struck air, then sliced into a tree; yanking it free, she felt a shower of wood chips rain on her skin. A roar tore itself from her lips, and she turned to bring her blade up and block the expected counter-attack.

It didn't come. Instead, someone tackled her from behind, shouting into her ear, their weight driving her back down. Her new assailant locked their arms around her shoulder and chest. She could make out his voice – yes, male, definitely male – as he shouted into her ear.

"Stand down! Amalia! Stop fighting!"

Her lips curled back in a snarl, and she drove her elbow backward, hitting steel, denting metal. The attacker grunted in pain, but held his grip, curling in at her back to defend himself from her onslaught.

"Amalia! It's me! Please!"

Somewhere in the core of her mind, the voice stirred memory. Sanity. Like hitting a cold pool of water, the shock cut off her rage at the root, leaving her stunned, confused. The pain she had blocked out hammered back into her, and she cried out, gasping, sucking in air. "Destrick?"

"What were you doing?" The knight-Commander held her still, his arms tight against any possible attempt she could make to leave. "It looked like you were trying to kill someone! What happened? What were you thinking? You weren't in control of yourself!"

"I was!" She turned and shouted it into his face, and he recoiled, almost letting her fall to the ground. "Greagor...he...he tried to..." She couldn't get the words past her lips, instead pulling on her torn garments so that Destrick could see the rips left by the huntsman's fingers.

"By the gods..." He released her, then stood; she heard the hiss of his blade leaving his sheath. "Where did he go? How did he flee that fast? Damn it; I should have let you finish him!"

The adrenaline and dragon-fire gone, Amalia found that her strength had left her. She couldn't muster the energy needed to pick herself up off the ground, instead curling into a ball and weeping. Her chest heaved as heavy, hoarse cries erupted from her lungs, growing louder by the second. Without the anger to hold her up, the true nature of the violation hit her full-force; she could feel him on her, in her, feel the echoes of the unnatural lust he had engendered and the disgust that had left in her mouth…for herself.

How could I have fallen for that? How could I have let it happen? She sobbed into the dirt, her cries transitioning to a high keen, despair taking hold of her senses. *What a fool. A pathetic, ignorant, naïve fool.*

"Amalia, are *you* all right?" She could feel him hesitate, feel his hands hovering just over her body, unsure as to where – or if – to touch her. "Did he…I mean, are you…?"

She didn't answer, couldn't answer. She just lay where she was, sobbing, crying out her pain, her shame, her weakness to the world. Eventually, Destrick wrapped his arms around her and held her close to him. He said nothing further, just held her.

"Where's Marchen?" The words were barely intelligible to her own ears, but she shaped them anyway. "Did…did Greagor kill him?"

Amalia waited for the bad news, felt it coming when Destrick tensed against her.

"He's right over there." The guard Commander turned his head, swiveling to take in their surroundings. "He's lying on his side, not moving, but he's breathing. Did Greagor strike him?"

Relief washed over her. *At least he survived.* She groaned through her sobbing. Destrick adjusted his arms, trying to make her as comfortable as he could.

After another few minutes, he whispered, "Amalia? Would you like to go home now? We need to decide what to do next."

She shook her head. "Not yet, Destrick. I'm not…I'm not ready. Just a little longer. Let me…" Another bout of sobs broke her words. "Just let me rest a few moments more."

"Of course, your Majesty." Again, he stilled, waiting. His breath slowed from his exertions, steadying. The tension didn't leave him, but he brought one hand up to the base of her neck, cradling her in his arms.

Even in her despair, Amalia felt something tickling at the back of her mind, like an itch under her skin.

Glorianna? Almost instinctively, she reached out to her sister. *Are you there?*

As she touched the Link, her head filled with a sound like a saw running against a steel barrel; it squealed in the recesses of her mind, and she brought her hands up to her ears in reflex. The noise resolved, slowly, separating into its component pieces – screaming from a dozen dozen voices, calling out for help, wailing in fear, shouting in anger. Sensory input from a hundred minds overwhelmed her system, throwing her into shock – her muscles spasmed, and she cried out once before falling, limp, blessedly unconscious.

CHAPTER THIRTEEN

"I never trusted him." Gorman paced around the room, rage and shame evident in every gesture, every line of his aged face. Each time his eyes landed on the fallen Queen, stretched out on her bed, attended by the medicus and his assistants, tears sprang up again and his voice grew rough. "I never should have trusted him. It was too convenient, the way he appeared."

Sighing, the aged advisor leaned against the wall. "But your man that saw them leave deserves a medal. Truly. He has done his country a great service."

Destrick nodded as he sat beside Amalia's bed, watching as the physicians ministered to her, changing compresses and force-feeding her spoonfuls of various colorful concoctions. "None of us are to blame for Greagor's deceit, Gorman. The fault is his, and his alone, and he will answer for it." Then his voice hardened. "And if his country refuses to hand him over to us, then they will answer as well."

"Hold a moment." The old man shook his head, plopping himself on one of the couches; blankets fluffed up on either side of him, and he smoothed them down. "You're suggesting war? War with the Outer Kingdoms?"

"If that's what it takes to exact revenge for what he's done to our Queen, yes." He leaned forward, his hands together, index fingers pressed against his lips. "Can you think of a more clear act of aggression? If his government will not accede to our demands—"

"These decisions must be made by the Queen, not by two worried men sitting at her bedside." The Councilor waved his hand as if to dismiss the whole issue. "Especially not when the attack is so near at hand."

Destrick opened his mouth to reply, but Amalia stirred, turning over under her sheets, drawing his attention back to her. "Lord physician, how is she?"

"As I told you before, her body is as well as can be expected." He leaned in and pressed the back of his hand against her forehead. "But she isn't responding to smelling salts or tinctures. I would have expected her to regain her senses by now, but nothing."

Destrick shared a look with Gorman; the older man licked his lips, and his eyes dropped to the floor. "Shock, then?"

"No. I've seen shock before." Turning to the other end of the bed, the medicus peeled back the sheets from Amalia's leg, exposing her knee, before reaching into his medical chest and extracting a small bludgeon. "But this…"

He struck her knee with the club, and Destrick flinched, expecting her leg to fly up of its own accord.

Nothing happened.

"This doesn't make sense." The doctor leaned back, rubbing his face with his hands. Dark circles nested under his eyes, evidence of the last day and a half of constant vigil. "It's as if…as if her wits are divorced from her body."

"Then why did she just roll over?" Gorman stood and came over, kneeling by the bedside. He reached out and took hold of her hand, feeling the warmth of her skin, but no muscle tone, no sign that she knew he was there. "How would she have done that, if what you say is true?"

The physician threw up his hands, knocking aside a plate of instruments and a glass of water, sending his assistants scrambling to contain the mess. "How should I know? This is outside the realm of medicine." He exhaled, his breath coming hoarse. "*Something* is certainly amiss; I've not known someone to lose their faculties so many times in such short order. And with the nightmares that you told me about, Councilor…"

Destrick glared, narrowing his eyes, leaning forward onto his knees. "Are you claiming that she's bewitched? That Greagor used some sort of enchantment on her?" His jaw tightened. "That gives me another reason to spear his head and hang it before the castle."

"You're asking the wrong person." Again the medicus lifted Amalia's arm, held her wrist, counted off the ticks of her pulse. "Everything that I can see says that she should be fine, she should be recovering. The injuries were not onerous; I've treated her myself for worse things. Even the penetration didn't cause serious lacerations or damage."

Destrick winced at the casual ease with which he referenced the near-rape of the Queen.

"But she's not responding to anything outside of her body. No stimulus, no treatment that I've tried has had any effect. I'm at a loss."

"No." Gorman shook his head, his voice rising an octave. "There has to be something you can do. Something you haven't tried." He put a hand on Amalia's head, on her hair, and tears gleamed in his eyes. "She can't slip away from us like this. Not for no reason. Not again."

"There's nothing more for me here." The doctor stood up, and his assistants began packing away his instruments, his tinctures and tonics. "If anything changes, feel free to call me back. Until then, I suggest that you make sure that the succession is properly planned out, or else you might have a civil war on your hands."

"We won't let that happen." Destrick spoke without looking up, his words low but carrying across the room. "Thank you for coming."

"I wish I could have done more." He nodded to the two men, then strode from the royal suite, his attendants closing the door behind them.

For a few seconds, neither spoke, gazing upon the unconscious Queen.

Gorman was the first to break the silence. "I can't lose her, Destrick. I can't."

"Nor can I." The knight nodded his agreement. "She's too important, both to this country and to me, personally. I'd die for her, if Nome would trade our souls."

"Yes. And me as well" Gorman sighed, then grunted as he hauled himself back to his feet; Destrick rose up and reached out, taking his hand. "But what can we do? I don't have any answers this time."

"If Greagor had something to do with this…"

"Leave your desire for revenge behind for now." Gorman pursed his lips. "We need to focus on what can be done for the Queen before Nome comes to claim her."

"But…" Destrick swallowed back the bile taste of his anger. "Yes. But if you don't know what to do, who would?"

The old man bowed his head, thinking, tapping his foot and sucking air through his teeth. "Before the battle in the Spring, when King Marcus was lost…"

"With the dragons?"

"Exactly. The Queen…well, Princess then, I suppose. Amalia. She and her father came to me to decide how best to go about the attack." His eyes narrowed, then he turned away, and seemed to be talking to himself. "Is it that? I had hoped that I was wrong, but…"

"Why you?" When Gorman glanced up at him, Destrick put his palms out toward him. "I don't mean to offend. But you aren't a military man. This should have been brought to the attention of tacticians and strategists, not scholars."

Gormal allowed a smile. "You'd be surprised at the tactics and strategy you can learn as a student of history." Then he raised his own hand, index finger upward. "But that's not the point. When they came to me…" He glanced back over at the Queen, took a breath. "They told me she had developed the ability to speak with dragons. In her mind."

Destrick's face dropped; the skin paled, and he stepped back, almost tripping over his own feet. He backed up into the wall, only stopping once there was nowhere else to go. "Then…then it's true? The rumors? She *is* a dragon-thrall?"

"No!" Gorman took two steps forward and slapped Destrick across the face. "And don't you ever claim otherwise! It…it wasn't magic. Not like that. Amalia never consorted with dragons, nor sold herself to them."

The blow rocked Destrick's head to the side, but, aside from the red site of impact, didn't seem to affect him much; one hand came up to rub the sting away, but he returned his gaze to the Councilor.

"But they wanted to know how to use it. How to control it, you see? So they could predict what the dragons were going to do. Anticipate an attack."

"And it worked." Understanding dawned over the knight's face as his hand came down from massaging the sore spot. "That's how we knew they were coming, how we were able to mobilize quickly enough to get out there before they arrived in the city."

"Yes. Exactly so." Gorman began pacing, raking both hands through his grey hair, his words picking up their pace as his speculation went on. "What if…the medicus said that it was like her wits were gone, removed from her body." When Destrick nodded, he continued. "What if...what if they used that connection? Stole her mind away, or locked it somewhere?"

Destrick nodded, the possibilities unfolding before him. "All right. But even if that's so...what do we do about it?"

The old man wrung his fingers together, muttering. "I found the key in my books before." Then he gathered himself up. "And I'm going to see if, perhaps, there's something else in there that might apply here."

"Wonderful." Destrick followed suit. "Then let's go."

"No." Gorman shook his head, putting his hand on the larger, younger man's chest. "You stay here."

"Why?" Destrick fell back a step, eyes wrinkling, face falling. "I don't understand. We can go through your texts more quickly if the both of us are searching. We don't have time to lose."

"You're right about that. But my books are..." He laughed. "Let's just say that you wouldn't understand the way they're laid out. Some of them are hundreds of years old and the language is archaic. Others are almost unintelligible."

Destrick blinked. "But—"

"But, nothing. You'd just be in my way. Also..." He lowered his voice. "If the Queen does come out of this, she'll likely be very disoriented. Shaken. She'll need someone other than Elsa here to comfort her if she awakens." Then his eyes burrowed into the younger man's. "Don't misunderstand; I don't want to leave her at all. But I can't think of anything else to do. So I'm leaving you in charge, to be here while I cannot."

After a few more seconds, Destrick conceded the point. "As you wish, Councilor. I'll remain here until you return."

"I think that's best." Gorman hurried out the door, opening then closing it again, leaving Destrick alone with the sleeping Amalia.

~~~

Amalia's mind drifted on the ocean of her thoughts. It was like a dream, the waves lifting her up and down, cresting and descending, but there was more to it than that.

Not the blood ocean again. The tell-tale scent of iron and copper stung her nostrils; flies buzzed above her head, their piercing whine aggravating, irritating, but she couldn't raise her hands to swat them away, nor kick her feet to escape them. Even though she knew what was happening, was aware that she was trapped in a dream, disgust and fear wrapped themselves around her spine, coiling upward to her brain and squeezing her heart.
~~~

Gods, why can't I stop this? Her breaths quickened; in her mind's eye, she could already feel the unseen force that would drag her into the depths, covering her head with the salty blood, forcing it into her lungs until she choked on it. *Am I being punished? Is that...*

Then her hand, floating above her head, bumped into something. Something hard, but mobile; the impact sent it bobbing away from her, sending tiny ripples through the surface of the blood. Scrunching her face, Amalia managed to push herself in the same direction, raising her hand out of the liquid and dropping it on the object.

Her fingers touched ridges, smooth spots bordered by sharp edges. It resembled leather, but tougher and more resilient than anything she was familiar with.

What is...

Her hands brushed across a bony projection, running from the leathery surface up into the air. About two feet from the object, it bent in an acute angle, joining a scaly membrane that spread out from the frame.

"By the gods..." Her mind expanded, her dream taking on visual form. She saw the whole ocean as if she were floating above it, saw her own body bobbing in the scarlet tide.

And saw that the dragon's body she rested her hand on wasn't the only one around her. The creatures lay in various tortured poses, the marks of slaughter still written on their flesh – open, bleeding wounds, swords and spears extruding from their skin.

Who did this? Amalia spun around, her perspective unchanging, panic rising. It felt as if walls closed in on her, pressing in, crushing in.

And that's when she noticed the sword in her own heart. A notched blade, grooved on the side, allowing her life to run down into the surrounding mass.

Greagor's sword.

~~~

"A fairy tale?" Cole, a callow youth, light of hair and build, arched an eyebrow, fighting to keep disbelief out of his voice. "You are seeking advice from a fairy tale?"

Gorman glanced up at the younger man, then turned another page. On the side of his desk, a fallen tower of similar texts threatened to complete its collapse to the ground. "They said the same thing. At the risk of sounding aged, it's almost as if you people have never seen what happens to history when it becomes legend."

"But where would these legends have come from?" Cole stepped to the other side of Gorman's desk; in front of him, the book revealed an illustration of a blue dragon, almost serpentine in shape. Its three pairs of wings were spaced along its body, and it had a similar number of legs.
~~~

An icy tornado spun out from its mouth, coating humans and ships alike in a slick, glassy coat. He shook his head. "This seems ridiculous. Dragons breathe fire, don't they?"

"The ones here do." Gorman didn't look up, immersed as he was in the text he was reading. His finger scanned through the words, skimming across lines of handwritten scribble. "But if our ambassador friend Lord Don is to be believed, there are other dragons in the world, throughout the Outer Kingdoms." He smirked. "I always wondered why these beasts were blue, not red. I thought it was a stylistic preference, or a fantasy. Consider also the different body shape." He reached out and traced out the contours of the blue dragon as Cole watched. "Why three pairs of wings instead of one? Why three pairs of legs? Its mouth is also much smaller, filled with finer teeth than the ones we're familiar with."

Gorman broke away for a moment, turning to the armarius and scanning down the metal plates until he found what he was looking for. "This is a diagram from the earlier part of the Dragon War. After the first few dragons were defeated, we took them apart, did a study on their anatomy." He unfurled the scroll and laid it beside the other. "Very different, yes?"

Cole rolled his eyes. "So what? They're all dead anyway, aren't they?"

"Weren't you listening?" Gorman slammed his fist down on the desk, making the papers and his assistant jump. "Who do you think murdered the High King? And Lord Don brings word of the monsters outside our own borders. If you think this problem is going to just go away while you bury your head in the sand…" He sighed. "Then you're a more hopeless case than I thought you were when I agreed to tutor you."

"But that was the last one, wasn't it?" Skepticism still shone on the young boy's face. "The King killed the dragon that killed him. We were all told—"

"What makes you believe one story rather than another?" Gorman snorted as he gathered up an armload of scrolls, piling them so high that they threatened to topple over his head. "Now move. I'm going to bring these up to the Queen's room."

"Of course, my lord." Cole hopped off of the stool and dashed to the door, holding it open for the aged scholar. "Lord Gorman…is everything going to be okay?"

Gorman stopped at the door. "Of course, Cole. It's going to be fine."

~~~

How long has it been? Time stretched out for Destrick like a blade; the uncertainty of it, each second half-
~~~

expecting Gorman to come back through the door with the joy of revelation, and each second being disappointed that it hadn't happened yet. He rocked back and forth in his seat, muscles filled with nervous energy.

"I can't stand the waiting without knowing *why*." He glanced over at Amalia, at Marchen. Both of them were stretched out on the bed, still save for their breathing. Occasionally, the hound would stir, quivering or shaking on the bed; once, his paws began to move as if he were running through the air, windmilling off the edge.

It made Destrick smile for a moment. Then his eyes returned to the fallen Queen, and the nascent amusement faltered and fell.

And turned into a snarl.

"What were you thinking?" He hurled the words at her unconscious body like a dagger, standing and spitting them out as he moved into a pace. "Running off alone like that, with...with *him*?"

He kicked a fallen cup across the room, hearing it smash into fragments as it struck the wall, then rounded on Amalia's bed, hovering over her, almost apoplectic in his anger. "You can't *see!* Maybe we've been coddling you too much, because of your father. Letting you act like there isn't something wrong with you."

Destrick turned away, his footsteps heavy on the ground, every motion filled with violence, rage. His muscles bunched and tensed, his fists clenched and unclenched, and his head pounded with the sound of his heartbeat. His mind played out scenario after scenario, imagining what must have happened with Greagor in that clearing. "How could you trust him? He's a snake of a man, if you want to call him that at all. Always watching you, always waiting for you…and you'd know this if you could see him! You wouldn't have been fooled if you could *see* him!"

Finally, in an angry scream, he slammed his fist into the wall. The stone refused to give, but his hand wasn't as lucky – Destrick felt his bones bend, and a stab of pain ran up his right arm. He hissed, shaking his injured limb, and the absurdity forced a bitter laugh from his lips.

"I'm sorry that I didn't get there sooner." He leaned forward, his head against the wall, rubbing the bridge of his nose with both hands. A moment later he flexed his injured fingers, speaking into his cupped palms. "I didn't know he was going to hurt you. I swear that I didn't."

He came over to her side again and knelt down next to the bed. He put a hand on Amalia's forehead. "At least you're still warm. You're always warm. It's like you've been lying in the sun for hours, even when you're inside." He pulled back, smiling a little. "Do you remember your first class? It was you, me, Kram, and Commander Narsom. You were the High Princess, so nobody wanted to say anything, but we were all looking at each other. I think everyone was afraid of being put up against you, to practice." A small laugh. "I know I was. But the Commander wouldn't have it. Said that you were the toughest thing on two legs he'd ever worked with and that you'd send each and every one of us to the medicus, given the chance."

Destrick let out a shuddering sigh, stroking Amalia's hair. Tears beaded in his eyes, and he blinked them away, refusing to give them the satisfaction of being wiped off.

"He was right, you know." He shook his head, staring into her face. "He was almost always right about people. I've never known anyone so strong. I'd have been driven into the arms of Ard, mad and lost."

His hand moved over to Marchen, rubbing the short fur. The dog shifted under his ministrations, his tongue lolling out in his sleep.

"Thank the gods you survived." Another sigh. "I don't know what she would have done if Greagor had killed *you*. Probably set all of us to war."

A loud *thump* at the door drew Destrick's attention. He got to his feet, giving Amalia's face one last, longing glance, then hurried to open it.

He was greeted by a mass of rolled scrolls so thick that he couldn't see who held them. Thinking quickly, he grabbed the most precarious of them, tucking them underneath his arm.

"Thank you." Gorman's voice was strained, tight. "Can you move? These are heavy, and I'm not as young as I once was."

"Yes!" Destrick jumped to one side, allowing the Councilor to enter with his burdens. Sighing with relief, he dumped the scrolls onto the couch, taking care not to let them crumple one another or fall to the floor.

"Did you find anything?" Destrick's eyes darted amongst the rolls, seeking any indication of hidden secrets. "A way to awaken her?"

"As if I've had time to look well enough, yet." The old man cocked an eyebrow at the guard-Commander. "I thought that I'd take your advice, let you help me dig through these. I hope your Ancient Realm is up to snuff?"

"I…" Destrick shook his head. "Who spoke that, again?"

"Erasminos preserve us all." Gorman massaged his temples with his forefingers. "I'll take those, then. You sort through the fables and legends, maybe get to the local histories if you manage." He leveled a finger at Destrick. "And don't ignore anything, no matter how ridiculous it might look. The smallest reference might be what we need to find out how to make her well."

~~~

"Where have my eyes gone?"

Amalia heard the voice coming from her throat, but it was not her voice. She felt herself move, shift in place, but her limbs were not her own – larger, more powerful.

And wrapped in blackness eternal.

"Mother?" She stood up, walked a few steps, slammed into a solid stone surface. The pain reverberated through her body and mind, staggering. "Amalia? Are you here? Can you hear me?"

Glorianna. Gods, what's happening here? Her sister's voice thrilled Amalia's soul, filling it with hope...and worry.

"Where am I?" The dragonling's voice quivered with fear. Her footsteps echoed, bouncing off the walls of what seemed to be a vast cavern. Water dripped from the ceiling into small puddles on the ground, a staccato beat of liquid on stone. "Is anyone out there?"

She can't hear me. Glorianna! Amalia called out with her mind, trying to pierce whatever barrier kept her from touching Glorianna's...but there was no barrier to fight, no obstacle in her way. For whatever reason, the dragon simply would not respond.

Another hesitant step forward. The smell of sea salt and blood touched her nose, winding tendrils into her
~~~

brain. Her feet slipped and slid over the moist rock under her feet, forcing her to fight for balance and to take each step with care. Unfamiliarity battered at her senses, each loose pebble and unexpected stalagmite sending her pulse into spasms.

The disconnected quality of the experience teased Amalia's brain; she found it hard to focus, felt a disparate reaction between the emotions Glorianna held and those in her own mind.

It's like other people must feel, watching themselves in a mirror. She tried to focus past the strangeness, to get a sense of where they (she? Glorianna?) were; on the edge of her hearing, waves crashed against the rocks, sending tiny tremors through the stone.

Glorianna struck another wall, but instead of rebounding off or stepping away, she attacked it, her claws striking, digging, chipping off shards of stone that bounced off her scaly skin. Her breath came faster, and she pushed harder…but the wall remained, even when her muscles gave out and she slumped against the ragged grooves she had made.

She began to weep.

Amalia felt her heart break; she ached for a way to reach out and comfort the dragonling, to be there with her, be beside her in her humid tomb.

"Why?" Glorianna breathed the word; there was no force, no power behind it. It dripped with despair, hopelessness. "Why can't I see anything? What's happened to me?"

"You're very strong." The soft whisper bounced around in Amalia's mind, coming from everywhere and nowhere, fading in and out from word to word. "It's been hard to restrain you."

Glorianna lunged in the direction of the voice, but her claws hit only air, and she tumbled onto her back from the momentum. A small spine shoved into her back, sending a tremor of pain through her nerves. "Where are you? What are you doing to me?"

"We'll talk about that soon enough, once the ship comes to take you home." Again the voice shifted, mutating from male to female and back, old to young and in-between. "You'll like it there. You'll be around your own kind, be given a place of respect. Not like the people here have been treating you."

Glorianna's thoughts clanged against the outside of Amalia's mind; the dragon's fear and frustration combined into a volatile cocktail of confusion; she couldn't focus on a single plan of action, a method to save herself. Her bodily aches and terror clawed at her, making every pebble a boulder, every scratch a sword-blow.

But Amalia paid attention from her place in the recesses of the dragon's mind.

"I know this is cruel. I do." The echo took on a compassionate, condescending tone, the voice of a man speaking to a hurt dog before putting him down. "But I don't have a choice. I can't let anyone else find out about you, or it'll ruin everything."

A hand touched the horns on the dragon's head; she snapped, but her jaws closed on nothing.

"You'll need that fight." Amalia could hear the grin in his voice; confidence and amusement oozed from every syllable. "We have a war to win."

~~~

Destrick reached for yet another roll of parchment...then threw his arm across the table, casting the entire pile to the floor. "There's nothing in here! We've been looking for hours!"

Gorman raised an eyebrow, then returned to his reading. "And we'll likely look for hours more, unfortunately. Research isn't a task that can be rushed. Unless the gods will it, knowledge does not simply rush into one's mind without effort." He sighed, spinning the roll to scroll down the page.
~~~

"We have to do *something*." Destrick rose from his seat and strode over to Amalia's bedside; she still hadn't moved, lying prone in perfect mimicry of a corpse. "She's not getting any better on her own. What if…what if he poisoned her when he attacked her?" He closed his eyes, took a breath and leaning his forehead against the wooden bedpost. "You didn't see her, Gorman. It made me sick. He treated her like street trash, common filth to be scraped off the boots. As if even the lowest deserve such."

Gorman didn't look up. "I imagine so. Assault is rarely a pleasant thing."

"How can you be so dismissive?" Destrick rounded on the old man, turning toward him with muscles tight, forcing his fists to unclench. *I don't want to hit him. I don't.* "You're acting like—"

"I'm acting like this is a problem that needs to be solved." Gorman exhaled through his nose, ruffling the papers on his lap. "When Amalia was poisoned at Catlin's castle, I didn't run around like a dismembered chicken, yelling and screaming for people to take action." Tapping his finger against the parchment, he leveled his eyes at the younger man. "I took my time to figure out what it was we needed to do. And because of that, she survived. We were able to determine what poison had afflicted her and take the appropriate steps."

"But—"

"I won't have you running off and trying something without knowing what you're doing. Not when the stakes are this high." He sighed, rolling up the scroll and setting it on the table to his left, picking up the next. "You're just as likely to get her killed as you are to solve the problem. Probably moreso."

"I can't just *sit* here!" Destrick stormed across the room, taking a place at the window, staring outside. "It just feels like I'm not doing anything to help her." He crossed one arm over the opening, propping himself against it. "It's just like the child said, in the village. 'Twice beheaded.'" His voice rose in pitch and volume. "And now I'm trapped in this room, with nowhere that I can go and nothing that I can do."

"Stop acting childish, boy. You aren't trapped." Gorman unfurled another text. "You're doing the only thing anyone can do right now. You're here with her, and you're trying to find a solution."

"I don't feel like we're making progress, Gorman." He turned back toward the interior of the room, then gestured toward the tomes. "The answer could be here, or not, but if it isn't, then all of our effort is for nothing."

"I wouldn't—" A knock on the door interrupted him. "Who is it?"

"Milord?" The main door opened, and a young messenger's curly head poked through. "Lord Don is wantin' to speak with you at your earliest convenience."

"Wonderful." Gorman grit his teeth, glancing back at the workload in front of him, then to Destrick. "I can't afford to ignore him. If he starts suspecting anything about Amalia's infirmity, then he might take that information back to his liegelord." He stood, facing the messenger. "What did you say to him? Did you tell him where I was?"

The young man's face lit up with fear. "No, milord, didn't even know that. I just told him that I'd run and get you as soon as I could. Had to ask five or six different folks where to find you, too."

"Thank you. You've done well." Gorman brushed himself off, straightening his robes. "Tell Lord Don that I will attend him shortly."

The lad dashed away, his footsteps fading as he sprinted down the hall.

"For the energy of youth." Gorman shook his head. "Can I trust you to keep going through these texts, Destrick? And not to run off on your own?"

"…Yes." He turned his head away. "I won't leave her. Don't worry."

"Good." He pulled the door the rest of the way open and stepped through the portal, cursing as he had to unsnag the hem of his robe from a loose splinter.

CHAPTER FOURTEEN

Destrick listened to him leave, his head still down, his eyes dancing from side to side. When the door shut, he ran over to it, pressing his ear against the wood.

Gone. Thank the Creators. He hurried to the bedside, kneeling down beside the Queen. "Amalia? I'm going to take you somewhere now. I don't know if it's the right thing or not, but I think that she might be able to help." For a moment, Destrick closed his eyes. "She knew this was going to happen, and she has to know how to fix it."

He slipped his arms underneath her. Marchen stirred, his eyes blinking open as the jostling roused him. He lifted her up; the sheet slipped off her body, revealing the thin shift that her servants had put her in.

"Come on, Marchen." Destrick kept his voice as low as possible. "She'll want you nearby when she wakes."

Destrick backed up against the door, pushing against the wood with as little force as he could muster. The door moved, inch by agonizing inch. Once he could stick his head through it, he turned, glancing up and down the hallway, looking and listening for signs of life.

There're some servants at the south end. The realization made him grimace. *And that's exactly where I need to go.*

"Marchen."

The hound perked up at the mention of his name, cocking his head and flapping his right ear. As always, his intelligence amazed the Knight-Commander.

"I don't know how much of what I'm saying you understand, but I need you right now. And so does she." His arms were tiring under her weight, but he didn't want to carry her on his shoulders like a sack of grain, so he shifted to try to compensate. "Can you go run that way…" Destrick gestured with his foot. "…and go bark really loud or something that will get them to chase you?"

For a few seconds, Marchen didn't move, just standing there with his head tilted and tongue lolling out.

"Fine. Damn it." Destrick thought, then his eyes lit up and he pointed down the hall. "Marchen! Play!"

The hound jumped up, bounding down the hallway with his nails click-clacking against the stone. He disappeared around the corner, and the murmur of servant chatter cut off.

"What's the Queen's dog doing here?" The speaker's voice sounded sharp, with just a hint of trembling. Destrick smirked. *He thinks she's coming down the hall. Wonder what he was up to that he wouldn't want her to see.*

Marchen gave a bark, then another, and metal clanged against the floor. "Damn dog! Go! Get away!"

"Should we catch him?" A serving-woman, the companion of the first, "The Queen wouldn't want him running wild like this…"

"That's not our business. Get DOWN!" He shouted at the hound, then yelped in pain. "He got my foot!"

The fatigue was showing; Destrick went down to one knee, using his leg to help support his arms. He took a deep breath.

From the end of the hallway, he caught a glimpse of the large dog with a middle-aged man's leg in his mouth, dragging him across the floor, away from the exit. The hapless servant scrabbled at the stone, trying to find purchase for his hands to hold him. His partner-in-crime, a woman of about the same age with her blonde hair tied up in a tight braid and pinned together, followed after him, her hands wavering from reaching out to holding back, as if she were unsure of what to do.

"Get him off me!" Marchen carried him off through the door into the next set of rooms.

"But…but it's the Queen's dog!" She ran after them, slamming the portal shut behind her. With growing discomfort and pain in his arms, Destrick grimaced as he hoisted himself back to his feet, his mind flashing back to the hours and years of training for his position.

"Here we go, Amalia."

He had only silence for comfort as he hurried down the hall, trying to outrun anyone else who might be coming in. His breathing quickened with his exertions, and by the time he was out the door, he was thanking his trainers for the grueling drills he had been forced to endure as a child.

Maybe I'll use this as an example the next time one of my own starts whining. He broke into the sunlight as his trembling arms threatened to fail him. As his feet crossed the threshold, he pivoted, kneeling to rest the unconscious Queen against the wall. Her head slumped into her chest, held up by a limp and lifeless neck.

"That part's done, then. Astrid's manor isn't too far." Destrick rolled his shoulders and massaged the burning out of each arm with the other. His head swiveled, back and forth, watching for any sign that someone had seen him, but no one was about on this side of the castle.

But that won't last long. At least, not if my guards are worth their pay. After a few more deep breaths, his muscles relaxed and the fatigue began to fade. He squared his stance and scanned the area for anything that he could use.

Nothing. He kicked the ground in frustration. *Of course not.* Another breath. *All right. What now? Think.* He scanned the horizon. *Maybe if I...*

"Is the Queen all right?"

The young voice froze Destrick in place. He blinked twice, his heart trip-trapping like a carpenter's hammer, then turned to the speaker.

"Midra? You...you're here?" He wiped his brow, glancing up toward the heavens as if some deity were playing an elaborate prank, then glanced behind her. "Is Lady Astrid with you? How did you know I was looking for you?"

"Why do you ask questions that you already know the answers to?" The girl shook her head. "I've never understood that."

"You knew, didn't you? That something would happen to Amalia. The twice..."

"Where is she?" The young girl interrupted as she squinted her eyes, her small feet bare in the grass as she crept forward. "I thought you brought her with you."

"I...I did." He managed a tremulous smile, indicating the fallen woman with his hand. "She's right over there."

"No she's not." Midra crossed her arms, shook her head. "That's not her. That person's nobody. Not even really alive."

"What do you mean?" Fear stole its way over Destrick's heart; his eyes skittered over Amalia, digging for signs of life. "She's still breathing, isn't she? She—"

"You don't know anything. Silly man." Midra reached Amalia, laying her hand on the woman's cheek. "Takes more than breathing to be alive, you know. Takes life. And she doesn't have any."

"You were right about what you said at the coronation this year." Destrick knelt down beside her, and her eyes followed him. "You told us that the dragon would be twice beheaded."

"And this is the second head." The girl nodded, sighing. "I didn't know then, not exactly, but it's good that you figured it out." She dug into the small pouch at her side, fishing out an old, beaten deck of cards too large for her own hands. "So I guess this is what you wanted?"

At the sight of the deck, Destrick's throat closed up, and he nodded. Before, he had felt a sense of unease on seeing them, a sense of weight; now that feeling was multiplied seven-fold, a blanket of fear that swallowed his courage and smothered it. It felt otherworldly, like a beacon of the gods' displeasure, and he found himself wanting to hide, or flee.

"This…this is real, isn't it?" He nodded his head toward the deck. "Real magic. Somehow."

"It is. But you already figured that out, or you wouldn't be asking me and I wouldn't be here." She allowed herself a smile, cocking an eyebrow at the guard-Commander.

"I just…I thought that all magic came from dragons." He rubbed the back of his neck, the unease deepening.

"It isn't free, you know." Midra licked her lips, and her hands moved, cutting and shuffling the deck between them. "It costs, every time. The first time, it was the guilt you'll feel when you think about how, if you had understood, none of this would have happened."

He took a breath.

"What will it cost this time?" Destrick gathered himself, lowering his voice and leaning close. "I'll do whatever I need to."

"That's noble of you." Midra riffled the cards, then neatened them up into an orderly, if worn, pile. "But it's not something that you can decide to give up. The gods will take it from you, when they choose, and nothing you do will stop it." She frowned. "Even I can't know what it is. But it's always commensurate to the knowledge gained."

A dark shiver caressed Destrick's spine. *Nonsense. The gods don't intervene in our affairs.* Then he swallowed. *But what if she's right?*

"Do you still agree?" Her words had the weight of doom on them, the certainty of one who has seen what she speaks of and knows its face. "I know you will, because I wouldn't have come if you didn't need me. That's always how it is."

"Who are you?" The words emerged from Destrick's lips in a low whisper, lost in the wind. "You're not just a noblewoman's fortune-teller, are you? Does Astrid even know you?"

"She doesn't, Destrick. I came here for you, and for her." Midra nodded toward Amalia's body. "And no, I am not. T'would be easier, I suppose, if I were." With delicate precision, Midra spun a small blue handkerchief from her belt, laying it on the grass between them and placing the deck atop the cloth. "As a teller of fortunes, there would be no need to hide truths in halves, or spin tales to disclose them. But it's been a long time since anyone rightly called me that."

Spellbound, Destrick sat across the cloth from the little girl. He couldn't tear his eyes away as she touched the top card, holding the edge between her index fingers.

"Say it."

"I will pay the cost." Destrick's heart trembled in his chest, and he cleared his throat to speak more clearly. "I will pay it, whatever the gods may demand. I swear."

"Good enough for now." Midra flipped over the first card; the art filled it from border to border, as usual. This time, the surface glowed red, more than two-thirds covered by a crimson sea. Within, a hand reached just above the surface, dripping the same red as its surroundings, fingers curled around a sword. At the edge of the card, the bone-white curves of a skull intruded, showcasing horns and sharp teeth in an elongated snout.

"She is trapped by Death." Midra caressed the card with her finger, tracing it along the contours of the images. "Imprisoned by dragon's blood. It dragged her down, holding her under the surface until it smothered her own life's spark."

"But she's not dead!" Destrick tensed and leaned forward, his voice spiking before he mastered it and brought it back down. He rubbed his hands together, sweat coating his palms and fingers. "She's breathing. I can feel the life in her skin. She's…"

"She's what?" Midra arched an eyebrow, and when he didn't answer, she smirked. "You can't tell me. So let me tell you."

Biting back another reply, Destrick nodded, settling back into his seat. He rubbed his sweaty hands on his breeches and watched, waiting for the next card.

"As you said, she is *not* dead." The next card came up, an attenuated cord lined with glimmering gems against the darkness; the wooden backing clacked against the painted face of the first as she laid it, crosswise, atop the sinking figure. "She clung to a single lifeline, a lone survivor. Linked by blood, the two of them remain bound together, but separated. Each has lost something within the other, and until they are together again, those things cannot be found."

Midra's words dug into Destrick's ears, and he fought against the urge to close them and leave. *It doesn't make any sense! Why can't she be clear?*

"Fortunately, the lifeline remains strong, as the two are close. This will change soon." Midra flipped the third card, dropping it beside the other two. This one showed a woman's hand reaching out from one side, and a dragon's claw from the other. The two limbs were separated by a short distance, but that distance was enough to cause them to drop the guillotine that they had been holding, sending it slicing into an unseen neck. Blood shot upward from the card's bottom edge, spraying across the hands in a fountain. "If the line becomes attenuated by distance, then the life of both will follow. If the distance grows too great…"

"Then they die."

"Yes." Midra sighed again, reaching out to gather up her cards. "And that's…"

"Wait!" Destrick gripped her hand; her skin felt…strange, almost false, not pliable or warm, but…

She removed her hands from his clutching fingers. "For what?"

He pointed at the third card. "How am I supposed to help her, help *them*, if I don't know where the…the lifeline is?"

"Ah, yes." She finished her action, scooping up the wooden cards and dropping them back into her satchel, followed by folding the handkerchief into quarters. "One more was on the road, bound to the Queen, when she was forced under the waters. She can follow the echoes back to their source. You'll have to ask her."

Midra's nodding gesture toward Amalia drew Destrick's attention that way. "What do you mean? You haven't done…"

When he turned back, the girl was gone, the only evidence of her presence the bent grass from under her knees. He stared, then searched around, his head swiveling as he hunted for a place she could have hidden.

"Just gone." Despite everything, his voice held wonder and awe. "Totally gone."

From through the nearby castle windows, Destrick heard the beginnings of an uproar; guards began calling for their fellows – and for him – and more and more running footsteps.

"We need to go." He scurried over to Amalia's resting place. "Come on. Let's hurry." Wrapping his arm under hers, around her upper chest, he hoisted Amalia up into an assisted carry. "Now…*where* do we go?"

He took a step to the south, toward the main village; in his arms, Amalia stiffened, her muscles tensing, and a small whimper escaped her. For a moment, Destrick's heart soared; he thought she was recovering, waking up. But when he turned to examine her face, what he saw took that momentary joy away.

Is she in pain? He paused, trying to think. Midra said that, didn't she? If we got too far away…

Then he tried again, this time retracing his single step, moving toward the north. At once, the discomfort on her face eased, and she relaxed back into the sleep of near-death she had been in since their return. Buoyed by this discovery, Destrick hurried out, glancing back toward the castle as he climbed the rise that led to the river, and beyond. Adrenaline fueling his actions, he picked up his pace into a run, sweeping the Queen up into a cradle carry and holding her to him.

After two or three minutes, just beyond the lip of the ridge, his already-exhausted muscles gave out and he tumbled. Rolling head over heels, Destrick did his best to cushion Amalia's fall, resulting in his taking several blows from small stones and projecting roots before they slid to a stop at the bottom. His back ran into a large tree, knocking the air out of him. Even through his attempts to regain his breath, a single happy thought penetrated the aches and pains.

I think we made it.

But he knew he couldn't rest. As soon as his weeping bones and body would allow, he was back up. Destrick took ten more steps, glancing back to make sure no one pursued.

And then his knee gave out, dropping them both to the ground again. Amalia rolled over three times out of his grasp, landing face down in the dirt. He scrambled toward her, flipping her over and brushing off her face.

"This isn't going to work." He curled up, overwhelmed by the combination of frustration and his injuries. "But it *has* to. Maybe I can…"

He trailed off as he heard the sound of hoofbeats behind him. A shadow fell over him, and he rolled over, his hand dropping to his sword even as he hissed from his bruises.

"Who's there?" He gave the challenge with as much strength as he could muster, hoping that his adversary couldn't detect the crack in his voice. The sunlight shone over the person's shoulder, silhouetting their slight figure on horseback, watering his eyes and forcing him to squint. "Identify yourself!"

The horse nickered, backpedaling to expose him to even more sunlight, then stepping forward again, shielding his eyes from it. He drew the blade and stood up, forcing his legs and arms to remain still.

"Always in too much of a hurry." Midra slid down the horse's side, landing on the grass with a soft *floomp*. She folded her arms, then reached up and patted Vivienne's flank. "Did you think that you would just carry her the whole way?"

"I, um…" Destrick's sword grew heavy, wobbling in his grip, and he lowered it to the ground, reaching up with one hand to massage the ache out of the other shoulder. "I didn't think it would be wise to head to the stables with the Queen."

"At least you *were* thinking." The young girl laughed, then stepped down the hillside, leading Vivienne down the thin traces of path worn into the grass. "That's worthy, in and of itself, in a way."

Destrick grunted, sheathing his weapon and leaning up against the side of the tree as she descended the hill. "Why didn't you say anything sooner? You could have gotten Vivienne while I waited…"

"I *did* say something sooner." She hopped down a small rise, the rapid drop fluffing out her brown hair behind her. "You just didn't know how to listen. I told you that someone else was with Queen Amalia and knew the way."

"Why couldn't you just say, 'By the way, go get Vivienne. You know, the horse? That Amalia had been riding?'" He shook his head again. "Why the secrecy?"

"Secrets are dreams wrapped in the realm of the living. When you expose them to the light, they become cold, sterile things…" She spread her hands. "And I choose to midwife them into the world, rather than murder them upon their birth." A sad smile crossed her lips. "I leave their deaths to others."

I have no idea what that means.

"And even if you don't know what that means…" Midra giggled when she saw the shocked look that crossed Destrick's face. "…Understand that I'm not your enemy. We just see the world differently."

She reached the bottom of the hill, stepping with care to avoid the projecting rocks and roots that the knight had tumbled onto, guiding Vivienne down the same way. She held the reins out for Destrick. "She never betrayed you. She never betrayed anyone. When she thrusts her claws through your chest, remember that."

Again, the force of Midra's words struck him hard; it was as if someone else, someone with more authority, more power, spoke through them, underlaid them with their own. Before he could reply, the little girl dashed off, scurrying up the hillside again.

"Wait!" He reached out toward her, taking a step in that direction.

"Better hurry. The sea is the Queen's death. And the tide goes out soon." Without turning around, she disappeared over the rise. In the sudden quiet, Destrick heard the increasing calls for the search, peasants and craftsman and merchants and servants all hunting for Amalia.

"Damn it. All right." He stumbled back over to Amalia, gathering himself for the effort before kneeling down and lifting her up. His legs shook and his bruises stabbed his nerves, but he managed to balance her on Vivienne's back. The mare danced in place, turning her head to examine what was going on.

"Good girl." Destrick stroked the horse's muzzle, putting his palm between her eyes and down. "The crazy girl said you know where Amalia needs to go. Can you get there?"

Vivienne didn't answer. *Obviously. What was I thinking would happen, anyway?*

"Right then." He swung himself up onto the saddle, behind the Queen. After slipping his feet into the stirrups, he checked everything to make sure she wasn't going to fall.

Or me. He rubbed the back of his neck. *Wouldn't enjoy it very much if I ended up with a broken neck, either.*

Then he gathered the reins back up and pressed his heels into Vivienne's flanks. "Let's go."

The horse bounded off, moving into a quick gallop that bounced both of them up and down. Destrick let go with one hand to brace Amalia's back, to keep her from shaking. He pulled back on the reins.

"Not so fast! You'll shake her to death!"

Vivienne fought against him at first, then relented, easing into a trot. The bouncing slowed, transitioning into a more manageable roll, and Destrick breathed a sigh of relief.

~~~

Glorianna? Can you hear me yet?

The dragonling startled awake. She didn't remember having fallen asleep, but at some point the fear and exhaustion must have overtaken her. Her head darted left, then right, then left again.

Amalia? The thought stumbled like she did, hesitated, tasted the word as if afraid she was wrong. ***Please? Is it you?***
~~~

You can hear me! She bathed in dual rivers of relief, her own and her sister's. *What's going on? What happened to you?*

I thought you were dead, like the others. Anger and fear mixed with the relief, forming a tide of blood in their shared mind-space. Unlike before, though, there were no visual images that went along with the Link, and the thought transmission was fuzzy, filtered through cotton batting.

The others? Amalia's throat dried up, her tongue heavy in her mouth. *How?*

Soldiers. Hundreds of them. Her words cut into Amalia's mind, lancing into her with the full force of Glorianna's fury and desperation. **They came with arrows that speared into our flesh and spears that pinned down our wings. They flooded into our caves, killing and killing and killing until there was nothing left.**

Why didn't I know? Amalia's heart felt cold, weak. *I would have come, would have done something...*

You didn't know because you were preoccupied with your own concerns. Amalia's mental avatar drew back at the harsh sting of her sister's reply. **I haven't felt you in the Link for many days. Since your coronation. Was the business of your human lands so important that you**

could not spare a moment to see what had become of us? You shut me out!

I did not! Indignation and hurt rose up in Amalia to match hers. *You didn't speak to me the whole time! Not even when I was being raped!*

The word shocked the fury from the dragon. The tenor of her thoughts shifted. *You...you were calling for me?*

Of course I was! More indignation. *And you didn't answer.* Amalia's bravado faded, cracking. *I needed someone. I needed you. And you weren't there.*

...I don't understand this. Who could accomplish such duplicitousness? The murder of our people and the...choking of our Link? Amalia could feel Glorianna shifting from confusion and hurt toward calculation, consideration. *Mother never told me of anyone. Nor our histories.*

That's for another time. Amalia sought to follow suit, choking down her own resurgent emotions, the terror and pain that had resurfaced at the remembrance of her own trauma. *Need...we need to figure out what's going on. Need to find a way to escape...whatever it is.*

I've tried everything. But I can't see. A sad mouse laugh drifted through Amalia's consciousness. *Even when I was Linked to you, I didn't realize how limiting it was.*

Feel sorry for yourself later. Exerting her will, Amalia dealt her sister a mental *slap*, feeling the recoil as if she had done it herself. *Right now, we have work to do.*

But what? The dragon reached up toward her face, her scales clacking under her claws. **I don't know what we can do. It's a cave. walls. Water. No exits.**

There are always exits. Again, Amalia struck the dragon with her will, trying to rouse her from her learned helplessness. *What's the matter with you?*

Everyone is dead, Amalia. Again, despair, weariness. **Until you, I had no one. I was alone. Just…just alone. Do you know what that's like? To go from everyone around you to no one?**

Do I care? Shock, pain. Hurt. *Your life is in danger, Glorianna. You can't afford to lay here and be a victim. It doesn't matter if you are one.*

…Why? Glorianna slumped to the ground again. **There's no point, Amalia. No one else to protect. No one to live for.**

Amalia's presence fell back, stunned. *She's given up. Completely given up.* For a moment, the threads of Glorianna's despair tickled her own mind. *What can I do, if she won't try?*

Then she firmed her will. *If you won't do it…*

With a supreme thrust that felt like it was bursting her skull open, Amalia forced herself past Glorianna's lethargic consciousness and into the dragon's flesh. The sensory input sparked to life; she could feel every cut, every bruise, every rock pushing into the scaly, leathery skin. She flinched back, then dug her mental fingers in deep.

What are you doing? The intrusion sparked some rebellion in Glorianna, and the High Queen could feel her sister begin to fight back. ***Stop!***

No! She pushed the dragon's limbs into motion, first clambering back to her feet, then stretching her wings. The muscles were strange to her, and she had several false starts as she put one claw out, then the next, stumbling forward onto one shoulder, then back up again.

How…The anger gave way to amazement, then awe. ***You're controlling my body. That…that shouldn't be possible.***

Shut up. Another step, then another. Amalia's strength grew, as did her awareness of her environment. Now she could smell fish, salt, blood on the rocks. She stopped herself just before crunching into one of the walls.

How did you know that was there? Glorianna's awareness tried to tap back into her senses, but Amalia rebuffed her, maintaining focus on her endeavor.

I asked you to stop talking. Please. She stretched out again; the fit was more comfortable, like a weight that rested on her shoulders rather than cradled in her arms.

The darkness greyed, and she scrunched up Glorianna's face. *I thought you said you couldn't see?*

I can't. When I awoke, I was as blind as you are. A pause. **My eyes were still whole, as far as I could tell, but not working.**

Little by little, the world brightened. *They're working now. Unless I'm just hallucinating.*

The cavern came into view; first, the edges of the rocks differentiated themselves from the environment through shades of grey. Then the puddles formed, reflecting the light, shimmering silver and white. Sharp edges thrust themselves from round blobs, and the space filled with sparkles and dust. At the last, Amalia found herself staring at tiny silver arrows dancing in a pool, to and fro at every disturbance.

What's going on? Can you see now? Glorianna clawed at the back of Amalia's mind. **Let me in!**

I...no. Not yet. She wasn't sure why, but it felt like it had to be her, that she would miss something if she receded to the back of Glorianna's skull, became a mere presence rather than an actor. She stepped forward, the light flashing off the crimson scales and claws. Several of those scales had been stripped, leaving bloody wounds that oozed onto the rocks, leaving thin, snake-trails behind.

Did they do this to you, or did you hurt yourself trying to escape? She raised her right forelimb, wincing at the tiny needles stabbing into her nerves.

Both, I think. Glorianna's thoughts throbbed with irritation; like the exposed wounds, they peppered Amalia's senses with pain. **They hit me with bludgeons and blades. I slew several, but…**

They weren't trying to kill you. Amalia kept up the dialogue as she scanned the pools and crannies of the cave. Even with renewed sight, the shadows were deep, thick, and it took attention to the details to make out what lay within them.

No. The thought carried ripples of shame, intermixed with low currents of sadness. **They want to use me for something.**

I think I might know what. Then Amalia's attention broke away from the conversation as she brought her sister's claw up, touching the rocks, feeling them against her scales. *Gods, how did they get you* in *here?*

I don't remember. It all happened so fast.

The human turned her dragon-shell's eyes to the cave's ceiling, feeling the muscles change their shape as she focused in, paying special attention to the cracks and crevices that allowed the filtering of light through them. *Maybe…*

She flapped her wings and kicked up with her legs, but her inexperience with the form led to her miscalculating the distance. Instead of latching onto the rocky face, Amalia slammed her chest into an outcropping, driving the breath from her and sending a spasm of pain through her body. She felt her grip on their shared flesh weaken and muscles slackened for a second before she firmed them again.

I'd think it would hurt longer. The stab had already faded, leaving a low burn in her bloodstream that moved throughout her body. *Do you feel that?*

I can't feel anything. Nor see. Frustration and spite underlaid each syllable. **Not with you in the way.**

Amalia barely noticed the anxiety in her sister's voice; instead, she marveled at the sensations running through her muscles, bones, and sinew. Her claws dug into the stone, carving deep, rich grooves into the surface, sending rivulets of pebbles down alongside trickles of water.

Water? She forced Glorianna's head up toward the small cracks, breathing deeply, doing her best to ignore the small particles that tried to make their way into her nasal passages. *Where...*

Then she recognized it - the salty tang of the sea. The smell brought with it the sound of crashing waves, so clear and forceful that she didn't know how she had missed it until then. The vibrations thundered against the rock, vibrating under her talons and against her scales.

What is it?

"We're near the coast. Or on it." The words sounded foreign, using Glorianna's tongue instead of her own, but the depth of Amalia's concentration prevented her from using the Link, instead reverting to the subvocalization that was so familiar. "Why would we be on the coast? Why here?"

I told you that they were planning something. They wanted to...to bring me somewhere. To help. Amalia could feel her sister's struggles to remember past the pain and fatigue, past the despair and hopelessness. *Maybe...maybe a ship? I think they wanted to put me on a ship.*

"Of course." The High Queen managed to get her rear talons locked into miniscule crevices, bracing herself well enough that she could apply force to the rubble blocking the light. "They...they want to…"

As she pushed up against the rock, she felt the stones give way, shifting and raining down pebbles and smaller debris. The dust and dirt attacked her eyes, forcing a reflexive blink from her dragon eyelids, the scaly membranes clearing the intruders before they could cause any damage.

In the sunlight, obscured and silhouetted against the day, a large, armored shape cast off the last rock in its arms, then paused in its efforts. Amalia recoiled, then threw herself forward in a desperate, screaming attack, extending her front claws as she launched herself with her legs and a strong beat of her wings. A sharp cry burst from the man's lungs as the two tumbled, rolling over and over on the rocky cliff, crashing against rock and dirt until they landed on the beach, the waves crashing into them where they struggled. The sudden exposure to daylight had blinded Amalia, leaving her to fight on instinct; with her empowered senses, she aimed for the center mass of her enemy as he rained gauntleted fists down on her back and neck, Her own screams and snarls shut out other sounds, but she could sense, on the periphery, the man struggling to draw his weapon, and so she dug her claws into his breastplate, crunching down through the steel until she could feel the mail links underneath, then further. Tucking her head under a wing to protect it from the blows, she concentrated her strength.

Not today! Tighter and tighter; she could feel the heartbeat beneath her claws as she tunneled through the steel fortifications, her rage building. *Not again, you bastard! Not ever!*

CHAPTER FIFTEEN

"By the Gods." The words tumbled from Destrick's lips as he tossed the last stone away from the blocked cavern. "It's…"

Before he could continue, the creature threw itself at him, its eyes blazing with madness and shrieking incoherent blasphemies. Its limbs scrabbled and flailed at his armor, the sound of talon on metal driving picks through his ears as he lost his balance, toppled by its added weight. The two of them went over, crashing against stones both sharp and smooth, and Destrick winced and cried out as the force reverberated through the steel covering his body. He had a brief moment, once the fall stopped and the collisions ended, to give thanks to the gods for its protection before the beast set on him again, snarling. Heat baked through the plate and mail between them, and the knight brought his left hand down in a fist between the monster's shoulder blades, a sharp surge of satisfaction peaking at the impact and resulting shriek.

The next sound, however, drove the nascent smile from his lips: crunching, protesting steel, twisting and bending under incredible force. A glance down revealed the source.

Nome's teeth! With his left hand, Destrick gripped the thing's clawed hand, trying to fight it back, to stop it from further rending his armor while his right reached for his weapon. *It's going to pierce straight through to my heart if this keeps up!*

The dragonling tucked its head into its wing, its vocalizations mixing with the squealing of steel. Destrick grew aware of his own throat growing raw with screams as the thing overpowered him; he could smell his own fear, taste it in his spittle, feel it in the accelerating beat of his heart. His hand closed around the hilt of his dagger, tightening around his last hope for survival.

Claws through the chest.

Realization drove a glowing spear of light through Destrick's fear, driving the fog and confusion and terror away into the shadows. Releasing his grip on his blade, he instead brought his hand up and, struggling to keep the dragon's talons from him just a few seconds more, freed his head from his helmet, tossing the steel encasement onto the ground nearby.

"Amalia!" He shouted the words down at the creature attacking him, praying to the gods he had not misunderstood. "It's me! Stop! Please!"

The words shook the creature; its strength slackened, and its struggles ceased. The dragon's head emerged from its cover, exposing its cracked and stripped scales, its bleeding wounds, and its catlike eyes.

"Destrick?"

~~~

Gods, I almost killed him!

Emotions ran wild in Amalia's blood - anger at herself, joy at the sight of her friend, confusion as to the situation. At the back of her mind, she could hear Glorianna struggling to be heard.

Why did you stop? What happened? Amalia!
Shh! Be silent.

The Queen took a deep breath, releasing the death-grip on Destrick's breastplate with great effort. As she pulled away, she felt the sting of the steel and blood seeped from the wounds left by the edges of the jagged metal.

"Amalia. It is you, isn't it?" The young man staggered to a kneeling position, the pain of movement writ large upon his face as he grimaced and hissed his way through the motions. "What happened here?"
~~~

"I...I don't know." Another breath, her dragon eyes skittering, unable to stay away from his face. They traced every contour, every feature, as her mind devoured the input and filed it away. *He's beautiful. More than I could have imagined. Even when I saw him through the Link, it wasn't like this.* "I...had a nightmare. Horrible."

The memory brought her back to herself, and she shuddered. "Blood. There was so much blood and death. Then...when I woke up, I wasn't in my own flesh any more."

You were in mine.

"How did you end..." Destrick extended a hand, then folded his fingers back into his palm. "How did you find yourself inside of a dragon?"

Oh, that's a question, isn't it? Glorianna's voice snapped at the back of Amalia's mind, a whip laced in venom. *Do you suppose this beautiful man will forgive you a dragon's birth? Or simply burn you at the stake for it?*

Be silent! Amalia shook her head. "That is for another time, Knight-Commander. For now, we need to seek remedies. And as quickly as possible, I should think." A small sigh. "I can only imagine that Gorman is...deeply concerned."

"He isn't the only one, your Majesty." Destrick joined her in her worry. "I'm sure that my kidnapping you has left them hunting vigorously."

"You…" Amalia turned; on the coast, prancing in place at the chaos, stood Vivienne, tossing her head and snorting. Draped across the mare's back, Amalia saw a woman's body, with raven-black hair streaming from her head, tied to the saddle to keep her from falling. She took a step toward the unconscious form, cocking her head. "I remember you. Remember the first time I saw that face, those scars."

"Your Majesty?"

"Have I been trying too hard to escape?" The words bubbled from below her conscious thoughts, from the Link, from deeper than that, so unbidden that she knew them not before she uttered them, but still recognized their truth. "Trying to leave myself behind?"

Of course you have. You've felt my wings, seen through my eyes. And now you have my talons, my muscles. Through the Link, Glorianna opened up her memories, flooding Amalia's awareness with images of Elise in full dragon splendor - a tower of strength and supernatural power, capable of destroying entire armies and laying waste to cities, of crushing through ships and stone alike with her jaws. *And this is what I will eventually become. Isn't that what you want to be?*

Another step toward her human body. Amalia felt herself shaking, even as she approached closer. "Is it? Am I so desperate to see, to fly, to *be* like you that I left my own flesh behind? That I've pushed everyone away from me?"

Then she turned her head, craning her head to appraise the man standing behind her, confusion and fear writ large on his features. "What have I done?"

"Amalia?" Destrick ran up to her, and she could hear the small fractures in both bone and armor, could hear him wince at every step. His gait hobbled, his armor torn and split like an overripe pear. "Is something wrong?"

"No. And yes." The Queen sat down on her haunches, and tears brimmed at the edges of her vision as she stared up into his face. "But I think I owe you, and Aetheria, an apology. You are better than I have given you credit for, and I have ill served you for the past three months."

"You were in mourning." Destrick waved away her concerns, shaking his head as he came down on one knee before her. "I would never—"

"Be silent." Unlike her communications to Glorianna, these words were spoken softly, filled with compassion and care. "And let me look on you for these last few moments, if you would. I do not expect I shall get to see you again, and I would take this memory with me either into the Crystal Palace or back into my own body, wherever the gods lead me next."

Destrick reddened under her gaze. "You speak nonsense, your Majesty. Come; let us find Gorman and explain what's happened. I'm sure that he's found something by now, some way to reverse this."

"I know how to do that myself, Destrick. The question is, simply, will I succeed?" Fear crept its way into her voice, setting the draconic timbres trembling. "So much, instinct. The knowledge of blood. But is it enough this time? I hope that it is. I do not wish to die today."

"Your Majesty, I…" Destrick trailed off, his eyes narrowing. "Do you hear that?"

Amalia nodded. "Oars in the ocean, and spray off the bow of a ship. Whoever came to capture us is here, before the tide goes out, I expect. Which leaves me no more time." Then she turned back to her Knight-Commander. "Destrick. Please understand that I never wanted to hurt you, or Gorman, or my kingdom, with this secret."

He furrowed his brow, but kept silent as she took a breath. *I must return.*

Reaching out with her mind, through the Link, Amalia found the hole in her consciousness she had left behind. The edges of it sung to her, a slow, siren call of loss and waiting, deep within the recesses of her soul. Stretching herself toward that wound, she gripped hold of those edges, feeling the same pain as she had on Destrick's steel breastplate as the sharpness sliced into her fingers.

With a final pull, she slid away from her fleshly anchor, separating from the scales and sinews of the dragon and filling in the emptiness in her own body. Her limbs tingled as her animating spirit took hold once again, and sudden thirst and hunger warred in her awareness.

Then her stomach clenched as nausea overwhelmed her. With only the barest awareness of her actions, Amalia strained against the ropes that bound her, snapping them like twine and twig before falling off Vivienne's back and crashing into the dirt, sending up her stomach contents like rotten eggs and festering meat had been simmering there for a week. Her muscles tensed as vomit and sputum flew from her mouth and nose, but she was spared the sight of it pattering onto the sand.

Welcome back. She lashed herself with her own laconic thoughts as the episode began to taper off into dry heaves and moaning. *I wonder if dragons ever deal with this.*

No. Glorianna shook herself as she flexed her wings and talons, coming back up to her feet. **We can eat whatever we want and never be sick.**

Wish that had passed over. Amalia gasped, spitting out the last few remnants of bile and raising her hand up to brush her hair from her face, only to touch the textured scarring across her eyes before encountering anything else. *Wait...*

"It's all right." A metal gauntlet tightened on Amalia's shoulder, bringing her awareness to it for the first time. "I'm here. I've got you."

*He...*Her senses reached out, tentatively at first, uncertain, then picking up on more and more nuances - the creaking of steel, the in-and-out of breath, the variations of heat. *He kept my hair out of the way. Why did he do that?*

As if you didn't know. Glorianna's mental voice carried with it a mixture of sarcasm and pity. **Or are you truly that blind?**

"The ships are getting closer, your Majesty." A note of concern crept into the young knight's voice as Amalia backed away from the puddle seeping into the sand and dirt. "What should we do?"

The Queen shook her head as she stood up, and she reached out a hand. "Marchen? Is Marchen here?"

"Gods damn it." Destrick cursed into the wind, then recovered. "No, my Queen. I...I neglected to bring him with me. I'm sorry."

Despite the current of fear that statement brought, Amalia raised her face and turned it toward the sea. "You never need apologize, Destrick. You saved my life today, and taught me something I will be loath to forget." Before he could reply, she extended one arm. "You said ships. How many do you see?"

You can just use my eyes, Amalia. Sight has returned to me.

She felt the mental beckon, felt the temptation to leave her own senses again, but she clamped down on the Link before she could do anything but imagine it. *No. And maybe never again.*

The sting of that comment echoed its way back to her, but she brushed it aside, focusing on Destrick's words.

"There are three ships, your Majesty; small, speedy rowing vessels. I expect that they'll make the beach very soon." A pause, and she could hear his words under his breath, counting. "I make four per ship. Two rowing and two sitting in each. Armed and armored."

"Have they seen us?" Amalia used Destrick's descriptions and her own senses to build a schematic of the beach - the outcropping of rock and cave that she and Glorianna had shared rose up out of the surf about five paces to her left, and the light from the sun slanted low in the sky warmed her face. From across the waves, she could hear something just under the sound of the surf, a low murmur, indecipherable but undeniably present. "Or is there still time for us to hide?"

Destrick's reply came slower than Amalia had expected, and she was about to turn her head toward him before he answered. "They're headed directly towards our position, your Majesty. If this were an attack, I would assume that they had seen us and know exactly where we are." He exhaled through his nose. "Though I would also wonder why they hadn't left a guard on the cave. Were they really so confident that...it...couldn't escape?"

Shaking her head, the High Queen focused on the problem at hand. "Then we have two options - fight or flee." Amalia reached down to her side, but her fingers grasped only empty air. *Damn. No weapon.* Then she shook her head, hair splaying out in all directions at the motion. "Glorianna, do you recognize them?"

Not from this distance. But their colors are similar. A pause, and Amalia could feel the dragonling pick herself up and launch into the air before gliding, almost crashing, to rest at the edge of the sea, spasms of pain lancing through her back. ***I...I can't, sister. I'm sorry. I can't fly just yet.***

The Queen ran over to where Glorianna had landed, extending her hands and running them over the multiple wounds and lacerations in the latter's hide. "I'm sorry. I didn't mean for you to…"

"Your Majesty?" Destrick's voice, confused, wary, approached as he did, his sabatons splashing in the surf with each careful step. "Are...is...it...all right?"

"She will be. Whoever it was that attacked us...that attacked her was not kind." Amalia grimaced. "Stay here. We will not let them take you."

I won't let you fight my battles for me. You've already had to do that once. Glorianna forced herself back up, into a sitting position, foreclaws on the sand in front of her and wings tucked in close to her body. Amalia heard her draw in breath through her teeth as she moved, but her mental voice remained steady and strong. *I will die beside you if that is what must happen. We two are the last of our family. I won't abandon you again.*

The wave of emotion that swept through the Link almost overwhelmed the High Queen. She reached out a hand to steady herself under the power of it all, fought to maintain her bearings as a child swept under by a powerful wave might.

"They're almost ashore, your Majesty." Steel underlaid the Commander's words, and she heard the whisper of the metal as he unsheathed his blade. "Here."

His footfalls approached once more, and then she felt her hand in his cold, metal one as he pressed her fingers around the hilt of a blade. She furrowed her brow, turning her face toward where his must have been. "Why do you give me this?"

"Because I think that you are better suited to it, my Queen. At least this time." A smile in his words. "Any foe of ours that crosses steel with you will regret it. And I am not helpless, myself."

Then, with less amusement: "But I must ask that you promise me, should we be overwhelmed…" He swallowed, then turned back out toward the sea. "That you will leave me, mount Vivienne, and flee. I will hold them as long as I can, if the worst comes to pass."

"I will not leave you—"

"Amalia." The use of her name brought her up short. "Please. I couldn't bear to see them cut you down, or capture you, It would destroy me more surely than their blades or arrows. Aetheria still needs you. You *cannot* throw that away."

The emotional power of Destrick's plea caught Amalia off-guard, closing her throat and tightening her grip around her blade. "I will not throw it away, my Lord. I will be High Queen, and do what I must."

"Thank you." The sound of wood sliding against sand, grating as it rubbed against joints and imperfections in the curve of a hull, reached her awareness, as did the impact of feet into the low surf, splashing each step. The newcomers called out to one another in a language unfamiliar to Amalia's ears, filled with strange digraphs and twisted vowels, the sounds curling in on themselves like serpents.

The Queen's senses spun in their efforts to keep track of the newcomers, sorting out one splash from another, one vocalization from the next. Subconsciously she drew her mental map, bringing up her blade to defend herself. Her muscles wavered, weakened by her inaction and her illness, but she pressed her lips together in a tight line and forced herself to stay steady.

No weakness, now. Three heartbeats passed; the last of the craft landed and disgorged its contents, and Amalia sensed Destrick's fear, his readied stance, and that both invigorated her and terrified her. *Even against Father, there was just the anger. I wasn't afraid.*

Glorianna's terror washed up at the shore of her awareness, leaving a thin film over her mind, threatening to seep in and pervade her thoughts. Instead, she scraped it away, visibly casting it off with a flick of her blade before leveling the weapon at the nearest group of intruders.

"Stay where you are. Come no further." The High Queen of Aetheria gathered all the regal mien and manner she had, bringing it to bear despite the trembling of her back leg. "Get back in your boats and go home, and this situation need not worsen."

The shuffling forward stopped, and Amalia heard murmurs, whispers amongst the group before them.

Twelve, as Destrick supposed. Her nostrils flared outward as the tension drew a bead of sweat on the back of her neck. *I wish I knew what they were saying!*

Then one member of the invading force came forward, two steps, then stopped. On the surface of her mind, Amalia felt a tickle, feathers across the skin of her forehead,

Then a voice, whispering, only audible as a sussurant caress, the words unintelligible but the emotions clear.

AWE. AMAZEMENT. FEAR.

Amalia shook her head, pushing the invasive force out of her thoughts; as she thrust outward with her will, she heard an exclamation, an exhalation of breath as someone in front of her tumbled over, splashing into the surf with a heavy, wet thud. Others scurried around the fallen one, their footsteps blurring into one another as she listened.

Glorianna growled, and Amalia braced herself for an oncoming attack. The stricken invader struggled to their feet, barking something to the gathered crowd before stepping forward again.

"Give us the Red, and we will leave you in peace." The words came slowly, forced through a tongue obviously unfamiliar, the woman who spoke them choosing each one carefully. "We have greater need of her than you do."

"You've already managed to offend me - not wise." The High Queen leveled her blade at the speaker. "Are you the leader? Leave my shores before I consider this an act of war."

Footsteps circling around the gathering brought Amalia's attention to Glorianna's maneuvering, and she heard the guards responding, some of them pivoting in place to keep track of the dragon's prowling. The leader took another step toward Amalia, and the ground trembled under the impact of her feet, sand grains trembling.

"You are outnumbered, and blinded." Again that strange tingling, like someone rubbing nettles over the surface of her scalp as the woman spoke. "Whatever strength you think you have is insufficient, even if you are Aetheria's Queen."

"I am the *High* Queen." Amalia lowered her stance, preparing to dodge or respond to attacks or threats. "And I am losing my patience with you. This is your final warning."

The first attacker came from Amalia's left, the sound of his footsteps crunching in the sand giving him away. The whistling of his blade came overhead, but Amalia's borrowed steel met it with such force that he stumbled backward, leaving himself vulnerable to the kick that connected at his sternum and sent him tumbling across the beach.

"Is this the extent of your strength?" The air pressure changed, and Amalia pulled her blade back into position as three others began to fan out around her. "Or is there more?"

"Why do you care?" Air propelled itself through Amalia's lips as she struggled with the sensory input, too many threats circling around, making small noises and tremors. To her right, Destrick pivoted by degrees, moving to cover her flank as Glorianna did the same. *I have to trust them. I can't focus if I don't trust them.*

"Because if there is more, you might be more valuable to us than the Red." The invader's voice firmed, and the others advanced two steps. "This is your last chance to surrender."

"I don't believe you." Amalia turned her head as Destrick spoke, his words startling her. "If we surrender, you will take the Queen and cut the rest of us down...assuming you don't murder her as well."

"Our oracles have told us that there was still one dragon-child of the first degree in the world, and that we would find them in these lands, but we did not expect you to meet us here." The speaker turned away from Amalia, the pitch in her voice and the grit of the sand on shoes broadcasting the action. "We sent our ambassador to make contact." A pause. "His last update told us that he had you under his control. Apparently he was mistaken."

Whore-son. Amalia tightened her jaw at the thought. *Greagor was one of them. A foreign spy, and worse.* "Apparently he was. I proved stronger than he thought. Perhaps you should take that into account and withdraw."

A pause, then murmurs. "We cannot withdraw without a prize. Give over your drake or yourself, and we shall leave your lands in peace, as you desire."

A flash of anger lit Amalia's blood aflame, and she swung her blade outward, the arc passing within scant inches of the other woman's face, cutting the air between them. "You shall have none of my blood, neither from myself nor my sister! You have walked into the dragon's den and its teeth shall close on you."

At the edge of her awareness, Destrick sucked in a breath, retreating a half-step. Amalia felt a pain in her chest as worry began to gnaw at her soul.

I said too much. Now he knows. Stupid girl.

The distraction almost proved fatal, as only Destrick's outcry gave Amalia enough time to dodge the arrow flying through the air at her; it grazed by her left hip, diving into the sand with a slide and crunch of grains. The landscape became a whirl of motion, with enemies and allies all moving at once, joining battle against one another. Destrick grunted as he slammed into one of the invaders, knocking both of them to the ground; she could hear his gauntlet crashing against flesh, over and over. A burst of fire, hot, almost liquid against her skin, sent its victims turning away mid-stride, stumbling over themselves as they made for the quenching waves.

Raising her sword, Amalia dashed forward, counting the breaths of her target; diving under someone's hastily-swung weapon, she reached the leader of the other group in less than two seconds, sending the two of them to the ground and bracing her borrowed blade against the other's throat. Through the steel, she could feel the woman's heartbeat, the trembling of her neck muscles; sweat-stink wafted into Amalia's nostrils, mixing with the salt of the sea and the metallic tang of armor and weapons.

"Enough!" The word burst from her throat, resounding over the beach. "Any further aggression towards me or my people and I will take her life." She turned her face to the left, then right, to encompass the entire foreign force. As some of them began to mutter to one another, she cut them off: "Do not test me on this. I have suffered enough of late that guilt over her death - and the deaths of you all - would be but drops in the ocean you would drown in."

An ocean of blood, threatening to drown me. The memory returned in full force, powerful, *present*, as if it were happening at that very moment. *How do I stay afloat?*

"I will not submit." The words came with difficulty, forced through a constricted throat and clenched teeth. "I cannot. My Lord will not permit it."

"Then I end you." With a sudden tensing of her muscles, Amalia pressed the sword into the woman's neck, severing artery and vein in a single motion. Coppery blood flowed over her blade, sending the metallic smell into her nostrils. "The rest of you? You have the same choice. But your end might not be as clean."

Four heartbeats. Would they take the deal? Or call her bluff? Amalia felt sweat trickling down the back of her neck, down her spine. Five. Six.

What are they waiting for? She imagined them looking at one another, maybe signaling with hand signs, planning their next move. *What if—*

"Withdraw, then." The voice in front of her brought Amalia back to reality, back to the immediacy and danger. "But-"

"Just stop." Amalia took another step forward, and the metallic scent changed, adding muddy sand to its mixture as her feet ground the blood into the shore. "I don't want to hear any last proclamations or threats. What I will allow you to do is to flee, with your tail between your legs, to carry word to your masters of what awaits them should they threaten Aetherian shores again. Or any of our kingdoms."

Again the invader tried to speak, but Amalia's sudden intake of breath cut them off. Instead, they scrabbled away, calling out in their native tongue to their companions. The whole group followed suit, retreating to the boats and setting back out into the water.

They're running, Amalia! Glorianna's communication seemed conflicted, tinged with anger and fear alike. ***Why...but...I...***

"Not vengeance, not now." Amalia shook her head, fighting against the urge to slump against the sand. "Not enough of us to win a fight if they kept at it."

"You went for her on purpose. It was a gamble." Destrick approached slowly from behind, telegraphing his steps clearly in the wet sand. "Otherwise they'd have killed us all."

"A wounded dragon, a knight with no sword, and a blind Queen?" Amalia turned her head in his direction, nodding. "We would have had no chance against all of them. It was the only thing I could think of."

"Well thought, then." Destrick sighed. "But we have a new enemy now, against us. What should we do, my Queen?"

Amalia allowed herself a small smile at Destrick's address. "We must return home and warn them. But the sun is low, and the darkness will soon overtake us." Weariness bore down on Amalia's soul as she realized how late it was, and how beaten her body had been by its trials. "I will not make it tonight, not without falling asleep on Vivienne's back. And she must be exhausted as well."

"She is." Destrick's words almost interrupted themselves as he tried to find the right things to say, the correct words to use. "I ran her hard to get here...and, if I may say so, your...dragon...friend? Doesn't seem in much of a position to get away from here alone, not today."

Save your sympathy, man-child. Glorianna limped away even as her thought burned into Amalia's mind. ***You take care of yourself, and I will take care of me.***

~~~

He won't sleep. The wind of Glorianna's breath brushed by Amalia's head, stirring the hair on her right side as the dragon approached. The High Queen stirred from her place, curled up underneath one of the trees; the humidity brought tiny splashes of water onto her forehead and cheeks, and she shivered under the caress of the wind. ***Too much on his mind.***

How do you know that? Amalia stopped herself from turning her face in Destrick's direction, instead tightening her grip on her own legs as she tried to find a comfortable position. *He has to be exhausted.*
~~~

He is. But his mind roils. He can't even close his eyes. Glorianna climbed up and settled herself on a nearby tree limb, a pulse of pain reaching Amalia's awareness as her sister brushed one of her wounds against the bark.

Will you be all right? Concern flowed out from the Queen toward the small dragon. *You're so injured.*

*I...*Now, instead of pain, it was a deep, open pit of despair, and Amalia teetered on the edge of it before Glorianna shielded her thoughts enough to hide it. ***I'll recover. I must. But don't worry for me now. You have more important concerns.***

The urge to join her mind with Glorianna's crept into Amalia's soul again, the desire to *see*, to examine with sight the camp and the environs. Instead, she focused on her mental map of the trees and the sleeping sites, standing and picking her way through the brush toward the small cluster of bushes where Destrick stood guard.

I wish I had Marchen here. Concern for the dog made her steps falter for a moment before she regained her focus and concentration. *I hate not knowing where I am.*

"Your Majesty?" Destrick whispered the words before leaving his station, striding over to her side in three quick steps. "Is something wrong?"

"No. I just..." Amalia swallowed. "I think that we need to talk. About...about what I said, and what they said, earlier."

"No, we don't." The firmness in Destrick's voice startled her, preventing an immediate response; instead, the silence filled with the conversation of the forest, the wind moving the branches and the insects chittering away around the campsite. The fire bathed Amalia in its heat, warming the right side of her body as she stood, stunned, until the Knight-Commander continued. "May I speak freely?"

"Of…" Amalia licked her lips. *I may not like what you have to say.* "Of course, Destrick. Please."

"Thank you." The young man took a breath, then reached out a hand, slowly enough that Amalia could track it, and laid it on her shoulder. "Amalia, I'm not stupid. Things have been...different...since just before your father died. You've been acting strangely. Angry. And your strength…" He shook his head, the sound of his hair moving through the air comforting and terrifying to Amalia at the same time; her senses wrapped around him at the expense of everything else, as she waited for the doom of his words, for what they would mean. "Your strength is incredible. Truly incredible. And that doesn't make sense, not in any rational way. None of this does." He laughed to himself. "I spoke with Gorman about it, about my concerns."

That statement drove a shaft of ice into Amalia's breast, but she did her best to hide it, giving him a tremulous smile. "And how did that conversation go?"

"I was worried, Amalia. Worried that something was...was wrong with you, with your outbursts, with your rages. But he talked me down from it. He knows you the best out of anyone, and he convinced me that you were just tired and strained from your new position."

"All true." The Queen sighed. "But not the whole story."

"No." Destrick tightened his fingers on her arm before releasing it. "But I think I understand better now, and it brings me only relief."

"Relief?" Amalia would have blinked in surprise, had she eyes to do it. "I don't understand."

"Of course you don't. Because you can't see yourself, not the way that we see you. The way those closest to you see you, the way Gorman sees you...and the way I do." His words softened, and he brought his hand up again, this time laying it on her cheek. "We'll follow you anywhere because we see the person you *are*. And if that person happens..." He almost choked, coughing and clearing his throat as Amalia stifled a laugh. "Happens to be part-dragon, then..." Another pause, and then Destrick breathed out. "Then I guess it doesn't really matter. You're still you. And I'd rather the reasons for the outbursts be that than some sort of disease or poison or curse."

"I…" Amalia paused to formulate her thoughts, her words; she was aware of the stirring of small birds in the trees, shifting as they moved to better shield their babes from the air. "I couldn't ask for a better assertion of loyalty, my lord." She brought her hand up to meet his, and they linked fingers, warmth passing between their skin. "Thank you."

Five breaths passed between the two before Amalia leaned toward Destrick, parting her lips as she moved. As before, the young knight met her embrace, but this time there was no fear behind the kiss; Destrick gave himself over to it entirely, the two pressing against each other as they wrapped arms around one another. Each kiss was broken by a short, gasping breath as they separated a hair's breadth before reconnecting. Gone was the desperation Amalia had felt before, the driving need for approval or acceptance.

Fire burned through the depths of her veins, lighting her limbs and her belly aflame as her hands moved over every inch of him that she could reach. He followed suit, pulling her tighter into him, pressed against the leathers and cottons that he wore. Every iota of her being, her focus, and her concentration latched onto the sensations in her hands, face, and body, and for those moments, everything else receded from concern.

Then they broke apart, panting as they pressed their foreheads together, mouths only inches apart from one another, breathing each other's breath.

Amalia spoke first. "It...it was better...this time."

"Yes." Destrick's smile burned through his voice into her ears. "I didn't break away from you like an idiot." Then he sighed, brushing her hair back from her forehead with his fingertips. "Did I tell you that Gorman about clubbed me over the head for that?"

"No. But you would have deserved it." Amalia pulled away a few more inches, her arms coming down to rest on his shoulders. "I should…"

"Yes. Sleep." Destrick leaned in and grazed her forehead with his lips before retreating. "I'll make sure no one approaches. You'll need your rest by the time we get back to the castle."

"Gorman won't be happy to hear what happened." Amalia felt her heart drop. "It was an act of war."

"Undoubtedly." Destrick's voice shifted in pitch and faded slightly as he turned his head away, looking back out into the darkness.

"But don't worry!" she continued, trying to lighten her tone. "I'll make sure to let Gorman know that you shouldn't be executed for treason. Maybe he'll just dismiss you from your post."

"If that is my only sacrifice, I'll consider it to be a blessing." The tone of his voice shifted, changing the implication of his words; there was a shadow behind them, a seriousness that caught Amalia off guard. "But I'm sure you'll be able to talk him out of it."

The pair separated further, their only contact now their hands as their words trailed away. Amalia smiled, unable to contain the emotion. "Tomorrow, then."

CHAPTER SIXTEEN

The sunlight crept over the horizon, sending its warming rays down on the small, makeshift campsite. Destrick stirred, his eyes narrowing as he stretched, shaking off the fatigue of hours of wakeful alertness.

And daydreaming.

Someone could have snuck in and away and I wouldn't have noticed it. His gaze swept the site, picking out the bumps and indents of Amalia's footsteps from the night before. *Thank the Gods she's still safe.*

A fluttering from above interrupted his thoughts, as the small dragon stood up on the branch it had perched in for the night, spreading its wings and shaking the dew off of them; the droplets splattered to the ground like a brief rain shower, Destrick glanced up toward the creature, then reached out and began gathering his armaments, beginning the process of fastening the plates and rivets of steel to his leathers and maille.

How much can I trust it? His eyes danced toward the bundle of cloth and flesh that was the Queen, and a smile tugged at the corners of his mouth. *She does. That'll have to be good enough.*

Then Amalia began to wake, reaching out her hand to her left side, groping, fingers opening and closing as if they were grasping an invisible something. Dropping his armor pieces, Destrick rushed over, taking hold of her hand with his own. She sat upright, her breath coming quickly, her face flushed, sweat pouring from her skin. Her black hair curled and matted, she turned her head in every direction it could manage, a songbird convinced that the hawk was bearing down on it but not sure from where.

"Get off! Get off!" She tried to wrench her hand from Destrick's grip, but he refused to loose it, even as her fingers closed on his with that monstrous strength she now possessed.

Gods...is it a nightmare? Is that what this is?

"Amalia! Wake up!" He brought his free hand up to her face, slipping his fingers into her hair and laying his palm against her cheek, feeling the rough texture of her scars against his skin as he did so. "Your Majesty!"

Her knee came up, smashing into Destrick's thigh and forcing a sharp grunt of pain and a sharper curse from his lips. Agony, like needles, drove into the wound, and it took all of his will to ignore it and keep his grip on the thrashing woman at his side. She lifted her hips, bowing at the waist as if to throw him away from her, and the force of it almost picked him up from the ground.

"Damn it, Amalia!" He gritted his teeth; on the periphery, he was aware of beasts fleeing, of squirrels and insects hurrying away from the commotion. "What is wrong with you?"

The small dragonling crept towards her, its full size only half again as long as Destrick was tall, its teeth flashing from behind strange lips and scales scintillating in the dawn's light. Destrick could only watch as it stepped up next to the writhing Queen, then laid its forehead on hers.

At that touch, Amalia immediately calmed, went quiescent. Her grasp on Destrick's fingers tightened, then relaxed, and she released a powerful sigh as her muscles slacked and the creature took a pace back, spreading its wings once, then pulling them back in close to its flanks.

What was that? Destrick's eyes flicked between dragon and woman, narrowing as he searched for some indication of what had happened in her face. Then he leaned closer, whispering into her ear. "Amalia? Are you all right?"

"Destrick?" She turned to him, bringing one hand up to rest on his face. "Is something wrong?"

He sighed, relaxing, flexing his fingers to restore feeling to them. "No. But I think it's best that you get up now. We want to get home by midday."

As the camp broke, Destrick found himself glancing her way, examining her behavior. She moved less confidently than he was used to, seeming to pause more often, to reach for things that weren't there.

I never realized how much of her ability was familiarity with our home. Then he rubbed his temples with the fingers and thumb of his right hand, trying to massage away the fatigue and stress building up in his muscles and skull. His eyes felt gritty, like sand had been trapped under the lids, and his arms and back ached. He rolled his shoulders and continued to watch as the Queen prepared for their travels.

Should I offer her my help? Indecision tore at Destrick's guts as his eyes strayed back to the Queen. She stepped, slowly, on her way to the edge of the camp where Vivienne stood tied to a tree, passing within five paces of the knight as he watched. *Or would she simply get angry that I didn't let her manage on her own?*

"Why are you standing there staring at me?" Amalia paused, crooking her head as he turned it toward him, her full lips curving upward as she pushed strands of long black hair away from her face. "Have I misplaced some article of dress? I usually have assistants for this, so it's entirely possible."

"No, Your Majesty. You look lovely." He stepped toward her and offered her his arm, which she took. Again he marveled at her features, eyes lingering on the curve of her nose and the transition into her mouth. He felt himself flushing, blood turning his cheeks a deep crimson and making his armor overly warm. "I was just concerned that you might need help."

"Thank you." Amalia turned to face front. "I didn't sleep well, and my concentration is...off. Your concern is appreciated, my Lord."

"It is a far cry from the palace and your bed, my Queen." Destrick stretched, his joints popping as he moved. "I miss mine, as well."

Amalia cocked her head, pausing...and the drawn-out silence made Destrick realize what he had said, and the implications made him redden again. *How does she do that to me so effortlessly?*

"How did you know where to find Glorianna?" He blinked at her sudden change of topic. "This isn't anywhere close to home. Where I was when...the separation happened." He picked her up, setting her on Vivienne's back, where she reached out for the familiar handholds and turned herself in the saddle. "How did you get here?"

"A…" The smile dropped from Destrick's lips as he remembered the strange pronouncement that had accompanied Midra's prophecy - a prophecy which had, again, proven accurate in its entirety. "A fortune-teller. She told me that you were lost and that I had to follow Vivienne to find you."

"Truly." Amalia's voice hinted at disbelief, or perhaps amazement. "Perhaps I should find this fortune teller and elevate her to nobility in thanks."

"I don't know how she'd respond to that." Destrick pulled himself up onto Vivienne, behind the Queen. "She is…strange, to put it kindly. But she was right, so I owe her much."

"We all do." Amalia turned round in her saddle, then pressed her lips to Destrick's for two beats of his heart - a heart that sped up considerably at the contact. Then she raised her voice. "Are we ready to move out?"

A nod of affirmation from the knight, and Amalia turned, putting her hands on her mare's neck. "All right, Vivienne. Let's go."

~~~
~~~

The castle gate opened as the pair approached, their arrival heralded by the guards they had met on the way, calling out that the search was over. The wooden gate creaked as pulleys and chains hefted its bulk out of the path. Amalia felt tension creeping its way back into her muscles and shook her head. She could hear Gorman's voice as he lectured her about her irresponsibility...or worse, about how worried he was.

You're the Queen, You'll take responsibility. It's no one else's fault. Her hand clenched on the reins as Vivienne trotted forward. Whispers from the guards and staff made their way to her ears, murmurs and rumors and questions about where she had been, what had happened. *But you'll have to address this at some point, or they'll think you're mad.*

Then the chatter stopped, went silent, One set of footsteps sounded out over the courtyard, and Amalia drew up Vivienne's reins, pulling the mare to a stop.

"Your Majesty. Destrick." Gorman's words dropped like the blade of a guillotine, sending adrenaline flooding through Amalia's body. "I hope that your journey found you well."

She swallowed, then straightened her spine. *He's being polite. He doesn't want to make a scene here.*

"It was unexpected, and there is much we need to discuss." The Queen gestured behind her with her right hand. "Have Vivienne stabled properly and summon the Council."

"As you command, your Majesty." Gorman's teeth bit off his words as he turned toward the gathered guardsmen and women. "You heard the High Queen. Make sure her horse is properly tended to."

"At once, Councilor." Metal clanged against metal as the guards saluted, and several sets of boots, both metal and leather, moved across the yard toward the eastern wing of the castle.

"Your Majesty, you said there is important business that we need to attend to. If you could make your way to the Lawgivers' Council chamber, I will."

"At once, Gorman." Amalia turned her head, addressing the man on the horse behind her. "Knight-Commander, I'll need you to…"

She trailed off as a new sound touched her ears, forcing her to face front. A smile creeping over her face, she slipped off Vivienne's side and knelt to the ground, extending her arms toward the growing two-beat gallop bull-rushing her. The mass of fur and muscle slammed into her chest, raining warm tongue-kisses over her face.

"I'm glad to see you too!" Amalia's voice changed to the sing-song she often used when speaking to her dog. "Did you miss me, Marchen? I missed you, I did."

Bringing her face down to nuzzle the hound's neck, she breathed out stress she hadn't realized she was holding, feeling her muscles relax and a feeling of near-giddiness descend on her mind. Marchen's breath calmed her, prompting a shudder and the tightening of her throat muscles around her windpipe. "I'm sorry that I left. I didn't mean to."

By the time Gorman cleared his throat, Amalia had lost track of the time passing. She started at the sound, bringing her face off of the dog's fur for the first time since their reunion. Nodding, she stood up, brushed the hair back from her forehead, then licked her lips. Before she could speak, she felt gnarled, wrinkled hands pressing a leather strap into her own.

"You'll want this, I think."

The level of gratitude that rose in Amalia's heart overshadowed any fear, any doubt that she held about coming back, any worry about Gorman's anger or annoyance. It so overwhelmed her that only the barest whisper passed her lips.

"Thank you." With trembling hands, Amalia threaded the strap onto the hound's collar, breathing deeply to balance out the raging fires of emotion swirling in her soul. Giving Marchen one last scratch on the top of his head, she stood, holding the leash in her fingers. At once, the dog leapt to attention, taking his customary place at her right side. With another shuddering breath, Amalia smiled at her mentor and Councilor. "I think I'm ready now."

"As you say, your Majesty." Gorman came around to the other side, threading his arm through his Queen's as they began to walk through the courtyard. The gathered attendants and functionaries began to scatter, their murmurs picking up steam as their leaders stepped through the doors into the main area of the palace.

"Are you very angry with me, Gorman?" Amalia kept her head forward, but was unable to prevent herself from asking the question; the echoing chorus of their footsteps on the floor drilled itself into her ears, demanding some sort of speech or other sound to drive it away. "I would expect you to be."

"Why?" Mirroring Amalia's lowered tones, the venerable advisor kept his words for her ears alone, tipping his head toward hers and breathing only enough force into his syllables to reach her. "The last I saw you, you were unconscious, trapped in a fit of near-death that the physicians could not identify. Other than concern, and the unfortunate tendency of some to let their worry turn into anger, why should I be cross with you?"

Why should you? Perhaps because I brought it on myself. Amalia bit her tongue. "Just that, I suppose. It still isn't easy to face the possibility of your disapproval."

"Now Destrick…" Gorman's voice hardened, sharpened to a blade that pressed against Amalia's ears. "I gathered from the way the two of you rode in that he's responsible for awakening you. Somehow. And I hope to hear how it happened, because my first thought is to have the man exiled for treason, at the very least."

Worry creased Amalia's brow, turning her head toward her companion. "You can't do that. He saved my life, Gorman."

The three turned, and Gorman's pace quickened. "Again, I gathered that. He couldn't meet my eyes when you two rode in, but you came in on the same horse, with no trace of acrimony between you." Then he tapped Amalia's wrist with two fingers, bringing them to a halt. "But your disappearance brought severe concern to the Lawgivers. It was no easy task keeping them satisfied with the excuses I summoned." He laughed. "Had you been gone any longer, we might have seen full-scale revolt from them."

"I suppose it's only understandable." Amalia paused as Gorman reached forward and the heavy doors creaked on their hinges. "Having their ruler taken so recently from them, and then my...spate of infirmity. Though I don't expect that such should happen again anytime soon."

Gorman sighed. "I'm sure that will lighten their hearts, your Majesty." The door closed behind them, and the

Councilor led his liege to her appointed place at the table. "No random ears about. Will you explain what it is that you feel is so urgent?"

"The issue is...complicated, Councilor. And concerning." Then she hesitated, took a breath; her heart seemed very loud in her ears, and her fingers closed tight on the arms of her chair. "Though...if you could see fit to summon our Knight-Commander, I should like him here. He was present, and can corroborate anything that I fail to explain well."

"It's that serious." Gorman nodded, his nails scratching at his beard as he moved, the fabric of his robes folding and brushing against itself. "Very well, then. I will have him brought here. Though I don't relish the anticipation."

Amalia pressed her lips together, Gorman's humorous tone failing to pierce her anxiety. "Gorman, thank you. I don't want to wait either, but I think it'd be best. He might have something to add or clarify."

The Councilor nodded, stepping out of the room to whisper to a passing attendant before returning. The sound of his steps surrounded Amalia's consciousness, blanketing her in volume, drowning out the thudding of her own heartbeat.

"He loves you, you know." The sentence caught Amalia off guard, "Destrick. Fool boy doesn't know how to deal with it, but he does."

Amalia felt her cheeks flush with blood, felt heat baking off of her skin and reflecting off her garments. The silence stretched out, Gorman no longer walking; the lack of sound brought her own thoughts and bodily murmurs into full relief.

"I...I know." The words slid out from between Amalia's lips, the release of a great burden. "I think we've finally come to an understanding about that."

"What kind of understanding?" The surprise in the old man's voice made Amalia smile. "I'm sorry, I shouldn't pry. And I know..."

The knock at the door interrupted them, causing Amalia's hair to whip around her face as she turned toward the sound. "You needed me, Councilor?"

"I understand that this is unusual, Knight-Commander, but the High Queen has requested your presence at this meeting." Gorman's garments ruffled as he half-turned, aligning himself such that he was facing both of them. The door closed behind Destrick as he stepped inside. "She says that you might be needed to..."

"Gorman." Amalia's voice cut in. "We are at war."

Three seconds passed. "Go on."

"Greagor was part of a larger plan to infiltrate our shores. Destrick and I encountered several others on the beach as they made landfall."

Metal grated on itself. "The Queen is correct, Councilor. There were a dozen of them, but we managed to drive them off. They were...very hostile, until Her Majesty managed to get a sword to their leader's throat, then cut it."

"Cut it. You mean...oh, no." The old man rubbed his face, fingers bristling over his beard. "Do you know who they were?" Gorman's voice spoke low, and Amalia could hear his skin brushing against the neck of his robe as he glanced from side to side. "Did they identify themselves, or did you take any dead?"

Amalia swallowed. *Now it gets uncomfortable.* "They did. They specifically referenced Greagor, and said he was one of theirs. And Greagor pointed out several times that he was from Hecval."

"The Outer Kingdoms?" Now Gorman picked up speed, beginning to pace, his words coming faster. "What about the ambassador? Don? Did he-?"

"I don't think so, Gorman, no." Shaking her head, Amalia took a breath, marshaling her thoughts. "He wasn't associated with...with Greagor. The huntsman-"

"The bastard," interrupted Destrick, under his breath.

"-sought to turn me against Don before…" Her voice began to shake. "…it happened. So I…I don't think…"

"I understand. Still, I'd have him watched, perhaps questioned." Gorman stopped, turned around. "What were they after, Amalia? There's been no diplomatic contact until Don arrived. And now this…this larger plan, of infiltration. The assassination could have been part of that, too." He tapped his foot on the ground, and Amalia heard his lips moving, teeth scraping over skin. "They wouldn't do this without something to gain. Some sort of…"

"They were after the dragons, Gorman." There it was. The words burst forth like Vivienne after being penned too long, "There were a whole family of dragons, red ones, on one of the islands off the coast. They…" She began to break down, her breath coming in great hitches and gasps. "They killed almost all of them, wanted to take one prisoner. Trapped her in a cave until the boats could come."

Seven. Eight. Nine seconds of silence. "Destrick?" Amalia could hear the strain, the desire for disbelief in Gorman's single word.

"All of it is true, Councilor. I saw it with my own eyes. Saw the wounded drake, heard them demand we give it over."

"A dragon. A horde of dragons." Gorman rubbed his face. "Amalia, what did they offer you for your allegiance that made it worthwhile?"

The Queen shook her head. "What? What are you…" Then the realization hit. *He thinks me a dragon-thrall.* A moment of indignation, then resignation. *Of course he does. What other alternative is there?*

"Is that what you think of me, Gorman? That I suborned my own will to another's?"

"Your mother died at their hands, their *claws*, and yet you fraternize with them? How long?" His words strained, he turned away; Amalia could hear Gorman's breath hitch. "They killed Queen Elise. They killed your father. Their daughter…I can't…"

"Gorman, stop." Destrick stepped forward, but halted his advance when Amalia raised her hand.

"I can, and will, speak for myself, Knight-Commander." She gave him a sad smile. "Gorman, I have not become a dragon-thrall. The truth…" Tension flooded her veins. "The truth is both more complicated, and much more dangerous, than that."

She heard his breath, heard his heartbeat in his chest. Time stretched out for infinity.

"Then tell me what it is. Please." He turned back. "I'll listen."

Thank the Gods. Amalia released her own breath, nodding as she did so. "Elise...my mother…" She licked her lips, bowed her head, then held it up high. "She was a Queen, but not in only one way. She was the matriarch, the ruling female, of the Red clan of dragons. And that makes me...a dragon-born child."

Silence.

"When I was born...my father saw what I was. And he thought that Elise had…" Swallowing, Amalia fought to continue; her throat closed into a near-stranglehold. "That I was a monster. He...attacked me." Her hands trembled, and she clenched them together; lost in her own imagination, she could see the disgust on her father's face...a face she had only ever experienced through the pads of her fingertips. "He threw me into the fire. The dragon that fled that day...was Elise. She thought I had died."

"The High King. Tried to kill you. And Elise. Was a...dragon." The stilted frame of Gorman's sentences struck Amalia as sharp contrast to his normal manner of speaking, elegant and educated. "That is madness, Amalia. Madness."

"Sometimes the truth is madness, Gorman." Amalia grimaced. "I didn't take it well when I discovered it, either. But there is no choice, other than to accept and use this."

"But you could be lying. Or, more likely, deceived." He turned back to her, and the change in volume and pitch made Amalia imagine him on the brink of tears. "I'm sorry, but I just can't accept that. I *knew* Elise, and Marcus, for longer than even you did. What you're saying doesn't make sense."

"But her strength, Gorman. And what you told me about, with the dragons' thoughts?" Destrick took a step closer, bringing the three of them into a smaller triangle. "How do you explain those?"

"Dragon thralldom. Come on, boy." The elder man shook his head. "You can't seriously believe that being born of...of one of *them* is a simpler explanation than that."

"Yes, I can. Because I know Amalia." Destrick shifted, taking a side step toward the Queen. "And you do too, Counselor. You say you knew her parents longer than she did, but you've been with Amalia for her entire life." He reached out, putting hands on the other's shoulders. "Please, Gorman, think. Reason this out. I didn't believe it either, until I saw what happened on that beach. The invaders knew." He took a breath. "Amalia didn't mean for me to know, I think. But I know that I trust her, that I believe in her."

Three breaths.

"Do you?"

"Yes, damn you. You're right." Gorman took four steps toward the young woman, then knelt onto one knee. "May Junandar damn me if I'm wrong, Amalia. But I do trust you. You're an uncommon woman, and I've seen the mistakes and the flaws and the tantrums and outbursts, and nothing has swayed me from your side. This...this shall not, either."

Reaching down, Amalia brought her long-time friend up and embraced him. Gratitude and love overwhelmed her, making it difficult to speak. He returned the gesture, and the two held one another for several moments.

"All right then." Gorman cleared his throat as he separated from Amalia. "If they want war, we will be ready for them. I'll notify everyone, begin mobilizing. Call up the commanders so we can discuss strategy."

"Very well, Councilor. Destrick?"

"Your guard will be ready on your command, your Majesty." Destrick reached out, and Amalia took his hand for just a moment. "Give us a few hours to prepare before we have to march."

"Hopefully it won't be that soon." With a small smile, Amalia turned away. "But still, don't delay."

CHAPTER SEVENTEEN

You're getting more and more nervous. Glorianna perched on the windowsill, hunched in the small space as she watched Amalia hurry from one end of her chambers to the other. *It's unlike you. Aren't you glad that he knows now?*

"I am." Amalia's flurry of motion prevented her from concentrating enough to speak through the Link, forcing her thoughts through her lips and tongue instead. "But something wasn't right. He was…" She shook her head, sighing. "Perhaps I'm overthinking it."

He was afraid. I could smell it on him. The dragonling jumped out of the window, stretching her wings out and scratching at the stone floor, a larger, scaled cat. *But why should that surprise you?*

"I suppose I…I just never thought he would be afraid of me." Amalia stopped her meandering, dropping down onto her bed. The room still smelled of her father's things, even after this time, and the sudden realization of that fact drove an icicle through her heart. "If this is what it means to rule a nation, it might be better if I abdicated to someone more worthy."

I doubt that you find such a soul, even if you wanted to. Glorianna crept closer to her sister, resting a claw on the bedskins. But you seem to be growing into it well.

"I don't think you're talking about the same person, then." Amalia put her head into her hands; from outside her room, she could hear the marching of guards from one end of the hall to the other. "I feel like I'm groping in even deeper darkness than I'm used to, with my senses dulled or stolen."

You're feeling what I feel. Lost. Loss. As the words came across the Link, they carried with them the weight of their emotions, pressing down on Amalia's will. No one left to speak with, commune with. No one's mind to share yours with, except mine.

Through the unceasing waves of sorrow that threatened to drown her perceptions, the young woman shook her head, fighting to speak. "How are you surviving?" The depth of pain astonished the Queen; it spread over her nerves, over her skin and under it, creeping into her lungs and stomach like a blanket of thorns, leaving bloody scratches on everything it touched. "It's…"

The feeling receded, the ocean of agony pulling back in low tide, only the crust of salt left in the wounds, leaving the woman able to catch her breath again.

Because I have no choice, Amalia. Now, instead of sorrow and pain, the incoming tide bore rage - ceaseless, red, bloody rage that stretched into the horizon. Because the other choice is to drown myself in it and die, and that leaves them unavenged. Which I will not do.

The Queen clenched her fist as Marchen tilted his head, his collar rubbing against his fur and the metal rings on it ringing against one another. "Nor will I. Not now, and not ever." More metallic feet clanged against stone floors, echoing up and down the corridor. "But what is the best way to help? To get that revenge? That's what I don't know yet."

But you think Gorman will be able to help? Despite his…misgivings? Glorianna breathed out in a loud exhalation, the air stirring Amalia's gown, warming her leg by several degrees. You have a great deal of faith in the man.

Nodding, Amalia allowed her memories to surface, bringing a smile to her face and a lightness to her heart she hadn't felt since the coronation…or possibly before.

"He loved my mother, you know. When I was younger, I didn't realize it, but before…" A nod, and she felt the dragon's understanding of her implied statement. "I finally pieced it together: the way he would talk about her when I asked. I caught a memory of his from when I was still in the womb, when she was telling him about me. That she could hear me." Amalia took a breath to still the shuddering in her vocal cords. "That is something that I think I've been overlooking. How hard it must be for him, with the realization that Mother was what she was."

A beast? The thought carried wry amusement, an almost mocking tone, as Glorianna crept over to the nearest table and pulled down the leftover mutton with her long tongue. *An animal?*

"Don't start that again, please." Amalia brought her hand up, cutting off the dragonling's snide comment. "You don't know what it was like for them...for us. I saw it, through his eyes - the stories, the legends. He fears you, so much. It's visceral, it's instinctual." She allowed her finger to drop. "So don't judge him."

Forgive me if I don't coddle your friends. They haven't been the subject of genocidal madmen attacking their home and family. The volume of footsteps outside grew louder; a veritable convoy of metal boots and low murmurs moving from one end of the corridor to the other before quieting. *They haven't lived for decades in fear.*

"Maybe they have." Amalia cocked her head, listening to the sounds outside, focusing on it for the first time. "Do you hear…"

Wood splintered and cracked, showering Amalia's face with fragments of her chamber's door. Marchen leapt to his feet, his barks and howls interposing themselves between his mistress and the invaders stomping their way into her room.

"Tie him down!" A loud, familiar voice sounded in the room, summoning forth a flurry of movement. Amalia backed up against the wall as she fought to regain her feet, her heart racing and slamming into her chest as adrenalin flooded her bloodstream. "And kill the creature!"

Swords and armor clanged as Amalia summoned her reason, trying to hold back the fear that threatened to cloud her senses. "What is this? Leave at once! You have no right—"

"No, your Majesty." Now she recognized the speaker - the Archprelate, all conciliation and compassion gone, his words instead filled with spite and bitter hatred. "You have no right to lead your people down this dark path, this road to blasphemy and desecration."

Glorianna's claws skittered against the stone, her emotions vacillating between fear and anger, between the fight and the flight. What are they doing?

Run! Amalia threw herself to the left, gripping her blade and swinging it in a wide arc that sent her attackers tumbling backward over one another. Get out of here!

More scrabbling as soldiers lunged toward the small dragon; reacting without thinking, Amalia lashed out, slamming the flat of her sword into someone's yielding flesh, driving them back with a shout and a scream. "Get out!"

A fluttering from the window and shouts of dismay from the surrounding soldiers told Amalia that her sister had successfully escaped. As she turned to defend herself, however, she felt the weight of several bodies slamming into her, metal edges digging into her skin through her garments. Grinding her teeth, she bunched up her muscles, hurling them off of her, sending metal and flesh crashing into the walls nearby. Her throat burned with her cries and screams as she fought against the attackers, her senses humming like her sword through the air. She felt her foot press into warm softness, and a half-second's introspection revealed that the ribs beneath the fur moved in and out with the hound's breath.

The realization allowed her anger to subside from flaming rage to banked fire, and she put her back to the wall, leveling her blade at those surrounding her.

Three, four, five, six… Footsteps sounded as they moved to flank her, stopping alongside her bed, in an arc just outside the reach of her blade.

"You consort with unclean monsters." The Archprelate moved behind the front line of soldiers. "You engage in magic, speak to them with your powers." His voice rose, turning into a rallying cry, speaking more to the crowd gathering outside in the corridor and the room than to her. "Their blood runs in your very veins, deceit perpetrated on your father, descendant of the Uniter! You spit on his legacy, and on the gods!"

"Stand before me and lay those claims, coward." Amalia tracked his steps with the tip of her weapon. "Present your evidence for my alleged crimes against my people and my father. I have done nothing but honor him and Aetheria."

"Evidence? I have none." A pause as murmuring bubbled over from the crowd. "But he does."

Metal moved as the crowd parted ways, making room for a slow, shuffling gait, lighter than any of the soldiers, uncertain, hesitant. The rhythm of steps resembled a stumbling drunk in their irregularity, but they moved forward, ever forward, rather than side-to-side or back and front.

"This is not what I meant to happen." Gorman's voice sounded like his steps - old, tired, and defeated. "I swear it to you. I just wanted to protect you."

Please, no. Not him.

The blow came from nowhere, striking her in the solar plexus and driving the air from her lungs in a single burst. Amalia fell to her knees, the pain a distant echo as her mind tore itself apart under the anger, fear, and sorrow. Hands gripped each of her limbs, holding them in place as she fought to breathe; she felt cold metal on her neck as someone clapped a steel manacle around it, then similar sensations on her wrists, bound behind her.

"He told me what you confided in him, Amalia. But I promise you it was in good faith." The priest knelt down next her, his words a whisper; his breath, hot on her skin, made her want to pull away, but her muscles would not obey her, as traitorous to her will as the man had been. "He wanted my advice, as a holy man. And I gave it to him, but he wasn't willing to follow through. Therefore, both of you have been placed under arrest."

The Queen began to regain some semblance of strength, but her struggles were contained both by the multiple soldiers holding her arms and legs, hundreds of pounds pressing on her muscles to keep her from throwing them off again, and the steel holding her wrists together. "You're...you've betrayed me. Betrayed Aetheria, and Junandar."

"No!" The condescending, practiced voice fractured, transforming into glass knives hurling themselves from the Archprelate's throat. "Your very existence betrays the Holy Father far more than anything I could ever do! This is in His name, to purify the throne He touched with his own hands."

He stepped back, standing, rubbing the back of his hand over his lips.

"You need to understand, Archprelate." Amalia fought to keep from letting her rage slip, fought to keep her voice reasonable. "What you are doing is treason, and you will—"

A sharp, crisp pain radiated across Amalia's jaw as the priest's hand made contact, knocking her face to the side as the blow landed on her cheek. The room went silent, save the sounds of breathing from the gathered attackers.

"You bastard!" Gorman's rage ignited in an instant, and he attacked, bound and tied as he was; the old man threw himself at Amalia's assailant, but he made it only two steps before she heard the sound of steel sliding into flesh.

His outrage vanished.

Then, so did his breath.

Amalia's senses followed him down to the ground, followed the last flashes of movement and life in his body, disbelief freezing her will in a block of despair.

The Archprelate stepped into his place, his presence a radiating pit of hatred and anger. "Men. Take the Queen to her cell. Four guards on the door at all times. No one is to see her." Then he laughed. "And keep her away from her pet soldier. I'm hoping to be able to break him of her enchantment and I don't want her influencing him."

"What if she tries to escape?" A voice from Amalia's right came, uncertain. "Or…"

"Stop her peacefully if you can. But if she attempts to use her magic on you…" Three heartbeats. "End her."

CHAPTER EIGHTEEN

Amalia's heart bled as the soldiers threw her into her cell. Her hands still manacled, she felt the cold of wet stone seeping through every pore of her body, smelled the musty odor of mold and metal. Her teeth ground together as she fought against the pain, brought herself to her feet.

I never thought I would be here. The thought came unbidden, like those that bubble up as the mind lulls itself to sleep. *I'd have had the servants tidy it up if I had.*

Through the small window (*barred,* she knew) Amalia could hear the sounds of nighttime - the chapels in town ringing their bells, the closing of doors and the stabling of animals - and the cool breeze dispelled some small amount of the stale air in the cell.

What have they done with Marchen? And Destrick? She didn't want to think about Gorman; as it was, her mental balance felt perched on the most precarious of footing. *Bastards, traitors all!*

She felt anger welling up in her throat, in her veins, turning her blood to flame...and this time she welcomed it. Anger was good. Anger would make her strong enough to break free from this confinement, and...

And what? She sighed and leaned against the cold stone, the wall draining the heat from her heart as well as from her body. *Run away? Take back my castle? How?*

The air grew colder; murmurs of conversation reached Amalia's ears from the stairs nearby, the low rumble of words spoken through stone walls and heavy wooden doors, indecipherable even to her acute hearing. Across from her cell, perhaps six paces away, a small, repetitive grinding sound, like a rusty knife cutting into thick rope, tugged at her awareness, refusing to let her drift off into restless sleep, maybe, or simply allowing her mind to wander.

"Stupid rat." She tried to put her hands up to her ears, but the sudden pain in her wrists reminded her of her situation yet again. "Go find somewhere else to chew." The steel dug into her skin, and her shoulders were beginning to ache.

She didn't know how long she had been there, how long since they had thrown her into the cell to rot, as the Archprelate had said. It may have been minutes. Or hours.

The bells had stopped by now, and the air continued to cool; it sounded as if the guards were running drills, perhaps, with muffled yells and swords clashing. Each passing moment made it harder for Amalia to focus, to do anything other than let herself sink into despair.

But she didn't let that stop her. She wouldn't. Instead, she lifted her mind, seeking her sister's thoughts, wherever she was.

Glorianna? Did you escape? The Queen affected the attitude of someone lost in despair, slumping onto the ground and bowing her head.

It was not a difficult pretense to adopt.

I did, sister. What about you? Why did you wait so long?

We were betrayed. Gorman was killed...and... Her resolve threatened to break, with the emotion rising high in her throat. She allowed herself a single sob - the better to sell the idea that she was truly suffering and lost, she thought - before swallowing it down again. *They killed him. He went to the priests for help and they...it doesn't matter. They threw me in a cell, under the castle.*

She flexed her muscles, channeling her dragon strength; the manacles held, but she could sense some weakness in them as the metal bent slightly. *I think I can get out, but I'm unarmed and there are at least four of them. They'd turn me into target practice before I could get through.*

What about your knight? For once, the mention of a human came from Glorianna's mind without any trace of sarcasm or belligerence; the only emotion Amalia could feel from her sister was concern.

And anger. There was that, too.

I don't know, but I'm sure it won't be good. Fighting her concern for Destrick, Amalia focused on the present. *They said they were going to try to break him of my enchantment, whatever that means.*

Then let's…

A sudden commotion in front of the cell drew Amalia's attention. Metal crashed and clanked, with strangled outcries mixed in; there were so many sounds, and so suddenly, that Amalia couldn't put them together and divine what was happening until it was over.

Leather boots. Large frame. Footsteps, taking care not to land on any of the fallen guards. *Who is it?*

"Your Majesty, a pleasure to see you again."

"Lord Don." She wasn't sure whether to be pleased or worried, so she settled for formal. "I'd rather it have been under better circumstances."

"As would I, Queen Amalia." He stepped forward, reaching through the bars; his hand landed on her shoulder, with a strong grip that belied Amalia's previous image of the man. "But you know that there isn't much time. Break free of those chains and I will unlock your cell."

"Why are you helping me?" She pulled, driving her elbows apart, the effort making her cry out as the manacles pulled at her skin. She forced the metal to bend, then to break, then to snap apart; the sudden release of tension made one fist crash into the wall and wrenched her shoulder with the other.

"Because this is not right, what happened here, if I may say so." He paused, the key hanging in the lock. "And because I think we can help each other."

"I can't leave my people."

"You don't have a choice. I got here as quickly as I could, but much has happened since they took you prisoner. The priest has whipped them into a frenzy against you, preaching that you betrayed Marcus and the other monarchs. He called you a murderer and a dragon-thrall. The whole place is in uproar, with factions splitting off." The lock turned, and Don stepped into the cell with her. "If you stay here, you'll either be executed publicly or killed, supposedly trying to escape."

"As opposed to actually trying to escape."

"Just so, your Majesty." Don's normally jovial voice carried none of its usual humor. "I can bring you to my country, offer you sanctuary there. You help us with our problem…"

"And then you come back with me, here, to end this rebellion and retake my throne?" Amalia shook the last scraps of metal off of her hands, rubbing her wrists where they ached. "How do you know I can help you in the first place?"

"Because you are the Sword of Junandar. And we need that sword now, more than ever." He put his hand on her shoulder again. "Come, please. Questions later. Even if you decide not to get on the ship, I'll at least know that you aren't trapped in this miserable place. They won't even give you any of the good food in here, you know."

This forced a small laugh despite the situation. "Very well, Don. And thank you." She stepped out of the cell. "But I…"

Be sensible, Amalia! Glorianna's voice broke in on her thoughts. *You know what he says is true. The holy man has had time to spin the story he wanted to use against you - and too many believe it. Go fight now, and you lose. Gather your strength.* A pause. *I don't know if this Don is to be trusted, but you cannot stay here, and his offer is as good as any until you know better. Flee. And I will follow.*

"What about Destrick?" Amalia addressed the question to both the visiting nobleman and the dragon in her mind. "Do you have news of him?"

"He is held under heavy guard in his own barracks, from what I understand." Don stepped gingerly over the fallen once more, holding Amalia's hand to help guide her. "And your hound is being kept there too. I think that he is being questioned, but I don't know why, or about what."

Yes. They do have them. On the second floor; I can see his shadow in the window.

Again, Amalia resisted the urge to leap into the Link, but the refusal came easier now, less painful.

"I promised him once that, if he were in danger, that I would leave him to safeguard Aetheria." Amalia paused at the stairwell. "But that was when I still had a country to protect. We rescue him - and my dog - before we flee, or we die trying."

"Your Majesty." She could hear the difficulty he was having in modulating his voice. "I really don't think that this is a good idea."

Neither do I!

"No, it isn't, Don." Amalia pushed past him, feeling the larger man's shoes skitter under him as her movement knocked him off balance. "But it's what I'm going to do, because the alternatives are worse. If I leave him to suffer…" She paused at the base of the stairs, shaking her head, her voice dipping. "…I would never forgive myself."

Don's footprints came behind her, hesitant. "Well, your Majesty, you won't find me any help there. A warrior, I certainly am not."

"Then make your way to the stables and get Vivienne and Lorne saddled, if you know how. We'll need to make quick time away from here." Lifting her chin, she projected her thoughts outward.

And I'll need you to watch my back, Glorianna. But don't engage; you're still too weak.

The return thought came as Amalia ascended the stairs, her feet moving quickly, one hand tracing the stone: ***I'll be my own judge of my weakness.***

A small smile creeping into one corner of Amalia's mouth found itself cut down in its infancy as she made her way through the prison's entrance. The sounds from outside, muffled by the stone of the cell walls, now rang clear in her ears - blades on steel, shouting and chaos; footsteps in unison a dozen yards or so to the left, and forward. Every which way there was activity and movement, and none of it was quiet.

Damn it. This isn't going to be easy, is it? Amalia took a breath to steady her nerves. *Nothing worthwhile ever is, father would say. Never is.*

Footsteps from behind and a hand on her shoulder heralded the approach of Lord Don. "Don't do anything foolish, your Majesty. Please. Our people - mine and yours - depend on your survival."

"I have no plans to die here today, Don. Get the horses. I will arrive with Destrick a... soon." For a moment, Amalia forgot that Gorman lay slain, cut down for his friendship and care, and her throat closed...until with a supreme effort of will, she banished the emotion.

"Then take my cloak, at least, your Majesty." Don presented the garment; it smelled of spices and perfumes, and Amalia had to steady herself against an instinctive recoiling. "It's a dark blue. It might help hide you, at least from a distance."

Swallowing, the Queen nodded and wrapped the cloak around herself. "Again, I find myself in your debt."

"Then survive." Don put a hand on her shoulder again for a moment before he turned; Amalia's senses tracked the padding of his feet toward the stables, the quickening of his steps as he began to run. Shaking her head, she focused every one of her senses, preparing to move.

Junandar, if I am truly Your sword, guide me now like the arm behind. She braced herself against the wall, sweat beading in the hollows of her neck, running down into the small of her back, soaking into her clothes. *Don't force me to leave a good man behind to die...for the crime of caring for me.*

With that final thought, Amalia pushed herself away from the wall, ducking low into a run. Her feet slammed against the ground with every step, her breath loud in her ears as her heartbeat quickened. In her haste, her own movements threatened to drown out her perceptions, narrowing her focus to the echoes bouncing from the stone walls ahead.

And the pair of guards that were turning the corner, shouting in outcry as she bore down on them, those same shouts strangling in their throats as Amalia's fists slammed with dragon's strength into their breastplates. She felt the metal part like silk, cutting small grooves into her skin while her knuckles crushed into bones, the impacts reverberating into her own shoulders.

The two guards flew into the stone walls behind them, metal and flesh colliding with one another, leaving them slumped over in quiet, breathless mounds, no further sound coming from their bodies. Bile rose in Amalia's mouth, quickly stifled as she reoriented her focus, shoving her nausea down into her gut as she stretched out her hands, searching for one of their weapons. Her fingers wrapped around the hilt of the still-sheathed blade, extracting it with a metallic hiss. The weapon felt light in her hand, smaller than her own, but its simple presence lifted some of the fear, the weight on her shoulders.

Her free hand felt for the door, moving down to the handle once she found it.

Locked, of course. A wicked grin slipped from between the High Queen's lips. *How unfortunate.*

Bracing her shoulder against the wood, Amalia shoved her way through the door...and kept going on, taking the entire thing off its hinges, leaving small splinters behind in the frame as the rest clattered to the ground with a raucous crash that rang in her ears. She paused, her nerves on high alert, but even her keen senses couldn't pull any signs of impending danger from the general din of the chaos around her.

What am I doing? She shook her head and dropped the fragment of wood still in her hands; her cuts stung, small rivulets of blood running down between her fingers and pattering onto the floor. *I'm going to get myself killed if there are any guards up there. I'm just lucky that they haven't heard me already.* Leaning back against the wall, she took a breath. *Think, Amalia, think.*

The best advice I've heard you give yourself. Too bad you didn't follow it before running out into the field! Glorianna's voice echoed in Amalia's mind, tinged with fear and fury. ***You were seen, you stupid fool. I count ten***

of them - no, twelve - on their way right now. You don't have long, so get on with it!

Her sister's anxiety and fear wound its way through the Link and buried its roots among the soil of Amalia's own adrenaline-laced terror. The Queen shook her head as she stood, back against the wall, fighting against the paralysis, to come to some sort of decision.

What am I...

The bark shattered her thought. Shattered the worry, the fear, and the hesitation; before she realized she was moving, Amalia had cleared the first flight of steps, her shoulder crashing into the wall as she misjudged its location. Pain radiated through her arm, joining the stinging fingers in singing the siren call of agony.

Wish dragon blood made me more resistant to harm. The thought crossed the back of her mind as she came around the curve of the stairs, taking the steps two or three at a time. Instead of slamming into the door, she brought herself up short as the tip of her toe brushed against the wood and warned her of its presence. Pausing, her breath moving in and out in scarcely-controlled gasps, Amalia leaned against the door, listening for any signs of what might lay on the other side.

The panting of a dog - a big one - with every other pant or so interrupted by a low, mournful whine, metal against metal, shifting from one second to the next in irregular patterns. Her mind fought to create sense of the sounds, to discern…

What is taking you so long? The mental shout made Amalia start in surprise, banging her head against the door.

"Damn it!" Amalia swore as the door creaked open, rubbing her head. "I wasn't…"

At the sound of her voice, Marchen's bark rang out clear and loud, echoing in the stone room. His chain rattled against the floor as he strained at the bond, sending daggers straight to Amalia's heart. She hurried across the floor, her ears picking out the presence of chairs and allowing her to duck past them, before she slid to a stop with the stone skinning her knees.

"Marchen!" Amalia's nose drank the hound's familiar scent; her skin soaked in the warmth of his fur and flesh. Overwhelming joy and love poured from the dog's mind into hers as they came together, her fingers running through his short fur and his tongue licking her face from chin to forehead, leaving trails of drool across her facial scars. "You're okay! I'm so happy to see you, I was so worried…"

"I'm all right too; thanks for asking."

Amalia froze for three heartbeats, her mind disengaging from her body at the sound of the other voice.

"Destrick." Amalia rose to her feet, taking tentative steps toward the young knight. Now that she knew he was there, she could smell the blood on him, the coppery scent that foreshadowed his injuries.

"Your Majesty." She could hear the pain behind those two words, feel the effort it took him to say them without his voice breaking. "I'm glad you're all right."

"We can talk later, Destrick. We don't have much time." Amalia pursed her lips, thinking, puzzling out the best course of action.

"Apologies. I simply-"

"Hush now." Amalia dropped her purloined weapon with a clatter and gripped two of the bars. Without another word, she braced her feet and felt her fingers moving into the metal like mud, the steel oozing over her skin as she snapped through the barrier. "There."

"I don't think I'll ever get tired of watching you do that, my Queen." Destrick's feet slipped a little against the stone as he adjusted his position; the smell of blood was stronger now, more fresh.

He must have reopened something. Amalia's fingers grasped as her hands moved into the cell, seeking the chains that bound Destrick. She stepped in, her toes dipping into pooled fluid and bringing another wave of nausea to her throat.

"I'm hanging from my wrists." Destrick's words came from a slightly elevated position from her left. "You need to reach up to get them."

"Yes." Another step and she could smell the sweat, feel the heat of Destrick's body hanging next to her. She lifted her hands up, leaning forward to grab hold of his arms, following them to the bonds around his hands. "Try not to fall on your face."

"I will do my utmost." Destrick tried to laugh, but it came out as a cross between a cough and a wheeze.

"I'm sure you will." Fingertips wrapped around chain links and, with one more tug, Amalia pulled the bonds out of the ceiling, sending a shower of stone chips and the knight himself falling down with a series of clitters and thumps. She stumbled backwards, trying to keep her balance as the force of her pull threatened to topple her; at the collapse, Marchen's voice chimed in with a chorus of barks, as if he could scare off the rocks with his voice.

"Ow." Destrick fell with a hard thump, sending small splashes of both pebbles and blood up onto Amalia's feet. "Thank you."

Amalia leaned down toward him, her hands grazing his shoulder before trailing down to his arm. "Destrick. Can you travel?" She braced herself to help him up, barely remembering to control her strength in her nervousness as she did so - she didn't want to send him crashing into the ceiling, after all!

"I can, my Queen. And I will. But I cannot…" He swallowed, the sound almost deafening to Amalia's ears. "I cannot fight. They crippled me, broke my hand."

They're coming! A clatter from below confirmed Glorianna's warning. *What's taking so long?*

"Destrick, you have to help me. I can't see and I don't know this room." Using her sense memory and the sound of his continuous whines, Amalia hurried back to where Marchen was still chained to the wall. "Come on, boy. Let's get out of here."

Metal scraped across the ground behind her, dragging for a half-second before ceasing.

"I have your sword, Amalia." Destrick came up behind her. "Can you get him out?"

"I was able to get *you* out." The High Queen gripped the chain with both hands, putting the links between her fingers and pulling in opposite directions. "As long as my strength remains in my limbs, I should be able to do this as well."

And with a small grunt of effort, she did just that, tearing through steel and severing the links from one another. Marchen leapt into her lap, licking and panting as if the pair hadn't seen each other in years.

"No time, Marchen! Off!" At her command, the hound withdrew, attentive and waiting for further orders. "We need to get out of here...and I don't think I can fight off ten or more at once."

"Whether you could or not, I'd rather not test it." Destrick's bare feet padded against the stone as he circled the room. "Here. Put the desk against the door to keep anyone from getting in, since the lock is broken."

Ah, yes. Amalia followed his voice and grabbed hold of the wooden edges. "Remind me to recompense my guards for the trouble I've caused them."

"I'm sure you can manage that." With Amalia providing the strength and Destrick the guidance with his one good arm, the two managed to get the desk to its new home, barricading the door as quickly as they could.

As Amalia pushed it into place, she heard the clanging and clinking of metal approaching the other side of the door. "She's in here!"

"Damn it!" Destrick swirled around in place. "We have to go out of the window, Amalia. There's nowhere else, no other way."

You took too long. Amalia's ears caught an impact on the roof above. ***But if you can get out of the tower, then there shouldn't be anyone close enough to catch you.***

"Fantastic." Amalia breathed the word in a low whisper. "Out the window, then?"

"It's about ten paces down, your Majesty. I don't know if we can make that jump."

The door shook as the assembled guards began to bang on the wood. The desk scraped slightly against the stone floor.

"We don't have a choice, Destrick. If we stay, then we die at the hands of our own people." The two approached the window; Amalia could feel the breeze stirring the air near the opening. "Don is supposed to be bringing us horses. If the Gods are merciful, he'll be ready when we arrive."

"As you say." Destrick's voice trembled; Amalia could smell the fear on his pores, through the blood and the pain he was still fighting, but said nothing. "I shall go first, then. If I make it down, I can try to catch you."

"With one arm? No." Amalia shook her head as another tremore shook the door. "We don't have time to argue. I'll go first."

"But-"

Before the knight could say another word, the Queen threw herself out of the open space, feeling the stone beneath her feet vanish as she flew into the air. For a moment, she remembered how powerful she felt while riding her sister's sight, how exhilarating flight was, with the vistas and seas rolling beneath.

Then gravity took hold, and she was falling, her stomach forced into her throat by the acceleration. She couldn't see the ground coming at her, but she knew it was, could almost feel it. Terror gripped her in the few moments it took to reach the bottom, and she braced herself for the impact, preparing to throw herself forward as soon as she felt solid earth under her feet.

At the very last second, Amalia felt a great heat well up in her body, like a sudden flush of blood flowing into her limbs and chest after intense exercise. The impact came hard, jarring Amalia's jaw and slamming her teeth together, sending a shockwave through her flesh. She tipped forward, pushing with her feet to absorb some of the force.

"That could have gone better." Amalia tested her limbs; though sore, nothing seemed broken. Blood leaked out from between her lips from her tongue, a stinging cut on the right side making itself known with sharp cries of protest. "Ow ow ow."

"Amalia!" Marchen's bark blurred out part of Destrick's call. "They're breaking through!"

Forcing the pain out of her mind, Amalia fought her way to her feet. "Marchen! Come!"

Without hesitation, the huge mound of animal flesh hurled itself out the window. Amalia focused her ears, raising her arms despite the wince in her shoulders, and the pounds of dog slammed into her and knocked her off her feet, hitting the ground again.

"Off!" Amalia pushed Marchen's muzzle away from her face. "Destrick! Come on!"

Wood splintered and the intruders' voices grew a magnitude louder. Destrick's bare feet scraped on the stone ledge. "Look out!"

A thump, then another two or three smaller ones in rapid succession, and Destrick lay groaning on the ground beside her. Amalia reached out for him, her fingertips dancing over his skin until she found his chest and hefted him by the armpits. "Are you all right?"

"Of course not!" Destrick's barking shout surprised her. "Damn, I wrenched my ankle. You'll...you'll have to leave me. I don't want to slow you down."

"I'll carry you before I do that." Amalia lifted him in both of her arms, then moved him toward her back. "Hold on as best you can. We're running."

I'm right above you, Sister. Go. Go now!

Amalia's hurried flight stopped Destrick's protests, and he slung his remaining good arm over her neck. The feeling was awkward, uncomfortable, but Amalia didn't care - she ran with him on her back like her father had run with her as a small girl. Marchen leapt to her side, his pants helping her to stay on track. The panic running through her veins and the need for haste turned her normally-precise internal map into nothing more than vague impressions and instinct. Four times, Marchen jumped into her path, using his own bulk to knock her away from obstacles or pitfalls.

From behind them, Amalia could hear the outcry beginning, hear the alarms and calls to pursue. Even with her draconic strength, carrying this much weight on her back had already sent burning spears into her legs, the fatigue slowly rising from a dull shout to a crowd of shrieking needles.

Now that they're after us, it won't be long until we're caught. Her foot came down on a small stone, sending a jagged bolt of pain up her leg.

"Amalia! I see Lord Don!" Destrick leaned further into her back and his injured arm came up, shifting his weight more. "That way!"

Amalia's breath was coming faster now, her heart breaking through her rib cage with each strong beat.

Marchen barked in response to the man's cry, keeping pace with Amalia's strides, crowding her left leg to guide her. On the edges of the breeze, the running Queen caught the smell of horse sweat and the gentle sound of Vivienne's whinnies.

They're getting closer. How far? Her voice gave words to the question boiling in her mind. "Destrick? How far?"

"Another hundred, hundred-twenty paces." She felt his weight move again as he turned his waist and craned his neck. "It's incredible, how fast this is! I can barely hold on!"

"I appreciate the praise, but…" She hitched in a deep breath. "…this might not be the best time for it."

"Apologies!" Despite everything, Amalia felt her lips curve in an unbidden grin at his jostled syllables. "He's coming this way, to meet us."

"Thank the Gods." Amalia's calves and thighs burned; only fear and will together kept her limbs moving at all. She stumbled, sending Destrick tumbling off her back and Marchen pulling up in a sudden stop. "Damn it all! I just…"

"It's all right, Amalia. It's all right!" Destrick's footfalls as he approached were uneven; he was still favoring his right leg, limping hard. "Don's almost here!"

Amalia could only nod at this point, chest heaving in and out; her limbs felt like jam, barely solid, barely *there*, and scarcely responded to her commands to support her weight.

"Majesty!" Don's voice called across the intervening space - no more than ten paces, now, and closing. "Hurry! They're closing in!"

"How…how far, Don? Destrick?" Amalia struggled to her feet, stumbling toward the horses. She heard fabric sliding across leather, then the impact of boots on the grass and ground.

Stop asking, damn you! And LOOK!

"We don't have long, Majesty." Don got behind her and slipped his arm under hers, guiding her to the horse.

"I won't. I'm sorry, but I won't." Amalia shook her head as Don led her. "Not anymore. I can't afford to."

"What was that?" Don leaned in closer; Amalia could smell his sweat, acrid and pungent, mixing moisture with mildew and fear. "Did you say something, Majesty?"

Need to bite my stupid tongue. "Nothing to you, Lord Don." Her breath was beginning to return, but the fatigue in her muscles had not lessened in the slightest. "My sister and I are having an argument."

"Now might not be the best time for that." They arrived at Vivienne's side, the heat baking from the horse's flank almost scorching Amalia's hands as she prepared to mount. "You need to flee."

Something in Don's tone made Amalia stop, her fingers gripping the saddle and one foot in the stirrup. "And what are you doing?"

"Your Majesty, I'm no good at fighting, but I can keep them from you for a few minutes, I think." He laughed; the sound was rich, warm, and without regret. "There is some dragon blood within me, too, after all."

"Please, don't." Amalia turned to face him, her throat burning. "I don't want to lose any more friends."

"Oh. Thank you." Don took her right hand and put it on his own chest, where she could feel the heartbeat. "But you must. Go."

"Amalia, we need to move. Now." Destrick had mounted his own horse by now, and he led it closer to the pair. "Nome watch over you, wherever you go, Lord Don. We won't forget this."

"I should hope not." The Queen heard steel hissing as Don unsheathed his own weapon. "Still shiny. Perhaps it is time to do it justice at last."

"I…" Amalia swallowed; she could feel Glorianna's irritation and sense of urgency. "I can't stop you. Goodbye, Don." She leaned and kissed him on the forehead; inside her mind, she had a brief flash

(Tell my children how I died)

that sent her mentally reeling. She swiveled at the hips, grabbing the saddle again before she turned fully and pulled herself up onto Vivienne's back.

"I will, Don. I will."

"Then get going." The nobleman slapped Vivienne's flank, sending the horse leaping forward. "Now!"

The two horses ran as their riders urged them on, Destrick taking the lead. Amalia leaned forward, letting her forehead rest on Vivienne's neck. She could feel the horse's nervousness percolating through her own consciousness, the worry at the darkness, at the noise and the fear in the air.

It's all right. Amalia tried to send reassuring thoughts through the connection, but they felt like lies to her. Nothing was all right - her oldest friend dead, her people in the hands of a scheming liar, and the only course of action open to her a mad dash from her home.

How had it come to this?

Foolish fear and idealism make the idealists fall and the fearful victorious. Amalia flinched at the anger, the thirst for vengeance inside her sister's thought as it flowed through the Link. ***Your idealism. Their fear.***

"Your anger at me is well-aimed." Amalia spoke the words aloud because it hurt too much to think about...anything. "But you can have at me later. For now, we ride, and we flee."

Disdain, fear, anger...so many mixed emotions ran through the Link, but Glorianna said nothing more. The sound of chaos and discord diminished behind her, and soon enough Destrick's pace slowed, which led Vivienne to do the same.

"We've left them behind, Amalia." The young knight's voice trembled with suppressed pain and fear. "I think we're safe."

The Queen shook her head, slowly, turning her head to face the way they had come. "No, Destrick. We aren't safe, not yet. And it'll be a long time before we are again."

END

ABOUT THE AUTHOR

Jason Patrick Crawford is a father of three rambunctious boys, one sweet-as-sugar girl, and has been happily married for over seventeen years. He lives in sunny California, where he constantly laments the lack of rain. He welcomes your feedback and hopes you will take the time to review this novel. Thank you for reading!

More from Jason P. Crawford

Chains of Prophecy: Samuel Buckland is a young man who has it all and is planning for the future. Gregory Caitlin is a businessman and politician. He has designs to bring hope back to a world in need...and he'll be damned if anyone gets in his way!

When the two cross paths, even the angels tremble.

An ancient magic has been rediscovered. Sam must overcome his lack of faith and accept his destiny, or the world he knows will suffer the consequences.

A skeptic who must harness the powers of demons and genies. A zealot who has begun to walk a darker path. Bound together by a stolen secret. Can any of them escape the Chains of Prophecy?

The Drifter: The drifter is a man out of time. Plagued by visions of historic events he never could have witnessed, he struggles to understand the strange abilities that seem so natural. When Death comes for him, he has no choice but to run. He must find allies who can protect him until he learns why he is being pursued.

The keystone of a terrible plan. A society of demigods buried in the rolls of history. Deadly schemes older than man. Welcome to the world of The Essentials.

Cycles of Destruction: A relic of unknown origin appears on Earth . . . and, through a series of coincidences, falls into unexpected hands.

A hidden organization guards the secret of the relic and will do anything to retrieve it.

Still grieving the loss of his wife, Army Veteran Cameron Mitchell must call on his military experience to piece together the mystery of the Alien relic before time runs out. all while protecting his greatest treasure - his son.

Seeking the Sun: Daphne Gianakos begins having strange dreams as she prepares for college life at the University of Florida. A chance encounter with a striking young man triggers conflicting emotions within her, but his identity challenges her entire worldview - he is the last surviving Greek god.

When he goes missing, Daphne must learn who she is, who she was, and the truth about what has happened to the gods...or the world will pay the price.

Dragon Princess: High Princess Amalia Therald was blinded at birth by dragon-fire, the last victim of a vicious war started by her ancestors. As she comes of age, doubts fly about her as to her capability and willingness to lead her country – and all the others. Determined to prove her doubters wrong, Amalia must come to terms with the truth of what happened on the day of her birth, and all the consequences that have followed.

www.ingramcontent.com/pod-product-compliance
Lightning Source LLC
Chambersburg PA
CBHW061615210726
48287CB00001B/137